Hindsight and Foresight

A Novel of the End Times

John Buckner

This book is a work of fiction. Names, characters, places and events are used fictitiously at the whim of the author's imagination. Any resemblance to real persons, alive or dead, is purely coincidental.

ISBN: 13: 978-0-9978949-0-5
ISBN: 10: 0-9978949-0-3

Chapter 1

As Charles Dickens said in the opening of his famous novel, A Tale of Two Cities, about the French Revolution, 'It was the best of times, it was the worst of times, it was the age of wisdom, it was the age of foolishness...'

In the current situation, the best of times were at hand for those who believed in the Lord Jesus Christ. The worst of times were at hand for those who were left alive on earth. The remainder of the quotation was equally applicable.

You see, the event spoken of in the Bible that most Christians call the rapture, had just occurred. It had happened just as the Bible said it would, in the twinkling of an eye.

It did not happen as many Bible scholars had thought it would. The majority opinion held that there would be total chaos when the event happened. Such had not been the case. Planes did not fall out of the sky, cars did not indiscriminately crash when the drivers who believed in the Lord were suddenly taken to the heavenly home.

Everything just suddenly stopped. Planes in the sky were miraculously landed, probably by Angels, and cars being driven by those raptured did not continue until they wrecked. Everything just stopped working for whatever reason.

That a large segment of the earth's population had disappeared without a trace was the only tangible fact which heralded the event. All those people had simply vanished into thin air.

Those remaining alive obviously didn't believe in the rapture, nor did they believe any other part of the Bible when the event occurred. Remaining world leaders, along with the less influential of the population were now searching for alternate reasons for the disappearance of millions of people.

Everything seemed just as it had been before the mass disappearances.

To be sure, there was a large number of people who had been exposed to Christian teachings at some time in their lives. Some might have even been leaning toward a true belief in Jesus Christ but had failed to make the necessary appeal to Christ for forgiveness. These people now had the proof but that was not going to help them avoid what was to come in the tribulation period. Their coming to a belief in Christ would assure them a place in Heaven as their final destination but that would not negate the consequences for their unbelief to that time in their lives. They would not have a bed of roses for the remainder of their lives on earth.

The President of the United States was among the missing, as were several other people in the higher official positions within the government.

The same held true for other countries around the world. The percentages in that category did not even approach the statistics for those in the lower strata of society. Did this mean that those without many worldly possessions were more favored than others? Not necessarily, but it was a fact that those with little seemed to appreciate more what they did have.

There's a verse in the Bible that says it is easier for a camel to pass through the eye of a needle than for a rich man to enter the kingdom of heaven. I believe this refers more to the fact that those in that category don't feel they need help to achieve their heart's desires, while those who believe in Jesus Christ seem to understand that what they have is directly from Christ.

Regardless, it was only the day after the strange occurrence and everyone left was trying to make sense of what happened. Those who had not been exposed to biblical teachings were especially confused by the event.

Had the event happened as many Bible scholars thought it would, there would have been little doubt that something extraordinary had taken place. But because there was not the chaos associated with the event it was difficult for those remaining to believe that Jesus had suddenly taken almost half the earth's population to heaven.

Their disbelief in the Bible made it impossible for them to understand what had occurred.

Those countries who had top level people disappear were scrambling to fill the vacancies. Others in countries who had no great exposure to Christian religions were not as affected, though there was not a single country in the entire world that did not have people suddenly disappear without a trace, most notably the very young.

Social media was going crazy. There were so many theories about what had taken place that it was difficult to even know how the theories had come into being. The primary driving factor was that there were no Christians left to espouse the true cause of the event.

Property, such as automobiles left unattended, that effectively blocked all traffic, had to be taken care of. The usual procedure for abandoned automobiles was that the law enforcement people called a towing company to have them towed until the owner could be notified or until someone claimed them. This procedure was fine when someone had trouble with the car and had to leave it along the road until they could make arrangements to have it taken care of. This situation was entirely different. Almost half the cars that had been on the road at the time of the rapture had to be removed from travel lanes before any sort of order could be restored to the highways. This number was in the millions. To add to the problem the towing companies did not have nearly enough storage space to park the cars they towed.

Establishing ownership was another major headache. In some cases entire families had vanished and there was nobody left to claim ownership of the vehicles. Towing companies took to using large shopping mall parking lots to store the cars, which did not set well with the owners of the malls.

After the first couple of days of complete chaos the tow truck drivers started looking at the registration and taking the cars to the location listed on the document. They of course took what they thought might be valuable from the vehicle before delivering it to the location. In some cases people were living in the houses where they delivered the cars, but in most cases the houses were vacant, which provided more opportunity for the unscrupulous to enrich themselves, assuming that the occupants would not be back. Some of the vehicles were pushed out of the travel lanes and left alongside the roads. In some cases those left alive found a car to their liking and simply got in and drove off. Nobody would file a complaint.

The automobiles were not the only major headache involved with the disappearance of so many people. Many of the people who disappeared had been employed in essential positions for the provision of utilities and emergency services. Hospitals were shorthanded, law enforcement units found themselves with less than half their normal numbers and utility companies were at half strength.

The effects trickled down to all levels of society. The chaos imagined by many biblical scholars with physical things was manifested in the everyday lives of those remaining. Society ceased to function in the normal manner. Crime ran rampart, because any with sound moral principles had been taken out of the world and those left were all for personal gain and more worldly pleasures.

Conner Frederick had been driving into the city of Washington, D.C. when suddenly his automobile ceased to function. It simply stopped dead in the fast lane of the Interstate highway he was on. It wasn't a screeching halt, but a sudden and complete stop. He didn't get thrown into the windshield, nor did the airbags deploy. The car just came to a sudden and complete stop. He glanced around to find that the same phenomenon had happened all round him.

He did notice very quickly that many of the automobiles traveling in the lanes around him did not seem to have occupants any longer.

It took him a few seconds to process the magnitude of what he was seeing and he immediately thought, "Oh Lord, I should have had more faith."

As they say, hindsight is always 20/20 and he knew what he had witnessed, or what had happened that he had not witnessed because of his unbelief.

Right then and there he prayed to God that He would forgive him for his unbelief and felt a sense of relief almost immediately. He hoped that his assumption that God had heard his prayer and forgiven him of his sins was correct. He would need to do more but he had been to church enough to recognize that the Bible had indeed been truthful when it said that all God's children would be taken to heaven in the blink of an eye.

Those still living on earth could only imagine what had happened. The rapture must have been a glorious sight to believers. The Bible says in I Thessalonians 4:16 For the Lord Himself shall descend from heaven with a shout, with the voice of the Archangel and with the trump of God: and the dead in Christ shall rise first...

The event had been witnessed by all those who were in Christ, yet unbelievers had not witnessed the great event.

Connor had studied the Bible enough to understand that two events had to happen before the 'day of the Lord' arrived. He remembered that a falling away from the Lord must occur, in other words apostasy on a great scale. The second item was a revealing of the Man of Sin, or the Antichrist.

Connor could readily see the apostasy, but he couldn't identify the Antichrist from his knowledge. To be sure there were a lot of candidates around the world but which would fulfill the requirements of the man talked about in the Bible as the Antichrist?

He thought that it would not be long before the Antichrist revealed himself to the world at large.

The Book of Revelation says that he will be given many supernatural powers. To Connor's way of thinking it would only be a matter of time before he emerged as the world leader.

Connor was not knowledgeable about what was supposed to happen next but he did remember that there was to be a seven year tribulation period. That supposedly started when the peace treaty was signed between the Antichrist and Israel, according to the Book of Daniel. It could be days, weeks, months or even years, but Connor didn't think it would be long before the event came to pass.

Once Conner was able to get off the interstate and make his way to his home he knew that his first task was to try to understand what was to come. He lived alone. He and his wife had divorced several years before, primarily because of religious differences. Connor now knew that his wife had been right and he had been wrong. That was little consolation to his current situation.

When they had been together he had gone to church with her to keep peace more than from any interest in Christianity. Enough had penetrated his thick skull to understand what Christianity was all about, but he had always thought that he was smart enough to make his own decisions about how he lived his life. Well, that had not worked out as he thought it would.

Now he was left in a world with those who shared what was left after what he was certain had been the calling home of God's church. He needed to learn what was required of him now that he was a believer.

There had not been any children in his marriage and the divorce decree gave the reason as irreconcilable differences.

He thought, oh if I could only do it over again!

Chapter 2

When he got home Connor immediately went to the bookcase and took down a Bible. He turned to the last book and sat down to read. He read through the first four chapters, wondering what was meant by the reference to the churches of Christ's days. That could wait until later. What he wanted now was some knowledge about what had happened and what was to come.

He couldn't find any reference to the rapture. He did not yet understand the 'rapture' was the way modern Christians referred to the sudden event which took believers home to be with God.

He began to get some indication as to what was to come when he got to the sixth chapter. He read about the seal judgments, which was bad enough, but when he came to the trumpet judgements he realized that if he lived long enough he would be going through some really rough times. He was now a believer and would witness the events with those who still refused to believe, but he knew that it was going to be tough for those who had come to a belief in Christ a bit late.

Even those who believed in the Lord for a long time had trouble understanding the Book of Revelation. The symbology was enough to confuse many who did not take the time to cross reference the other books of the Bible for parallels.

As Connor went through Revelation the second time he tried to find something that explained what had taken place. It was not until he saw the reference to I Thessalonians 4:16 that he made the connection.

If, as the Bible said, all believers had been taken up in a cloud then he would not have any knowledgeable people left to help him understand his new-found faith and his responsibilities.

He wondered about the sealing of the 144,000 mentioned in Chapter 7 of Revelation. If there was to be that many believers within the Jews alone then he could not reconcile that with what had just happened.

He went back again and looked at the verses in I Thessalonians to see if there was any exceptions to those raptured. He could not find any reference to substantiate that and wondered how that was to happen.

There were too many things he did not understand. The only thing he was absolutely sure about was that Jesus had indeed taken the believers to heaven. That was simply an indisputable fact that he had not witnessed but the aftermath was enough to solidify his belief.

After Connor had read the Book of Revelation through twice and looked up the referenced verses that he could identify, he moved to the computer and looked at religious web sites.

He found that there were many different interpretations of the last book of the Bible. Some believed that the events envisioned by John had already happened just after the time Christ was on earth. Others believed that some of the events had happened while others were yet to come. Still others believed that the entire book was about things yet to come that had started that very day.

Conner tended to allay himself with the last group. With all those who believed in God having left the earth the remainder of the populace would be fair game for the Antichrist. He idly wondered how many of those left had been like him, exposed to the truth but too stubborn to accept it as truth.

He was confused by the 144,000 who were supposed to be sealed by God against the events that would take place within the next seven years. Were they heavenly souls returned to earth, or were they people like him who had come to belief because of the rapture?

The fourth chapter of I Thessalonians very clearly stated that those who were dead in Christ and those who were believers and still alive would be taken to heaven in a cloud. He had to assume that the 144,000 were like him and came to belief in Christ after the Rapture.

He was so immersed in his research that he skipped supper. It was midnight before he decided to go to bed. He did something that was not part of his normal routine, he prayed, fervently. He again asked God to forgive him for his previous unbelief and to help him through the times that he now knew were going to be unlike anything the earth had ever seen. He even mouthed an apology to his late wife for being unwilling to accept the truth of the Bible. He asked for guidance to learn the things that he was sure would be the key to his newfound faith and his very survival in the times coming.

He was still praying when he fell asleep.

He dreamed that he was in the presence of God and that he was being given instructions about what he was to do with the rest of his life.

When he awoke he couldn't remember all the details, but two things stuck with him vividly. God told him that his sins were paid for by the death of His son, and that he was to make contact with those in Israel who were to be sealed against the Antichrist. Did this mean that they were immune to harm? He thought about this and it didn't seem logical. It was clearly stated that Christians would be martyred during the tribulation. That none of the 144,000 would suffer at the hands of the Antichrist didn't seem to fit the pattern. They would preach the gospel during that period and the Antichrist would be hot on the trails of all who did so.

He thought that it meant instead that their faith would be unshakable no matter what horrors were visited upon them.

He wondered if this had simply been a dream, or if God had indeed given him instructions. Time would tell, but he first wanted to learn how many others there were like him who had heard the word and not believed until now. The obvious first step was to check the churches and see if they were getting any new business from others like himself. That was on his agenda for the day.

The roads were still clogged with cars that had not been removed. Most had been driven to the side of the road and abandoned in order to make room for cars to travel the roads. It was still like a pinball machine moving from one side of the road to the other to avoid the stopped cars.

Connor found the church where he and wife used to go and pulled into the parking lot. There were nearly 50 cars there but some of those might be where the abandoned vehicles had been stored.

He locked his car when he got out and went to the door of the church. He found it unlocked and opened the door and went inside. He discovered about twenty people sitting in the pews, most reading the Bible or religious pamphlets. Some were talking in low voices. He made his way toward the front of the church and one of the people sitting in the pew asked him, "Are you the pastor?"

Connor had to smile at this. "I think the pastor is in heaven already. Those of us left here didn't accept the truth of the Bible. I suppose you are all like me, wondering what is to happen now that all the believers are in heaven. I am talking about those who didn't need the rapture to convince them that Christ was real, and that the Bible is truly the word of God."

Someone else said, "What are we supposed to do now. How do we know what God wants us to do?"

"I'm just as new to this as all of you. Some of you were obviously exposed to the word of God and refused to accept it, like me. I don't know the story of each and every

13

one of you, but you're being here today means that yesterday you didn't believe in God. Maybe you believed but didn't accept the instructions for the way you were supposed to live your lives, and you certainly didn't believe that Jesus died for your sins. Is that about the gist of it?"

Some said yes and others nodded.

"How many of you went to church regularly at some point in your lives?"

Twelve people raised their hands.

"How many of you believe that God was responsible for the mass disappearances that took place yesterday?"

Every single one raised their hands.

"I know enough about the Bible to know that every single believer in Christ was taken to Heaven yesterday. Those of us left might have been close to a belief, or maybe far away until something happened to open our eyes to the reality. What that means is that we have no pastors left to give us guidance. We have no structured way to educate ourselves about what God demands of us. I went through the Book of Revelation twice last night to try to understand what is coming. I don't claim to be an expert but if you wish I can relate my thoughts on what is coming."

Everyone seemed to agree to the offer and Connor said, "First let's get closer together. I want everyone to be able to contribute to this since I am not an authority. I remind you again that what I tell you is my interpretation of the final book of the New Testament, and the actual meaning might not be in line with what I get out of it."

There was some milling around as everyone moved to the front two pews. Connor took the time to find a water fountain.

When he came back he moved the table beneath the pulpit over so he could read from the large print Bible kept there.

"Okay, what happened yesterday was the harvest of all believers in Jesus Christ. Most of those now in heaven

14

referred to the event as the Rapture. All the references I could find use the 'Day of the Lord' phraseology. I suppose that the word Rapture didn't exist when the Bible was written, but it amounts to the same thing. According to I Thessalonians 4:13-17, the dead in Christ was first to arise and then all those who believed in Christ followed, in the twinkling of an eye, other verses say. One says 'like a thief in the night', but the meaning is the same."

"All those people missing were taken to heaven?" one of the group asked.

"That's how I see it. I can't find any other explanation for what happened. If that wasn't the rapture then where are the members of this church who would certainly be here among us to try to explain what happened?"

Several heads nodded assent to this statement.

"Okay, now that all believers are in heaven, what is to happen to the rest of us?"

"Two things that were to definitely happen before the rapture are detailed in the Bible. One is a great amount of Apostasy, which I think means false teaching or unbelief. Many religions were to rise and not teach the true word of God. I think that has been happening for many years now. The second thing was the rise of the Antichrist. I think this is happening now as well. There are certainly enough candidates around the world to fill that role."

"The most important factor for those of us who have come to belief in Christ is that seven years of what Revelation calls the Tribulation period is coming. The Tribulation period starts when the Antichrist signs a peace treaty with Israel according to the Book of Daniel. Let me read to you what is to take place from the Bible. I will start with Rev. 7."

Connor read the chapter aloud. This was the chapter that dealt with the sealing of 144,000, 12,000 from each of the tribes of Israel. When he had finished he asked for some discussion about the topic.

One lady asked, "If all believers have gone to heaven, then where are these people going to come from? Will God send them back down from heaven?"

Connor had to laugh out loud. "Excuse me mam, I am not laughing at the question. I am laughing because I had the exact same thought the first time I read this. I don't believe that God is going to send anyone back except for the two witnesses mentioned later on in Revelation. I think the 144,000 are going to come from people just like us. In other words they will be new believers and will have a tough time understanding enough to become witnesses for Christ. I don't know if they will be protected from physical harm, but they will be given unshakeable faith. The Bible says that many will be martyred because of their refusal to renounce their faith. If the 144,000 are given divine protection then their converts will be the ones martyred during the tribulation. I don't know any of this for a fact, but that's how I interpret that chapter."

"Who is the Antichrist?" an older man asked.

"Someone who will rise up to become the de-facto ruler of the entire planet. I have heard enough about this to know that most Bible scholars thought the man would come from somewhere in southern Europe or Asia Minor. He will unite the world as a peacemaker but will make war once he is in control. The Middle East has been a battleground since the days when Christ was alive on earth and I don't think it is unreasonable to believe that the Antichrist now rules one of those nations."

One of the others said, "I certainly want to know more about what is coming, but I want to be absolutely sure that my faith if secure. I want to be baptized."

Connor looked around at the group, who all nodded assent.

"Okay, after lunch we will have a communal baptism. Since we don't have anyone who has performed that task before I will give it a try."

Connor had witnessed enough baptisms to know where to look for the applicable Bible verses.

"Are any of you familiar with the church offices?" he asked.

A couple of people raised their hands.

"Let's see what we can find in the offices that will help get us on the right track. Considering the time when the rapture occurred there must have been people in the church, otherwise the doors would be locked."

Chapter 3

The computers were still on but in the sleep mode. Connor brought one to life to see what the secretary was working on. He found the church bulletin for the coming Sunday on the screen.

He moved to the pastor's office and did the same. The pastor had been working on a sermon, ironically enough, on the Book of Revelation. He called that to the attention of the others with him.

"That might be a good place for us to start. Let me see if I can print out what he has developed so far."

Connor keyed the document to print and several pages rolled out of the printer. He looked them over rather quickly and found that the sermon was an explanation of the sequence of events that were foretold in Revelation.

He showed them to the others and told them that it might be a good idea to use the outline for a starting point to try to understand what was to happen.

"Another thing we should do is get on the internet and see if there are others like us looking for answers," he said.

One of the others went to the key locker on the wall in the office and found the keys for the area that housed the baptismal. "There are robes in the bathrooms for both men and women. I think they had to heat the water before they used it though."

"We might have to just shiver for a while," Connor said with a laugh.

Connor and several others went out to lunch at a nearby restaurant. The place was not nearly as crowded as normal. That stood to reason because they had lost over half of their customer base.

While they were eating they talked with the waitress. "What do you think happened to all the people who disappeared?" Connor asked her.

"I don't know, but I have a theory," she replied.

18

"What's your theory?" one of those with Connor asked.

"I believe the Russians, or maybe the Chinese, must have discovered some way to break down the basic elements which make up the human body. They somehow got all those who disappeared to ingest a substance that caused them to just revert to the base elements."

"What about the fact that they all disappeared at the same time?"

"I don't know how they managed that but it seemed to work that way."

"You don't believe this might have had something to do with the Bible?"

"I don't know much about the Bible, but I don't see how that could have anything to do with it," she said.

"The Bible talks about all Christians disappearing at the same time at what is called the Day of the Lord," Connor said.

"That's just as likely as anything else. It sure makes my job easier. I guess the down side is that I won't make as much in tips."

Connor was astounded at the lackadaisical way the waitress seemed to take such a momentous event. If the majority of those now living thought along those lines it would not be a surprise that the Antichrist could arise so quickly.

When the group got back to the church the others were already there, and the numbers had grown by five. Connor asked one of the men who had mentioned that the baptismal had to filled and heated if he would see to that.

While that was going on he gathered the remainder near the front of the church again and told them that they would wait for the water to heat up a bit so they wouldn't freeze during the baptism.

He took out the sermon notes he had found on the pastor's computer and asked if they wanted him to go over them. The majority wanted to learn as much as they could about what was to come.

He started with a prayer that God would give him the ability to present the material in such a way that all could understand it.

He had heard some of the sermons dealing with Revelation and was not totally in the dark.

"The first thing to understand is that Revelation was written by the Apostle John and was based on a vision he had while on the island of Patmos in the Aegean Sea. The entire book is based on what he was told to write down while in heaven in the spirit. The contents of the book were dictated to him by Christ, or an Angel speaking for Christ, so these are not John's words, as some believe, but are the actual words of God, through Christ the son."

Looking at the pastor's notes Connor said, "The pastor explains that the symbols in the first chapter of the book, which are seven golden candlesticks and seven stars represent the seven churches in biblical times, and the seven angels of those churches."

Still using the pastor's notes Connor said, "He says that the following messages to the churches represent successive eras of the church which span the entire period of the New Testament. That means from biblical days until now. Please don't ask me to break those down at this point because I can't. I haven't studied enough to even attempt to do so. We must however, assume that the pastor was smart enough to know what he was talking about since he is no longer among us. It is important I think to understand that the sequence will not be complete until the second coming of Jesus."

"If my thinking is correct the next thing we will see will be the rise of the Antichrist. I think we should all research the most influential people in leadership positions around the world, with special emphasis on southern Europe and the Middle East. It might also be a good idea to check the social media and let people know that we are a functioning church."

"Should we keep our jobs?" one man asked.

"Unless you can provide for your needs in some other manner I think it is essential that we try to act as normal as possible. Remember, most of those remaining are in the other camp. That's one reason we need to identify other believers in our area. Once the Antichrist rises he will start persecuting those like us who have turned to Christ."

"We will not be immune to the judgements God sends during this period will we?" someone asked.

"No by a long shot. We are going to have to weather the storm just like everyone else. If anything it will be harder on those who have come to a belief in Christ. The Antichrist will be trying to turn us into his followers at every opportunity. With all that is going to happen during the seven years of the tribulation period we are going to be in for a really rough time. There will be wars, famine, earthquakes and other calamities that the world has never seen. I believe we will be well advised to stockpile non-perishable foods someplace against the time when it will no longer be available," Connor said.

"My dad was a member of this church when it was built back in the 1950's. He told me they included a bomb shelter. That was in the days when everyone was afraid the Russians would launch a nuclear attack. I don't know that it would have helped much at that time but it might be a good place for us to start looking to the future," one of the older men said.

"That's a very good idea. After we do the baptism we will see if we can locate it and see what condition it is in. Let's head to the baptistery and do that first."

The group made their way to the stairs leading to the raised baptistery. "Women use the dressing room on the left. Men on the right."

There were not enough robes to outfit everyone at the same time so they did it in small groups. Connor did the honors with help from some others and by the time everyone had been baptized he was quite chilly. He asked everyone he baptized to affirm their faith verbally.

Once everyone had dressed and warmed up somewhat Connor asked the man who had mentioned the bomb shelter to lead them to the basement.

The basement was quite large. It had apparently been used as a social hall in the early days. It was now used mainly for storage and to house the HVAC system. There was still a lot of room and it could be made larger by organizing the material stored there. The man who knew about the bomb shelter led them to the area that had been boarded over.

"This is it. I don't know what shape it is in since I have never been inside, but I believe it is quite large."

"See if there are any flashlights in the building. We will tear the boards off and see what kind of possibilities it offers," Connor said.

The walls were of course concrete and it appeared that the basement was the same size as the building above it. One of the men found a tool chest and broke out a couple of hammers and a pry bar.

They methodically tore the plywood off the opening and discovered an area about half as large as the main building. It had cement walls and the ceiling was also cement. It had a musty smell and was totally devoid of furniture. In one corner was what appeared to be a stack of folding army cots. They would need some light to explore thoroughly. All the light available was what filtered in through the opening they had made by removing the door covering.

When someone returned with flashlights the group looked around inside the room. To Connor it didn't appear that it would provide much protection from an atomic bomb, but for the purpose he envisioned it was ideal.

With the flashlight he discovered a venting system near the back of the room. He had no idea where it terminated on the other end, nor did anyone else in the group, but that could be crucial to their use of the space. It didn't make sense that the original builders would not have provided for a supply of fresh air. The opening might have just been covered over. They could get measurements from below and locate the place above the vent pretty easily.

He also discovered that there were lights in place in the ceiling, though they didn't work when someone tried the switches. All the wiring seemed to still be in place so it should be fairly easy to connect the wiring to the existing breaker panel.

He said to the group, "We are going to be facing the most hectic seven years in the history of mankind. We need someplace to hideout and this looks pretty promising. It will require a lot of work but I think it is worthwhile. I don't want to seem to be pushing my own ideas, so if someone has anything to say then speak up."

There were a few comments, mostly positive toward using the area.

"Where's the money going to come from for the project?" someone asked.

"From us I suppose. There might be a bank account for the church but I don't know if we will be able to access the funds. I think we should do the work ourselves so as to keep what we are doing secret. I don't think it will take a lot of funds. The major expenses will be a sturdy door, concealed if possible, and reworking the venting system. We can move furniture from other areas and set up the workspace. Are there any among us who opposes the project?"

Nobody did, so Connor continued, "Any of you got any construction experience?"

Several hands went up.

"Let's see if we can identify where the venting system comes up outside. Once we locate it we can start listing the materials we need for the project. I don't want to seem to be putting the cart before the horse, but once the Antichrist starts his rise to power we are going to be pressed for time. Those who are in his camp will report us for sure."

"I don't believe it is a good idea to have everyone outside looking for the vent. Someone will notice a large group for sure and might remember it later."

A middle-aged man by the name of Larry Elliott was in the construction business and volunteered to handle the materials list. When four of them went outside to locate the old venting system it was not as hard a job as they thought it would be. They paced off the distance they had measured inside the church and found that an outside storage shed was in the location where it should be. The shed of course was locked and Connor sent someone inside to find the key.

Once in the shed they didn't see any evidence of the vent. The walls were made of concrete blocks but the floor was wood.

Larry said, "I'll bet they built this shed to disguise the vent from the start. I don't know how old this is, but it looks as if it could be old enough to have been built at the same time as the original building. I will bring some tools tomorrow and we will tear the flooring up and see if I am right."

They all went back inside and told the others what they had found.

"I think we should all meet in the morning and try to get better organized. I think we should plan for the long term and we need to have someone responsible for all the functions that are needed to continue the mission of the church. I think first and foremost we should be spokesmen and women for Christ. There are going to be a lot of people who need to hear about Christ and that should be our foremost purpose. All of you make a list of the things you think we need to do and we will refine the list tomorrow. We can then get on with making preparations," Connor said.

It was nearing 4:00 p.m. when they broke up.

Connor noted the number of cars in the church parking lot after everyone had left. Some of them probably belonged to church employees who were there when the rapture occurred. He made that the first item on his list. It might have seemed a convenient place to store the cars that were towed and the towing companies had no room for.

Conner was an investment broker by profession. He didn't see much need for that particular skill in the time remaining. He had enough money saved to see him through the seven years unless something devalued the dollar. He knew that a one world government was coming and when that happened he would probably lose everything anyway. He would use what they needed to keep the church going and stockpile food and other necessities as a first step while the money still had value.

He went out for pizza that evening and worked on his list while he was waiting for his food order.

Accessibility was the first item. What that meant was they had to have some way to reach people who needed to hear the word while not revealing the secret space until they were sure about the person's conviction. That would require a lot of thought to get that procedure established.

He listed a food coordinator who would be responsible for acquiring and storing food items. They would want to shop at the warehouse type store, COSTCO, SAM's CLUB and the like, never buying in large enough quantities to call attention to what they were doing.

He listed a security coordinator who would be responsible for maintaining a watch on the church. This was an area that would require a lot of discussion because he felt very strongly that they needed to be armed to combat those sent by the Antichrist to eliminate their activities.

They would not require a nursery coordinator since the little ones were now in heaven.

Information coordinator was another position he felt was necessary to get the word out when there was an emergency of any sort, and as time passed there were sure to be many.

As he devoured the pizza he continued to work on the list.

There was a lot he didn't know about the structure of the church staff. He knew that a minister was required, and preferably an assistant. They would need a secretary, probably two to work on the internet material. There was sure to be a lot he hadn't thought about.

When he got back home he turned on the television to see what the rest of the world was saying about the mass disappearances. The newscaster continued to report on crime, government functions, and local opinions about what had happened.

Without fail all those interviewed mentioned conspiracy and science, even others government involvement. None brought up the Bible as the document which foretold the event.

It appeared to Connor that the majority were indeed going to be like the waitress thay had talked to at lunch.

He heard an interview with a Jewish Knesset member who disclaimed the religious aspect of the disappearances. "I have believed in God and kept his tenets for my entire life and if the disappearances were orchestrated by God then I would no longer be here. No, there's some other explanation that we haven't discovered yet. It could possibly be that aliens beamed up those who are missing to their space ships."

That interview gave Connor pause for worry. If those who lived according to Talmudic laws or were followers of

Judaism were all still alive then the verse about the only way to the Father being through the Son had to be the explanation.

Those who believed in the Old Testament but did not believe that the New Testament was God's word included a lot of Jews. That might be one reason that there would be 144,000 who made the connection based on the rapture. In that light it made a lot more sense to Connor that the 144,000 would make the leap of faith.

The President of Turkey was interviewed and tried to assert a calming influence. "Whatever has happened it is imperative that world leaders come together to assure the safety of all of us. I propose that a summit be convened by the United Nations to address the issue and bring order to all law-abiding nations."

The interview was a pretty long one and the Turk handled the questions in what was on the surface a logical and thoughtful manner.

Connor's opinion when the interview was over was that he had just possibly gotten a glimpse of the Antichrist. He was charismatic and seemed to want to help deal with the situation but that was the very characteristics that the Antichrist was supposed to have.

He jotted a note on his list to discuss him when they got together the following day.

The local news dealt with an upswing in lawlessness. Since the disappearances thieves were ransacking the homes of those no longer around. The homeless could pretty much choose a house where no one was home and have shelter, as well as food left in the pantries and refrigerators.

There were not enough police to respond to all the calls and even the cops who responded were likely to help themselves to anything that appealed to them.

That part of the aftereffects of the rapture Biblical scholars hit closer to the mark. Some of those left had a sense of right and wrong but had no moral compass to govern their actions.

This situation is only going to get worse he thought, and it isn't going to be long before it starts to affect those who have become believers.

It was going to be essential that they organize properly from the start. While the people had still not come up with an explanation for the disappearances it would not be long before a definite split between those who had become believers and those who had not could be seen. When that happened the lines would be drawn and life would become that much harder for those like himself.

He made a note to discuss cyber security at the next meeting. Since the righteous had been raptured those adept at hacking would have a clear field to locate computers and that could spell real trouble for the groups of believers that would come into being over the next few years.

Connor spent some more time on the computer trying to get a feel for the Israeli situation. It was too soon yet to draw any conclusions from what was on the social media, but since the Jewish people had historically been believers in the Old Testament they had a belief in the Godhead figure. Because those remaining didn't accept the New Testament they didn't have the necessary belief in Christ until the rapture. With the foundation in Bible belief they could make the jump to the truth of the New Testament much easier than those who had no foundational beliefs. That helped explain where the 144,000 sealed by God would come from. It made sense to him from that standpoint.

That there were posts on all the social media sites talking about the possibility that the disappearances were religiously based was more than he had heard on the television news stations.

The list he started had grown considerably and he went to bed thinking about all that needed to be done.

Chapter 4

Life in the nation's capital slowed to a crawl. The usual news of Senate and Congressional actions came to a standstill. There were not enough of the elected officials left to carry out the functions for which they had been elected. The newly sworn in President was not the sharpest knife in the drawer, as the saying went, and had a tough first week trying to deal with a bad situation. His charisma was the reason that he had been chosen as the running mate for the now disappeared elected President. His former boss had not given him a lot of responsibility, and nothing that required any degree of analysis or decision making ability.

He now became a pawn of the heavy hitters in the Senate and Congress who were left, as well as the special interest groups. It would take almost a month for the newly appointed officials to fill the roles of those who had disappeared.

In the meantime it was not safe to be out after dark unless you were with a group, or carried a weapon. Lest I paint a picture of a city in desperation you must remember that all those left were ones who did not believe in Christ. Not all of them were crooks or thugs. Some had been law abiding citizens with good moral values and good intentions. What separated the two groups eluded Connor. He supposed that some of them were very similar to himself in their life styles. They were basically good people who simply had no spiritual values.

When Connor awoke the following morning it was the third day after the rapture. He had a quick breakfast and drove to the church where he had spent the last two days.

He thought he would be early, as it was not yet 8:00 a.m. but the number of cars in the lot told him that many were already there.

He locked his car and went inside. There were now close to 50 people there. The ages seemed to represent those from teenagers to geriatrics.

One of the people sitting in the pews he heard say, "Here comes the pastor now."

He didn't know whether to be pleased by the comment or if he should straighten the matter out forthwith. He did not have the traditional calling that most pastors talked about, but the situation that had been thrust upon him almost demanded that he accept the position as the best qualified to try to put the church back together. There were others who could probably do as good a job, but Connor had some definite ideas about how to proceed in the trying times they were about to endure.

He shook the thought off and moved to the front of the group. He looked the group over and said, "I notice a lot of new faces this morning. Why don't each of you tell us why you are here?" He pointed to a middle aged man in the second pew.

The man stood and looked around at the others. "I guess I am here for the same reason as everyone else. My wife and children disappeared, along with a lot of others. I concluded that those missing were the ones usually in church on Sundays, and sometimes more often. I was preached to enough by my wife and kids that I recognized immediately what had happened. I think those who disappeared are in heaven now and I decided that I wanted to be there as well when my time is over here."

Connor pointed to another of the new ones.

"I'm kinda like that gentleman. A lot of my friends are gone, and all of them were church people. I decided that what they had been trying to tell me for so long was true. I don't like the alternative of being here with non-believers so I want to do what is necessary to be with them when I die."

The stories that came out as all the new arrivals told of their background and experiences were very similar. It took the better part of half an hour to get through them all.

When they were finished Connor said, "All of us here were in the same boat a few days ago. None of us believed the Bible, and in particular, none of us believed in Jesus Christ as Lord and Savior. Each of us here equate the disappearances to Christ calling his children home. Is that enough to convince us that belief in the Bible will get us to where we need to be to satisfy God's requirements? I don't know the answer to that question yet, but I am going to study the Bible and find out. I know that the New Testament says that the only way to the Father is through the Son. I take that to mean that you must believe that Jesus came to earth, born of a woman, and died for the sins of the entire world."

"If any of you believe that you are taking the easy way out, let me disabuse you of that notion right now. If anything you are making your lives harder by accepting Christ. The next seven years are going to be unlike anything the earth has ever known. What's left out there," Connor said waving his arm at the outside world, "are those who have no belief in Christ, or God for that matter. The last book of the Bible tells us what to expect and when to expect it. But, the bottom line is that if you profess a belief in Jesus Christ, then you are open game for the Antichrist and his followers. Having said that, I believe it is too soon yet for the Antichrist to try to plant spies in our midst so we will accept you at face value."

"I want to pray and then have some discussion about how we are going to organize ourselves."

He launched immediately into a prayer for guidance from God and for protection of the group. He prayed for wisdom and the ability to recognize what God wanted the group to do.

"Before we get too far into any plans we need to address a couple of issues that might be critical to our survival. I know that some of you will be against firearms, especially in a religious setting, but the other side, once they organize are going to try to root us out. I believe our very survival is going to depend on our ability to defend ourselves at some time. What I propose is that we establish a small arsenal of rifles and pistols here at the church, and that we always have access to a weapon, whether on our person, or in a vehicle."

"Do you think that is really necessary?" one of the woman asked.

"Let me read you again what Revelation says from the seventh chapter on." He read it aloud to the entire group.

When he had finished he said, "Now, is there anyone here who wants to face any of that without some way to defend yourselves. As believers in Christ you will be persecuted by the forces of the Antichrist. You will be forced to worship him or bear the consequences. Many of us will not live to see the end of the tribulation period, and some will succumb to the false teachings of the Antichrist. With a weapon you can defend yourselves to some degree."

Many of the men in the group were nodding their heads affirmatively as were some of the women.

Connor went on, "Once we acquire the weapons we will need to make sure that everyone knows how to use them. I suggest some firearms training within the next two weeks for everyone."

"The next item is cyber security. For those of you not familiar with the term it is the ability to exploit communications, when you use your cell phone, i-pad or computer. You might also remember that most cars have GPS locators in them. It is a simple matter for anyone with the knowledge to locate any car, phone, or computer to a very narrow area. In other words, when the other side comes into power they will use those devices to track us. I am not knowledgeable enough to even give you a good explanation about what all that entails, but I believe it is essential that we find a believer with those skills to make sure we don't do something dumb."

Heads nodded and one of the new people raised his hand.

Connor pointed to him and he stood.

"You are right on the money with all that. That is how the CIA traced the bad guys in the Middle East for years. I worked in that field and can help out with some countermeasures that will make their job harder. I'm not sure we can eliminate everything that they might exploit, but we can make the job a lot harder for them."

"Okay, if there are no objections you are now our cyber security chief. Start working up some lesson plans to educate us all."

"You new folks I assume are here because you have come to a belief in Christ. That being the case you will want to be baptized. The rest of us did that yesterday. If you want to be baptized today raise your hands."

Everyone raised their hands.

"Okay, while the preparations are being made we can go on to the other organizational things we need to think about. Did all of you give it some thought last night?"

Heads nodded yes.

"Our first responsibility, according to what I read is to bring others to Christ. In order to do that we are going to have to have regular services until it becomes impossible to do it openly. We will need to keep the church web site up and running, and we will also have to print brochures explaining what happened and why. It is going to take several of us to do that. I suggest that we form an outreach committee to deal with that consisting of at least four people, maybe as many as six."

Three ladies raised their hands and commented that they would be willing to help with that.

"Does anyone else have anything we need to do?"

The carpenter, Larry Elliott stood. "We have the bomb shelter in the basement that looks like it will make a good hideout if we design it right. I want to conceal the entrance is such a way that it will be hard for anyone who doesn't know about it to detect it. I think we also need some alternate locations to meet if things go really bad quickly. I suggest we modify some homes with enough space to move to if we are discovered here. I want to start on the basement today and I need several men who know a bit about the building trade. You don't have to be experts, just know how to use hand tools. How many of you have pickup trucks?"

Three raised their hands.

"You guys are going to go to three different stores to pick up materials. I have started a list and we will refine it before we send you on your way. We are going to need somewhere around $1,000.00 to start this. It might take more than that but I think that will be enough for starters."

Connor turned and picked up one of the collection plates, took his wallet out and put what money he had in the plate and passed it on. Everyone else did the same and when it had made the rounds it looked like there was enough to get started.

Larry told the three with pickups to divide the money three ways and to do the same with the list of materials he had made out.

Connor asked the three ladies who had indicated that they were willing to help with the administrative chores to come with him to the offices.

"There are three functional computers here. Once the room is finished in the basement I want to shift all this stuff down there. We can set up a couple of dummy positions to look as if this is where we conduct business, but the real work will be done in the basement. We will set them up to run off the WIFI from the main computer. That way we only need one computer line going to the basement. Think about what we need in the way of printers and office supplies."

Larry took a group downstairs to start the clean-up that would be necessary to start the project. The first thing he did was trace the electric lines from the bomb shelter to find out where the wires terminated. He discovered that they had simply been bundled and tied off from the live wires. It took less than an hour to get the power back on in the shelter. With light they could better see what needed to be done inside.

Although there was a somewhat musty smell he did not see any evidence of water, which was a very good sign. He had a closer look at the venting system. It was a one way affair that only brought air into the space. He needed some way to vent the stale air. In the event that someone set fire to the main building those inside the shelter might be able to survive with a two way system.

He looked the vent over and determined that he could split the opening and have one side taking air out and the other side blowing air in. He would need to devise a ducting system to pull the stale air from a distance away from where the fresh air would be coming in but it was a pretty simple job. He took out his notebook and started making a material list for what was needed.

Some of the ladies had come down and were now searching for cleaning materials to get rid of the dust and musty smell.

The pickup trucks returned soon and the material was brought down the back steps to the basement and Larry showed them where to place things. He then went to his own truck with a couple of helpers and carted his tools to the basement.

When Connor came down he was amazed at the size of the room. He had only had a flashlight the night before.

Now the overhead lights were on and he could see the size of the room. It was easily sixty by eighty feet.

Larry told him his idea about the ducting system and Connor nodded his approval.

"I want to make the door out of steel and have it mounted on rollers with dead bolt locks going into the concrete from both sides. It will be electronically operated but the control will be hidden on the opposite wall in some way. I haven't got it all worked out yet, but if we can get someone to paint a biblical scene on the metal it can be disguised as a large painting. If I can get the seams to match up good it will not be noticeable. Even if someone sees the small cracks at the edges I don't believe they will be able to dislodge the door without some serious pneumatic tools. Also, if the venting system works out we should be able to survive a long time if necessary. The only drawback is the lack of restrooms in the room. As long as things are normal we can exit the room and use the regular bathrooms, but if we are under siege we will need to think of something to use."

"How about the chemical toilets they use in recreational vehicles?" Connor asked.

"That's a good idea. We can buy a couple and just leave them dormant until there is a need to use them," Larry said and scribbled a note in his pad.

"You don't think I am being too paranoid about this do you?" Connor asked.

"Not by a long shot. Just from what you read to us we are going to be in for a really rough time and everything we can do now to increase the odds for survival when things get tough will be time and money well spent," Larry replied.

"Listen, I have a pretty substantial bank account. I think the money will be almost worthless when the one world government comes into being, so we might as well spend what we need to in order to make this room as secure as possible," Connor said.

37

"I was thinking along those lines. With my wife gone on I don't have much need for what I have either. I will kick in whatever is needed to get the job done. I also think we are at the point where we don't want to advertise this unless we are absolutely sure about new converts."

"I agree. We are 47 strong with the new additions today. I want to appoint someone as security officer to keep an eye on things. I also believe it would be a good idea to install the spy cameras so popular on the outside and inside of the main building. We can have the signals sent to this room and monitor it whenever someone is here."

"That's a good idea as well. When I install the lines for the door I will add enough extra line to bring the signals in from the cameras."

While Larry and his crew were working on the interior of the bomb shelter Connor went back to the sanctuary and called the others together.

"I think we have a pretty good start on what needs to be done now. I want to caution everyone not to broadcast anything about this to outsiders. All it will take is for one wrong person to become aware of what we are doing and it will all be for naught. Remember, those who support the Antichrist will lie as a matter of routine. They will profess to be believers in Christ just to tear us down. The consequences will not be a slap on the wrist, or a few days in jail, but will cost many of us our lives. We really need to be security conscious at all times. Now, those who want to be baptized let's go to the baptistery and get on with it."

The new members were baptized and everyone got back to work.

The social hall, which had been erected as a separate building after the original construction was well stocked with tables and chairs. They were going to need some way to cook, or at least warm food in the bomb shelter after it was finished and Connor told Thelma Burgess, who was the lady he appointed as secretary, to organize a team to bring some of the chairs and tables to the basement of the old building so that when the changes were finished they could move them in for use there. "Make sure you get some of the cooking gear as well. If we get stuck in the room for any length of time that will be a welcome addition."

Connor went back to the basement to see what he could do to help with that project. He asked Larry to make sure he ran some 220 Volt lines to handle stoves or ovens.

Larry made another note in his notebook.

The work inside the room went very quickly. The item that gave them the most trouble was to be expected. The door had to be fabricated from sheet metal and they had no welding equipment, but one of the men with the pickup suggested that they rent a welding set. Larry quickly agreed and that was done the following morning. The panels that would form the inside and outside of the door had to be welded in place and only one man from the group had any experience with welding equipment. The end product had to be ground to smooth out the welding marks and the bolts which would slide into the concrete facing had to be exact. They also had to be mounted on a sturdy bar on the inside of the door to work properly. It took four of them the entire day to get it right but the end product was passable. The outside was smooth and fit snugly into the opening.

While the others were putting the finishing touches on the door itself Larry ran the wires to the control panel.

They waited until the next morning to mount the door and that gave them almost as much trouble as fabricating the thing in the first place. The door was on rollers and was easily moveable once the sliding bolts were disengaged.

Larry mounted the control panel about halfway down the opposite wall behind a framed picture. When the proper code was entered the door didn't move. The lock simply disengaged. The door would have to be pushed within thirty seconds or the lock would reengage. He explained the system to the others and they nodded understanding.

"I'm going to put mounting brackets on the inside so that a bar can be slid in to keep the door closed in case anyone discovers the control panel while we are inside. That won't be as effective as the sliding bolts but will require a lot of force to dislodge the brackets holding the bar in place."

The rapture had occurred on Monday and by the end of the week they had all the construction changes made.

One of the women was an amateur artist and volunteered to paint a scene on the door if she could get some help.

The venting system worked pretty much like Larry thought it would. He mounted an air scoop on top of the storage shed with a screen to keep bugs out and oriented it in the direction from which the wind usually blew. He installed an electric blower, just in case it might be needed in the future. He also mounted a small electric blower in the bomb shelter to push the stale air up the duct. It was very quiet and would help to pull the fresh air into the room.

Once all the modifications had been made they moved the chairs and computers into the room. They also brought some movable screens to section off the areas for sleeping if it became necessary, which was almost a certainty before much longer.

Their numbers grew by another 15 before the week was over. No one mentioned what was going on in the basement to the new arrivals until the following week. They interviewed them very carefully before letting them in on the secret.

They started buying up consumables. Paper, printer ink, food, whatever they could think of that they might need in the future.

Larry installed the cameras at strategic points and ran the lines to the basement.

Norm Layne, the computer guy hooked them to a television screen and they were in business.

Only one computer line was brought into the space, and that from the cable outside the church building.

They had a brief worship service each morning before starting to work. Several of the men still worked regular jobs and were not there until evening time.

They slowly settled into a routine.

Connor had started to inject scripture from other books of the Bible into his talks to try to give everyone a better understanding of the entire Bible. He especially concentrated on the Books of Daniel, Isaiah and Matthew to make everyone aware of the earlier prophecies that Revelation concerned.

They decided to continue to have Sunday services and Connor was to fill the role of pastor. He would concentrate on the New Testament for these talks to try to make people aware of the path to belief in Christ.

Nobody knew if they would even have anyone show up on the first Sunday, other than their group but felt they should follow the scriptures in telling others about Jesus.

Most of those in their group had invited friends to Sunday services and surprisingly a number showed up. It was nothing like the numbers that routinely attended the church, pre-rapture, but there were enough to encourage the others that their efforts were worthwhile.

Connor concentrated on the scripture dealing with coming to faith in Christ. He only touched on the Book of Revelation during the last few minutes of his talk. (He hesitated to call it a sermon)

"All of us here are new believers. Why is that you might ask?"

"We believe that the mass disappearances were in fact the rapture prophesied in the Bible in several different

41

places, but nowhere as graphic as in the last book of the Bible, Revelation. We believe that we are in for a really rough time in the next seven years, which is called the Tribulation in the Bible. I don't know the reason for your being here today, but I have to assume you have questions about the disappearance of so many people simultaneously. You have to suspect that the root cause might be something supernatural, and of course you are right. We will have a brief time now for those of you who want to be sure about your own salvation to come forward and talk about it."

One of the ladies was a pianist and she played a hymn as most of the newcomers came to the front of the church. Only three of the newcomers did not come forward.

After the hymn was finished Connor said a prayer and dismissed the service. "Thank you all for being here today. If you have any spiritual needs in your life please don't hesitate to call on us. Those of you who came forward, if you would remain for a few minutes we will get some additional information from you and hopefully answer any questions you may have."

Only the three who had not come forward left the church.

Chapter 5

It was in the second week after the rapture that the president of Turkey made the appeal for a worldwide summit of heads of state. He proposed that the meeting be held in Rome, with the concurrence of the new Pope. The ranks of the Catholics had been thinned considerably by the rapture and only a small number remained in the Vatican. They had agreed to house all the world representatives who would come to ease the burden of transportation and housekeeping.

The proposed summit was for the following Monday. The Turkish leader had already gotten verbal commitments from half the world's countries and expected that most of those he had not coordinated with beforehand would show up as well.

When the church group met the following morning Connor brought up the possibility that the Turkish President might very well be the Antichrist.

"Why do you think that?" asked one of the ladies.

"Well for one thing, the Bible says that he will arise to become the one world leader by proposing peace. That is essentially what this man is doing. No one else has stepped up and the Bible is very clear that it will happen, and very early after the rapture, which is where we are right now. Remember, all those who will be at the summit are non-believers and probably don't have the foggiest idea about what has been prophesied. If he is the Antichrist it will be fairly simple for this man to assume the leadership position because he is the only one at the meeting who will know for sure what happened to all those who disappeared."

"I guess it makes sense in that light, but how can we be sure he is the Antichrist?"

"By what happens at the summit. I don't have the answers to those questions. All I can do is wait for events to unfold and see how they line up with the Bible. The single thing that will signal the beginning of the tribulation is the signing of a treaty with Israel. No one except a head of state will have that authority," Connor said.

The number of people at the church had grown to over 100 and they still had the morning meetings for discussion and reinforcement. Connor was doing an admirable job for one who resisted the Lord for so long. Others were stepping forward as well and the web site had new information each day. The site was getting a lot of action as far as people accessing the site, but they had no way to gauge the impact of the information they were putting out.

Norm had set the site up with a bogus address, but it would be a simple matter for anyone to copy the address of the church and locate it that way. As a matter of fact the first Sunday after they got the site running they had visitors at the morning service who said they had gotten the address off the web site.

Norm talked to Connor after the services that Sunday and suggested that they try to make the web site more anonymous before it became general knowledge that they were the sponsors. "If we take the address off the site the opposition will have no way to locate us. I used a fictitious address so when they look at that location it will not tell them much."

"I kind of like the idea of reaching people in the area who need to hear the word, but I understand what you are saying."

"We can list a cell phone number as a point of contact. I can disable the GPS function in the phone and it should be safe to use," Norm said.

"Okay, let's do it that way. What will happen when someone tries to locate the phone and finds out that they can't do it?"

"By that time the Antichrist will have arisen and they can probably just have the phone taken out of service. We will then do it over again with another number. I want to get a new phone under a fictitious name so they cannot tie it to anyone here," Norm said.

"You know a lot more about that kind of thing than anyone else here, so have at it."

The group was using the bomb shelter for the work while keeping someone in the office in case anyone stopped by.

They were all learning on the fly. They had to become more adept at the shady side as well as try to learn what God required of them.

When the weekend before the summit rolled around all the television stations started to carry almost continuous coverage of the coming event. It appeared that most of the world leaders would be in attendance. News reporters put the question of all the major countries and didn't find any who would forego the meeting.

The media carried almost continuous coverage of the Rome airport beginning on the Sunday before and a steady stream of jets delivered the world leaders to the summit. Limousines were lined up to ferry the groups to the Vatican and did so on a steady schedule. The biggest problem was the national anthems of the different countries. The band seemed to be a bit on the light side and it was obvious that the regular band leader was not in attendance.

The Vatican requested that only one camera crew do the filming within the grounds and that all other news outlets use the same video.

The news people didn't much like it but reluctantly agreed to the procedure.

The largest room in the Vatican was used for the meetings and that is where the camera was set up. There were meetings between individual leaders not available to the media, but that would have been the case in any event.

When the news coverage of the meeting got underway they said that only two countries were not represented and that there had been travel difficulties for those two countries, one in Africa, and one in the Far East.

There were three female heads of state, Romania, India and Taiwan.

The Turkish President, whose name was Ahmet Demir, chaired the meeting, since he had been the major force behind setting it up. There were no opening prayers, no moment of silence, nothing to recognize the large number of people who no longer called the earth home.

He got right into the meat of the matter with his opening speech. "As you all know, something extraordinary happened just two weeks ago. Many of our fellow citizens vanished from the earth. So far as placing responsibility, there has been no indication of involvement of any country on earth. I suppose it is possible that some alien civilization might be responsible, but the more likely event is that it had to do with retribution by some God or Gods not happy with the devoutness of their worshippers. I think we should put that behind us and try to get on with our lives. The only thing that has changed is that there are fewer inhabitants now on our planet. For better or worse our planet has undergone a huge change and we are going to be faced with a lack of ability to even feed everyone unless we take some drastic action to make sure the food supply continues to be adequate. I would now hear any comments from within this group as to how to deal with the problem."

One by one the representatives of the world's countries made a statement. Some were simply agreeing that something should be done, while others waxed philosophical about what might have happened to those who disappeared. Most of the theories reflected the kind of stuff available on the internet and not a single person talked about the possibility that the disappearances might be in fulfillment of Biblical Prophecy.

That pattern continued until the Romanian President, Madam Gonzorov came to the podium.

"Unlike most of you, I have a pretty good idea about what happened to those missing from our midst. Have you noticed that those who are missing are mostly people of the church? I hate to have to say this, being in the presence of the major faith of the Bible, but it seems to me that the people who worshipped the Biblical God must have been less than faithful to their calling. I think their God got so upset with them that he simply wiped them off the face of the earth. My God would never do that. He wants us to be peace loving and helpful to each other. That's why it is so important to come together in this time of crisis and act in one accord. We need to help our less fortunate brothers and sisters and the way to do that is to bolster the economies of the more fortunate countries and get us all on an even footing."

She went on for almost thirty minutes and as the camera panned the members in their seats one could see a lot of nodded agreement.

Connor was fascinated by her speech. She was in her forties and boasted a very appealing figure. Her unblemished skin was very photogenic and she seemed totally at ease in front of the camera. She was the first of the entire group that had made any mention of the Bible and her hypothesis for the disappearances seemed to be well received. That she acknowledged so many people of the faith could be punished by God validated the existence of the object of their worship. The spin she gave to the event made it seem that the Biblical God was washing his hands of the world and her God, who she had not identified, was more benevolent and understanding.

Connor sat deep in thought in front of the television. He had thought that the Turkish President was setting himself up as the Antichrist but now had to rethink that assessment. Was it possible that the Antichrist could be a woman? What he could recall from his reading always referred to the Antichrist in the male form but that could just be a linguistic nuance. He would discuss this with the group the next day, especially if the Romanian leader wound up at the top of the heap from this summit.

The summit was to be a three day affair and not all the proceedings would be televised. Connor thought that he would give a lot to be privy to what went on at the private meetings.

There were obviously a lot of private meetings because from the start of the second day the direction of the summit could be discerned by those who had the advantage of being believers in Christ. Most of the second day's discussion dealt with coming to some agreement about worldwide cooperation in some format other than the United Nations. Those familiar with the history of the U.N. would know that the organization had never been very effective in dealing with world problems in any substantive manner.

Connor felt sure that the results of the summit would give them a clear indication of who the Antichrist actually was. Admittedly he was interpreting the situation from a shallow knowledge of what was prophesied to occur but all he could do was try to fit the pieces together with what the Bible said would happen.

The discussion at the church the day after the initial meetings was very lively.

Connor started off by praying. He then asked if everyone had watched the proceedings at the Vatican summit.

Everyone had watched at least some of the news coverage.

"What part of the proceedings impressed you the most?"

"I thought that most of the theories of the disappearances were taken directly from the social media," one woman said.

"I was kind of thrown by the Romanian President who said it was the Biblical God who was punishing his worshippers. That was the first time anyone had even mentioned the Bible," Thelma said.

Several more made comments but nobody mentioned what Connor thought was the most important aspect of the day's activities.

"Did it occur to any of you that the Romanian President might be setting herself up as the Antichrist?" he asked.

"But that couldn't be," someone said. "Doesn't the Bible talk about the Antichrist as a man?"

"I don't know if it does or not. I know that the reference always seems to be in the masculine, but nowhere does it definitively state that the Antichrist will be male, at least to my knowledge. I was struck by her carriage and charisma during her speech, and the others at the meeting seemed to be in agreement with the points she made. She was also the only one to mention the Bible and acknowledge the existence of our God. Maybe I am way off base, but I think that before the summit is over she will end up being top-dog."

"I did notice that she was very attractive and carried herself really well. She didn't seem to be ill at ease in front of the camera and doesn't Satan use women a lot to get his way? Look at Adam and Eve and Jezebel," Larry said.

"There's a lot of truth in that," Connor said. "I just think we are going to have to look at this with an open mind. Remember, the Antichrist is not Satan, but Satan's henchman, or woman."

"In this situation a woman might fit his needs better," one of the women said.

During the second and third days of the summit Madam Gonzorov seemed to be everywhere the camera was. She and the Turkish president were seen together a lot with smaller groups. Toward the end of the second day the Turk called everyone together in the meeting room and made an announcement to the worldwide television audience that the group had voted to disband the United Nations in favor of a stronger coalition of world leaders. The facilities of the U.N. would be left in place to act as the action arm of the new World Coalition. This meeting would be the initial gathering of the members and the new charter would be drawn up while they were all still together at the Vatican.

In the afternoon of the third day the announcement was made that Madam Gonzorov had been elected as Chairperson of the new group. She came to the podium and talked about the new charter and how the organization would work.

"The new organization will have greater power to enforce the laws of the world. It will provide observers to nations having weapons of mass destruction to ensure that weapons are not used. Each nation will provide up to five percent of their population to support the coalition thereby distributing the responsibility evenly throughout the world. Part of the charter deals with the equitable distribution of foodstuffs and a separate division of the coalition will deal with that."

"The current U.N. building in New York will serve as our headquarters for the present time with plans to establish other regional facilities. Only the general outline of the responsibilities has been developed at this meeting. The first and most important chore of the group will be to finalize the charter's powers and constraints. Because of the fears of the Jewish people based on their religious beliefs the committee agreed to sign a treaty designating Israel as a neutral ground and Coalition forces will be dispatched there to insure that no country violates that tenet. World commerce will continue but the World Coalition will provide a blueprint for distribution of food to guarantee that all countries receive adequate supplies of foodstuffs. If necessary, all of us will contribute to a fund to make sure the needy are not ignored. There are a lot of details that need to be worked out but we will do so as the first item on our agenda. I will step down as President of my country to devote all my energy to the Coalition."

When Connor heard the speech he thought, "Well, there it is. If she isn't the Antichrist then the real item is waiting in the wings."

Chapter 6

Connor had not even bothered to let his company know that he was still among the living. He had simply stopped going to work. He made sure he could access the money in his retirement plan and had it transferred to his regular bank account very early after the disappearances.

As one week became two weeks, then a month, the operation of the church smoothed out. He spent a lot of his time there, studying and preparing his talks, which he still didn't refer to as sermons. The painting the lady did on the door was very good, and the areas around the perimeter of the door had been sanded and filled with putty to further smooth them out. After a coat of paint was added it was very difficult to recognize that the painting was actually a door. Other paintings were done in other areas very similar so that the door wouldn't stand out.

All the men, and even some of the women had purchased guns and ammunition, in some cases multiple weapons, so that the armory inside the bomb shelter would provide a weapon for everyone. The weapons were stored in a cabinet built for that purpose by Larry. They didn't have to worry about the young accessing the weapons because there were no young left. The youngest in their group was 13, and he looked as big as most of the adults.

Two or three car loads of the group would travel to a desolate part of the countryside to practice with the weapons until everyone at least knew how to load and fire them.

As they got around to looking at the cots they found that most were dry rotted. They were made of canvas and the material had rotted over the years. Instead of trying to repair them they visited camping stores and bought new ones, a few at a time.

Connor suggested that they develop a watch list to have people in the shelter at all times. One of the upper middle-aged men volunteered to simply move into the shelter and keep an eye on things at night. That was accepted as a short term solution. As the situation changed they would change their mode of operation to fit the needs.

The web site was getting thousands of hits each day. There were apparently a lot of people out there still looking for answers.

Norm had added a section to the web site of frequently asked questions and also added an e-mail address for personal contact. Nobody thought they would get a lot of action on the e-mail side but they were getting hundreds of e-mails a day. A lot of them were from other parts of the world, especially Europe and China.

The traffic from Israel in particular was also heavy.

Connor remembered his dream the night after the rapture when he had thought God had told him to contact the Israeli converts.

One of the e-mails was brought to his attention by Thelma.

"I think you need to read this," she said, handing him a print-out of the e-mail.

Connor did so and got a chilling sensation in his gut. The e-mail said, 'My name is Ephraim. I live in Israel and have been watching your web site since the rapture. I had a vision from God telling me to contact you. I know this might sound strange but would it be possible for you to come to Israel, or for me to come to you? You obviously are a new believer and I think it would be beneficial to both our groups to establish a regular means of communication for the coming times. I am including a phone number where you can reach me as well. I look forward to hearing from you soon.'

Connor said to Thelma, "The first night after the rapture I was so overwhelmed that I couldn't even think straight. I went to bed and prayed for God to give me some guidance and help me make the right decisions. When I awoke the next morning I had a faint recollection that God had told me to contact the remnant in Israel. I thought that was a rather large presumption on my part and didn't know if it was really God telling me something or not. I guess this verifies that the directions came from God."

Connor did the arithmetic for the difference in time zones and found that it would be the middle of the afternoon in Israel. He called the number given on his cell phone.

Ephraim answered on the second ring.

"This is Connor Frederick in Washington. I received your e-mail."

"Thank you for calling back so promptly. When we noticed your web site some of my group talked about it. It was there so soon after the disappearances that we thought you might have biblical background. Then last night I had a vision from God telling me to get in touch," Ephraim said.

"When the rapture occurred I knew right away what had happened. I had gone to church when I was married to my wife, who is now in heaven, and enough rubbed off on me to recognize what had happened. I became an instant believer. When I got home that evening I read Revelation through twice and cross referenced some scriptures. I worked until almost midnight and prayed before I went to sleep. When I awoke I remembered God telling me to contact your group. I didn't know if it was a dream or if it really happened. I got so wrapped up in our church efforts here that I didn't give it much more thought until I got your e-mail. What is it that you want to do?"

"I would like to make some plans for the hard times that we both know are coming. I believe it is essential that we witness to as many non-believers as possible in the time we have before things start to get really rough. If we could sit down and talk for a couple of days we should be able to come up with the essentials. Would it be possible to host a group from Israel at your church?"

"Certainly. We have over 150 members now and we can put you up in private homes. I too believe that the better we are prepared for what is to come the better off we will be. Aside from that I now take the Bible seriously when it says to go forth and make disciples," Connor said with a chuckle.

"I have your number on my caller ID. Can I get together with my people to discuss it and call you back later today?"

"Of course. The number is my cell phone so you should be able to reach me at any time."

The web site was generating a lot of inquiries and it took two people almost full time to respond to the phone calls. Their efforts were doing a lot better than Connor thought they had any right to expect. At least there were others out there searching for answers. The third weekend after the rapture they had over 250 for the Sunday morning services.

Connor followed his instincts and tried to teach the basics of a belief in Christ as the Son of God and that the way to the Father was through the Son. He always talked some about the Book of Revelation and pointed out that the mass disappearances were fulfillment of the scripture. He basically wanted to put the word out that the only way to eternal life was God's way.

He was working on a series on Revelation but was still searching for supporting scripture. He really didn't have a good grasp of theology and needed to search for scriptures that most theologians would know from their studies.

When Ephraim called back later that evening he asked if they could house a group of five.

"As many as you want to bring. We need all the help we can get," Connor told him.

"We will make flight arrangements as soon as possible and I will let you know when and what flight number we will be on. I assume you are at the address you had on the web site earlier in Washington?"

"That's correct. Once we know when you are to arrive we will arrange transportation from the airport. I suggest you fly into Dulles if you have a choice in the matter. E-mail me a picture so I will know who to look for."

The next morning at the usual meeting he told the others that a group from Israel would be coming to visit and make plans. "I believe there will be five and we will put them up in our homes. I believe this is part of the group referred to in Revelation as the 144,000 who will be sealed by God."

Even the morning sessions were drawing almost 100 people now. Some were members they had picked up during the Sunday services, but others showed up as first time visitors. Some were just driving by and saw all the cars in the parking lot and decided to see what was going on.

Some of the younger people in their midst were producing pamphlets inviting people to church and going door to door and leaving them.

The time they were in now would be the best time to reach people. The results of the rapture made everyone aware that something monumental had happened and once the foretelling was pointed out to them it was much easier to believe than it would be in even a short few years. It is much easier to believe in something that you can see than in something that people have told you, and the disappearance of so many people, all from the churches, gave testimony to the reality of what God taught in the Bible.

Connor always carried a 9 mm pistol with him now. He carried it in the car during daylight hours and on his person after dark. The news was reporting on loosely organized gangs operating in different areas of the city and he felt safer with the weapon.

The group from Israel arrived two days later and Connor asked for volunteers to put them up. They could always rent hotel rooms but it would be better if they kept a low profile, both for them and for the local church members.

Connor took them to the basement and showed them how they operated.

"I'm glad to see that you are thinking toward the future. This arrangement is going to come in very useful in the years to come I think."

"Those were our thoughts when we showed up here after the rapture. Tell me about your group," Connor said.

"Most of us were followers of Judaism. There are many differences within the faith, just as there are many Christian denominations. One basic of Judaism is that the Messiah has not yet come. We did not believe that Jesus was the fulfillment of the prophetic scriptures in what you call the Old Testament. The rapture's occurrence shattered that belief and those serious about their religion had to recognize the disappearances as fulfillment of New Testament scripture, which meant that the rest of the New Testament was God's word."

"So how many are in your group?"

"I believe that we are part of the 144,000 spoken of in Revelation. Keep in mind that we are as new to the faith as you are in terms of belief in the rapture. Our focus has always been on what you call the Old Testament and we are having to reconcile our newly found faith in the same manner as you."

"How many of you are there numbers wise?"

"The number is in the thousands already, and more are coming every day. I believe that the 144,000 will be scattered around the world and that we are to continue to preach the word in some manner. Some of your group might even be descendants of our ancient tribes."

"What are your thoughts about the Antichrist?" Connor asked.

"At first I thought it was going to be the Turkish President, but now I just don't know."

"What if the Antichrist is a woman?"

"You mean Madam Gonzorov?"

"Yes. She is now the chairperson of the One World Coalition and practically has a license to do as she pleases with the group."

"My interpretation of Revelation is that it is supposed to be a man, but I don't recall that the scriptures say it will be a man, though all references are to the masculine."

"It will depend on what happens in the near future, but for now my money is on her," Connor said.

"According to the scripture we in Israel will be left alone for the first portion of the tribulation period after the treaty is signed. I think we are going to be able to operate openly for that time. Also the two witnesses have not appeared yet and I suspect that will be happening soon."

"I imagine the One World Coalition will be formed before that happens, but they will certainly make your job a bit easier with the proof at hand."

"Have you had any trouble from government officials?" Ephraim asked.

"No. So far they have not been a problem. I don't think they will even bother with us until after the rise of the Antichrist. Once the coalition tries to institute the one world religion is when it will start to get rough," Connor said.

"I believe we should try to coordinate our activities. I am talking about ways to reach the unsaved. I have been following your postings on the internet and I think you have a good grasp of what we will be going through. Do you mind if we put some of your information on our own site?"

"I am honored that you think it is worthwhile. I just try to remember that all those who knew the most about our situation are no longer around. I try to keep things as simple as possible so people at every level can understand."

"Our meetings are well attended but we are starting to have protest groups show up as well. They seem to want to blame us for what happened. The police do nothing about it and sooner or later we are going to have a physical confrontation. So far we have not done much to prepare our people for the rough stuff but I notice you have a lot of weapons," Ephraim said pointing to the gun shelf.

"I decided early on, just from reading Revelation a couple of times that we are going to have to defend ourselves at some point. The gangs have gotten worse around here since the rapture. I think it is a combination of the gangs seeing easy pickings and the police not caring much what happens as long as it doesn't destroy public property. Keep in mind that the police left are non-believers as well."

"How many of you know enough about guns to use them?"

"Everyone here has gone through a short familiarization to learn to load and fire them. We went to a deserted area in the woods and all had a turn with both handguns and rifles. We may not be expert but anyone here knows how to handle a firearm," Connor said.

"Have you tried to reach any other churches in the area?"

"No, and that is one thing that we need to do. Once the persecution starts we will need to stand together. Right now we have no way to know how many converts there are, other than those who came here. I know the web site gets a lot of hits but I don't know how effective the information is. Some have showed up here and told us that they came because of the web site. Since we took the address of the church off the site and substituted a phone number we have two people who do nothing but answer phone calls."

"Pardon me if it seems I am telling you how to do the job you have been thrust into, but you seem to have a knack for organization, and you understand what is at stake. I think a beneficial use of your time would be to visit other churches and try to point them in the right direction about how to prepare for what is to come," Ephraim said.

"Maybe we can do that while you are here, at least with a couple of trial churches. I'm sure the new believers will be happy to hear from someone from the group spoken about in the Bible. I can try to lend a hand in helping them prepare. Let me see if one of the ladies can contact other people like us. If they are agreeable it certainly is part of our calling," Connor said.

He passed the word to one of the outreach people and explained what he wanted. She got right on it and before the afternoon was over she had four places lined up for them to speak."

It was apparent that most of the churches she had contacted had a group similar to theirs because the first presentation was set up for the following day.

Connor explained that their job had been made a lot easier because the bomb shelter was already there and all they had to do was make the modifications.

"We have bomb shelters all over Israel because of the situation. All the countries near us are historical enemies and when we resettled the land in 1948 many of the dwellings, especially the government buildings were built with shelters in the basement, not necessarily for nuclear weapons, but our enemies can hit us with conventional weapons much easier than anyone could do to you. I guess it is just an inbred point of view for us."

Connor's church was located on the south western side of Washington and the group they would be speaking to was on the north east side. Enough of the cars had disappeared from the roads that travel was much easier than it had been just a few weeks before.

When they arrived they were met by the person filling the same role as Connor did for his church. He had not been ordained or elected, he had just stepped into the breech as Connor had and been accepted by the others.

For such short notice they had a very good turnout. There were more than 100 people there.

Connor started the meeting with a prayer and then a brief description of how his own group had come into being. "I imagine that the same circumstances happened here. After all believers were raptured those of us with any Biblical knowledge at all knew exactly what had happened. In my case I had a lot of exposure to the scripture but thought I knew how to live my life better than God did. I lived comfortably and thought I pretty well had my stuff together. When all the believers disappeared it was a wakeup call. Are you familiar with the Bible verse where Jesus is talking to his disciples and tells them that they had an easy way to testify to his resurrection because they had seen him but blessed were those who believed without having seen Him? I guess that's where most of us were just a short time ago. Since you are here I assume that all of you are believers now. Is there anyone out there who doesn't believe that Jesus is the son of God and that a belief in his birth, death and resurrection is necessary to follow those who disappeared a short while ago?"

Nobody raised their hands.

Connor continued. "Now those who believe that since you have accepted Christ you are home free, let me disabuse you. If your physical wellbeing is foremost in your minds then you have made the wrong decision. Your new belief in Christ will make your final days much harder that anything you have ever experienced. Just reading the Book of Revelation will give you an idea of what is to happen. After the rise of the Antichrist a one world religion will be instituted and everyone will be forced to worship that God, or symbol, whatever it turns out to be. Failure to comply with the order to worship the new God will mean death. There are so many calamities that God is going to send down that might do in new believers as well as those who don't believe. Our failure to accept the word of God until we saw the proof makes us susceptible to the things that will happen during the next seven years of what is known as the great tribulation."

"I don't want to preach a sermon but I think you all should be intimately aware of what is going to happen and in what sequence. Since none of us here knew much about Christianity until just recently there are no recognized experts on interpreting the scriptures. I kind of fell into the leadership role in our church because I had heard the word enough to recognize right away what had happened and why. While it is important to bring others to Christ we have a responsibility to look after our own physical well-being as long as it is possible. Remember, you can't follow God's command to go forth and make disciples if you are dead. We are at the very beginning of the hard times and no one is persecuting us now, but that is going to change. When it does, we will all be fair game for the Antichrist. What I want to do is give you some suggestions for survival when times get rough. I will allow Ephraim to say a few words and then I will give you some suggestions about your future survival."

Ephraim took the podium and talked about how things were in Israel. "I am part of the 144,000 that the Book of Revelation talks about. God says that 12,000 from each tribe will be sealed against the Antichrist. Just as a matter of information, the people I am talking about are new believers just like yourselves. The major difference between you and us is that most of us believed that what you call the Old Testament as the word of God and disregarded the New Testament. We all believed that God was coming back but not in the way the New Testament teaches it. Like you, when those who truly believed disappeared we knew instantly what had happened and that we had been wrong.

At least we knew enough about the Old Testament to make the jump of faith more quickly. We have a rather large group of new believers, I am talking about in the thousands, and because of the way Revelation is laid out we believe we are not in much danger for some time. The two witnesses will soon appear and the one world government will execute a treaty with Israel, which they will honor for a short time. The two witnesses will be there for three and one half years, then will be slain and lay in the streets of Jerusalem for three days, then be resurrected. After that we will be in more danger than any other peoples on the earth. I came from Israel for the express purpose of getting to know this man," he said pointing toward Connor. "God told me in a vision to contact him. I suspect that the reason is to devise ways of reaching unbelievers. My group has a web site that you might find interesting. For now we are simply putting out the word that Christ is the answer. In coming times we will be sort of like an on-line newspaper to get the word out about what is really going on in the world around us. I don't want to limit Connor's time but if you have questions I will try to answer them."

When Connor got back to the podium he told them that what he was about to suggest to them was his own views based on what he got from the Bible.

"Just a cursory knowledge of the Book of Revelation should be enough to convince you that as believers in Christ you will be fair game for the other side. The Antichrist will be accepted as God by everyone except those of us who recognized the rapture for what it was. Worship of the new world leader will not be optional. It will be mandatory. The penalty for refusing to worship him will be death. Now the Book of Revelation clearly states that many new believers in Christ will change their allegiance to the Antichrist. Many more will be martyred who refuse to worship the Antichrist. I don't believe God wants us to meekly accept the death sentence. I believe he wants us to resist with every fiber of our bodies and souls. In that regard we at our church have established an armory and had familiarization training for all our members, both male and female. We also believe that a famine is going to occur and we are preparing for that by stockpiling non-perishable foodstuffs. We have also built a hideout where we can continue to worship and put out the word of God electronically. It is still very early in the chain of events and all we can do now to assure our safety in the future will be time and money well spent."

Connor spent another 15 minutes telling them the things that his group had learned from experience. He did not reveal the location of their hideout though.

After the formal presentation there were many questions. None of the group had undergone baptism and some asked about it.

Connor baptized the entire group while they were there and they didn't get away until well after supper time. They exchanged phone numbers and other electronic addresses.

On the way back to Connor's house Ephraim said, "For a new convert you are a pretty good pastor. Think what you might have done if you had become a believer earlier in your life."

Connor did and said, "The really significant difference is that I would not have to go through the seven years we are facing now."

They repeated the performance at four more area churches over the next five days. Connor now had a loose coalition of churches in the area that could rely on each other to some degree.

When the group got ready to head back to Israel Ephraim called Connor aside. "I don't want to seem melodramatic, but I worked with Mossad for most of my life. You do know what Mossad is?"

Connor nodded affirmatively. "If what I read in the spy novels is truthful then I know it was to Israel what the CIA is to us."

Ephraim nodded. "I want to stay in close touch and once they start to mess with our communications we need some way to know that each of us is talking freely. In other words not being coerced to say something under duress. What would be easy for you to remember?"

"You mean like a single word?"

"It can be a short phrase if you wish, just something that you will definitely remember."

"How about, 'better late than never'?"

"It's kind of a common saying but will probably do the trick. I think we need to think about encrypting our cell phones and data exchanges. Do you have anyone capable of doing that?"

"I don't know. I have a guy who worked with CIA in that regard and he might know someone who can do it if he can't."

"When can you come to Israel?"

"Soon I would think. I want to wait a few days to see what comes out of the new world coalition group. I will give you a call in a couple of weeks."

They were leaving for the airport when Connor noticed a couple of cars behind him that appeared to be pacing him. He slowed to allow them to pass. One did and moved back over in front of him causing him to slow down. The car behind got close enough that Connor had no choice but to stop. He opened the center console and took the 9 mm out.

When the cars had all stopped two people from each of the cars got out and approached Connor's car.

Connor looked for weapons and didn't see any guns. He did see a couple of knives and as they came close he raised the pistol and said, "Are you guys really sure you want to do this?"

They all looked at the pistol Connor was holding, then looked at each other. One of them moved toward the car with the knife in front of him. Connor didn't wait. He shot him in the leg."

He fell down screaming and the others stopped their approach.

"Get him into one of your vehicles and get out of here. If I have to shoot again it will be to kill."

Two of them got the injured man to the car in front of Connor and drove off. Connor jotted down the license numbers of both cars, just in case he should see them around again.

"I must say, you handled that admirably. Any nerves or regrets?"

"I don't think so. It was just something that had to be done. It is going to get a lot worse, and being squeamish at the beginning does not bode well for the future," Connor said.

"Do you think it was a random act, or did they target you specifically?"

"I have no idea, but I got the plate numbers from both cars. I don't know that it will help because of the preponderance of vehicles available from those who have gone on, but I can keep an eye out for them in the future."

Chapter 7

The next morning Connor told the congregation what had happened with the attempted robbery. "That's just a little of what we are now facing. I didn't hear from the cops, so I assume they didn't report it, but you just don't know when you are going to run into a situation where you need to defend yourselves."

"Ephraim mentioned that we should encrypt our cell phones and internet communications. He used to be with Mossad so he should know what he is talking about. What about it Norm? Can you handle that or know of anyone trustworthy that we could get to help us out?"

"It's almost impossible with cell phones unless you have keys produced so that all users can have access to them. About the best you can do with the cell phones is disable the GPS function. I can do that to all our phones and it will keep us from giving away the location. The computers are easier to encrypt and I will get some instructions on the procedure and get us all onboard with that."

"I would like to have you and Larry make the rounds to the churches we visited this week and see if you can get them started in the right direction with what we did here. Don't under any circumstances reveal what we did here," Connor said.

The two agreed to that and planned to start on Monday.

The service that Sunday morning saw the largest attendance that they had witnessed since the rapture. The church was almost full. They had close to 200 members and these were full time members, not like before the rapture when a church's roll might have five hundred and only have half that at Sunday services. These were all serious people.

Connor was becoming more comfortable in the pulpit and was beginning to plan the services, especially the Sunday morning one to emphasize specific points, much as pastors were taught in seminary. On this day he used the life of Saul, later known as Paul, to demonstrate that most of them were in a similar situation.

Saul had been a persecutor of Jewish Christians and a dramatic meeting with Jesus on the road to Damascus had caused him to do a complete turnaround. After his conversion he exhibited the same zeal in proclaiming Christ as he had in his persecutor role.

"If you want to stretch the imagination a bit it is easy enough to see a parallel to what happened to Saul that day. He not only didn't believe in Christ but went out of his way to torment those who did. It took the direct intervention of Christ to turn him around. With us it took an event that could not have happened without Christ's direct involvement to show us the light. The Bible is very specific in proclaiming that the only way to God is through Christ. That means that you must accept the basic tenets of the New Testament which say that you must believe that Christ was born of a virgin, was without sin, and died on the cross for the sins of all mankind. He then ascended into heaven."

He went on to explain that the disappearance of all believers was foretold in several books of the Old Testament. He quoted some of the scripture dealing with the event and cross referenced them to the Book of Revelation. Some of the references were almost word for word and even those with a very fundamental understanding of the Bible could see the similarity.

When he had the altar call most of the visiting people came forward. There were more than 25 and he told them that they would need to talk more in-depth so they could fully understand what the profession of faith meant, both now and in the coming times. He asked if they wanted to stay and do that on Sunday afternoon and the decision was unanimous to do it then and there.

Connor had instituted a procedure to do background checks on all new converts. It was still early and from his understanding of the Book of Daniel the tribulation period had not actually started yet, but he didn't want to compromise the location of the safe room until they were relatively sure about the sincerity of new people.

The ethnic makeup of their group was diverse. There were several Asians and a good number of blacks. Washington has a high percentage of blacks and it stood to reason that that segment of the population would be searching for answers as well.

One of the middle-aged black ladies was working with the outreach group and had a tendency to sing softly during her chores. It seemed so natural that nobody mentioned it but Connor asked her if she would be willing to provide some music for their services.

She agreed and the move made a world of difference to the tone of their services. While the message was still about the dire situation in which they found themselves it lifted the spirits to 'make a joyful noise unto the Lord'.

Connor also had the outreach people contact other church groups that they could identify and he visited several other churches in the area over the next two weeks.

The same familiar situation existed at each location. Some had no leadership at all since no one stepped forward as he had. At every stop he emphasized the hard times that were coming and warned them to prepare as much in advance as possible. Only one of the churches had performed any baptismal services and he did that at those who had not.

He told them that he would have a couple of his people visit and help them outline what they needed to do if they had to go into hiding.

Nothing happened with the One World Coalition for three weeks. It was not even in the news very much. The world leaders then met in New York at the old United Nations building and within a couple of days a news conference was called to outline the plan that had been generated.

Israel was the only nation that refused to sign on to the new mandate. That was settled by a treaty between the One World Coalition and Israel. Each vowed not to attack those of the other camp without extreme provocation. The last phrase was not explained further.

The basic tenets of the mandate was that the leaders would attempt to bring the world to a more equitable footing. Within six months, the codicil said, the group would take over all distribution of food to assure that everyone worldwide had adequate nutrition. All religions would be allowed but would be closely monitored by coalition representatives. Within one year the inequitable wealth distribution would be addressed by changing to a one world currency.

Madam Gonzorov had been confirmed as President of the One World Coalition and did all the presentations of what they hoped to accomplish.

The levy for troops to support the coalition would go into effect immediately and training would commence within a month. Each country would provide facilities for training and the coalition would provide instructors.

Once that happened Connor started to get more calls from churches farther away. They were hearing about his work and wanted to have him come speak to their groups. Many offered to pay for his expenses and he ventured as far south as North Carolina, and as far north as Pennsylvania. He still had not called Ephraim to settle on a date to visit Israel and he should do that soon now that he knew more about how the new world system was supposed to work.

Connor's church had gotten more members every week and they could barely hold the crowd for the Sunday services. He chose half a dozen of the more knowledgeable members and started breaking up into smaller groups for the weekday discussions. There were still a lot at the church but the smaller groups lent themselves to discussion more readily.

When he called Ephraim to discuss the trip to Israel he learned that the group in Israel had to break into smaller groups as he had. They were still getting protests from non-believers but only minor skirmishes had occurred thus far.

Connor left Washington on a Monday. He had to fly to Paris and change planes to get the rest of the way to Tel Aviv, then a car to Jerusalem.

On Wednesday, which would be the first day of their discussions, they were sitting around a conference table when the door suddenly burst open and an exited man started jabbering in Hebrew, which Connor could not understand. Somehow he knew that the news was that the two witnesses had made an appearance.

Soon a cart was wheeled in which had a 17 inch television on it. Once they got it hooked up the scene at the west wall, or Wailing Wall as some call it, was on every channel. It was hard to tell much from the small television screen, but the plaza in front of the wall was packed with people.

Enough could be seen that it was obvious that the two were not dressed in twenty first century clothing. They both wore robes that must have been popular in the old Biblical days.

Both wore flowing robes and the headdress popular among the Arab nations, what they call a keffiyeh. Both had long flowing beards that were almost totally white. Their faces were weathered, as if they had spent much time in the sun. The robes were white with flecks of what appeared to be gold thread in the pattern woven into the material.

They stood before the wall, not talking even to each other. The camera angle of the station they were watching was not very good but at least allowed the viewers to see over the heads of the many people now packed in the plaza. The camera was mounted atop a van and as the people jostled for position around the van and bumped it the picture wiggled and it was hard to tell what was going on.

Ephraim provided a running commentary of what the newscaster was saying.

"He says that they just suddenly appeared at the wall. Some men tried to have them removed but didn't seem to be able to even touch the two. Nobody seems to know who they are or what their purpose is for being there. He says that their clothing is hand woven and is not nearly the quality of today's manufacturing process."

"I don't imagine it would be," Connor said with a chuckle. "I sure would like to be close enough to talk to them."

"As would I brother. We will wait until the furor dies down somewhat. I suspect the police and military will be arriving soon to try to restore some order."

As if on cue a siren sounded and flashing lights could be seen approaching the wall. There was no way that they would be able to get close enough to do anything worthwhile. The crowed plaza was too packed to allow much movement of anyone. Finally the two police cars stopped and men got out and made their way to the wall on foot. That was quite an accomplishment because the people simply didn't want to move any farther away from the scene, though most of them didn't know what it was all about.

"As much as I would like to be there now I think we will be wise to bide out time until things settle out somewhat," Connor said.

"I think you are right, though I will send some people to find out what they can. My employers will have people there and I will get a pretty good read from what they report."

Any plans that they had were placed on the back burner until they could learn what the two witnesses would do.

For now they were simply standing in front of the wall. No one was within ten feet of them, though they could not determine the reason for this. When the police came they drew nearer and could be seen talking, though the microphones could not pick up what they were saying.

When one of the uniformed policemen reached out and touched the arm of the nearest to him he immediately collapsed to the ground. Other policemen drew their weapons and pointed them at the two.

The voice of one of the witnesses could be heard even over the clamoring of the many people packed together in the plaza. It was as if they had a public address system. "Stand aside those who fear the Lord, for we are his witnesses and nobody can harm us. Turn aside from your wicked ways and seek the way of the Lord. The day of the Lord is at hand and you will not have much longer to wallow in sin and the wicked ways of the world."

Strangely, Connor heard the voice in English. He thought it odd that they would preach to the Jews in English and commented about it to Ephraim.

"To me he was speaking Hebrew. I think any who hear them will hear them in their native language. Isn't it amazing what the Lord can do?"

The policeman who had collapsed started stirring and was soon back on his feet.

The other witness said, "Be warned. There are those among you who would do us harm, but it cannot happen because we are protected by our God. If you should attempt to do us harm you will die."

The police started trying to move people back but they were packed so tightly that those behind had no place to go and the ones in front could not be moved.

The two took turns speaking. The message was that people must turn from their sins and turn to God. "The way to God is through Jesus the son. Whosoever believes in the Holy Scriptures that Jesus is the way to the Father will be assured of eternal life. Those who continue in a life of sin will be damned to eternity. Do not believe the false teachings. The Bible says that 'many will come in the name of the Father, but you must resist their teaching."

As they continued to watch the scenes on television Connor asked, "Who do you think they are? I mean, I know they were sent by God, but who are they?"

"I have been researching that very subject and I cannot tell you. I don't believe they will be any of the old prophets returning. From what I can learn they are probably helpmates of God in some form or other. I don't believe they were here on the earth in body before now. I have read some thoughts that they are beings that God created like the angels. I do know from what the Bible says that they cannot be harmed until God decides to allow it, some three and one half years from now. Fire is supposed to come out of their mouth to devour anyone who tries to harm them."

"I wonder if they will have special powers to warn them of impending danger," Connor said.

"Maybe we will get a chance to ask them," Ephraim said.

"I don't see them spending all their time in front of the wall. They will have to sleep sometimes and they will need to eat as well, at least I think they will. Maybe we should try to talk to them after some routine is established."

Ephraim had a larger television set delivered to the conference room and hooked it up to the satellite receiver. That way they could check the world news and see how they were reporting the happenings.

One of the cameramen had gotten brave and climbed atop the wall so he could get better coverage of the two witnesses. Since he had the best location others news reporters were using their feed.

Ephraim switched the channel to CNN and they listened to what was being reported there. They didn't have a reporter on scene yet but were pirating the good pictures from the cameraman on the wall.

The announcer said, "We don't know exactly what is happening in Jerusalem just yet but something extraordinary is going on there. Two old men appeared apparently from out of nowhere as we have the story and started preaching from the west wall in Jerusalem, which most of you should know is considered a sacred site by most of the religions that were founded in that area. Those include Muslims, Christians and Judaist, as the major brands of religion. There are many sects within each of those categories and right now we can't tell you which of the religions seem to be the sponsor of these two. We have people enroute to the site and will bring you live coverage as soon as possible. As you can see the plaza near the section of the wall seen as the most holy place is teeming with people. Even the streets and alleys leading to the area are so packed that it is almost impossible to move. The police even had trouble getting to the front of the crowd."

"We have Madam Gonzorov of the One World Coalition on the line now. What is your impression of what is happening in Jerusalem right now, Madam Gonzorov?"

"I do not know much more than you do, but if the situation does not stabilize the coalition will send troops to assist the Israeli's in dealing with the situation. As you know, we agreed not to interfere with Israel unless their situation destabilized and our assistance was obviously needed. This might be one of those times when we can be of assistance to them. So far there has been no violence, but any time you have a crowd as large as the one there is you will have some people who do not abide by civilized rules. We will monitor the situation closely and let Israel know that we are available if we are needed."

The announcer pressed his earpiece into his ear to hear what someone was saying though the headset.

"I am just told that they have declared that they are witnesses from God and that no one can harm them," the announcer said.

"Did they say from what God," Madam Gonzorov asked with a chuckle. "As to being able to harm them, I believe the crowd will trample them if they stay where they are. I apologize, but I must get back to my task and I have every confidence that Israel will be able to handle the problem."

During the next few hours Israel did indeed deal with the problem. They sent the army to the area and systematically removed the people from the area and by nightfall had an area within about 50 yards from the wall roped off. They also had soldiers and police on duty with weapons to prevent anyone from getting nearer to the two witnesses.

You must remember that other than the new believers that Ephraim represented, the entire Jewish population were not believers of the New Testament, so it stood to reason that they would use whatever means necessary to keep order. The earlier incident with the policeman who collapsed when he touched one of the men was seen as a sign that they must be very careful about dealing with the two.

"I want to be watching this when darkness comes to see how they handle sleeping arrangements," Connor said.

"I suppose if they are heavenly beings then they won't need sleep," Ephraim said.

All the same, when darkness fell the two moved along the wall to a corner where perpendicular masonry had been added and sat on the ground with their backs to the wall.

Many of the crowd had disbursed and though there were still a lot of people it was nothing like the chaos of earlier in the day.

"What would you think about making an approach in the middle of the night?" Connor asked.

"It might be the thing to do instead of waiting until it will be more difficult to get to them."

"It might also be a good idea to try to arrange some decent sleeping arrangements for them too. We might take a tent and a couple of cots and see if they want them."

"Since I am still with Mossad I might be able to make arrangements for us to pay them a visit officially," Ephraim said. "I will need to go out for a while. I will be back very soon."

There were a great many new converts in Mossad, including Ephraim's boss. When he told him what he had in mind the skids were greased with the police and military to allow them to approach the two.

Ephraim had an 8 X 10 tent packaged so that he could carry it on his back like a hiker. The cots were collapsible so that Connor could carry them in the same manner.

Just after midnight they made their way to the plaza. One of the military officers escorted them to the area where the ropes had been mounted. They stepped over them and walked up to the two huddled in the corner. The weather was very chilly. It was autumn and the really cold air had not moved in yet, just the same it was uncomfortable in the elements.

As they got closer the two stood and greeted them.

"Welcome brothers. You are new converts?"

"Yes we are, but as my friend says, 'better late than never'," Ephraim said. "We did not know if you needed sleep and food, but it stands to reason that you will and we want to help however we can."

"We could manage without either, but it will help people identify better with us if we conform to their ways. You two are part of the remnant and you will have a lot to do," one said.

"He is part of the remnant," Connor said, "I am from America."

"Yet you are still part of the remnant. Nowhere does it say that all the remnant will be from Israel. You are a descendant of one of the original tribes," was the reply.

"I didn't know that, but I guess it makes sense. What are your names?" Connor asked.

"I am Mordecai. He is Benjamin."

"May we set a shelter up for you?" Ephraim asked.

Mordecai nodded approval.

Connor and Ephraim took the tent out of the bag and set it up against the wall where they had been sitting. Ephraim had enough foresight to bring a hammer and pegs.

It was difficult getting the pegs into the ground since the area was paved with stones but he managed. Having the rear of the tent against the wall helped to stabilize it somewhat.

Connor set up the cots. "We will bring blankets later," he said.

"Why not let me call and have someone bring them while we are here?" Ephraim asked.

He made the call and told the police that someone would be bringing blankets soon.

"What kind of food would you like?"

"Bread, fruit and cheese, plus water?"

Another call got that order put in.

"May I ask what happened to the policeman when he touched one of you?" Ephraim asked.

"I suppose you could say he fainted. When a non-believer touches one of us his system stops working momentarily, just long enough to render them unconscious."

"What happens when a believer touches you?" Connor asked.

"Try it and find out," Mordecai said.

Connor reached out and laid a hand on the man's arm, just as he had seen the policeman do. Nothing happened, but he felt a warmth not consistent with the situation and the weather.

"I guess that's one way to know who is a true believer and who isn't," Ephraim said.

"Will you two remain here for the entire time?" Connor asked.

"No. We will move around the city, but we will not leave Jerusalem. This seemed the best place to start because it is sacred ground."

"What else can we do to help?" Ephraim asked.

"You two have your own flocks to lead. You will be quite busy and unlike us you will need to travel a good deal," Mordecai said. "Things are peaceful now and you need to make preparations for the time when you will be persecuted every minute. The Bible refers to us as witnesses, but you two are witnesses as well. You will endure many hardships before the Lord comes again but your faith will see you through. Remain steadfast in your belief and the Father will see to your needs. Satan is on the prowl now and he will tempt you in every way possible to convert you to his side. Resist with all your body and soul," Mordecai said.

"The Father has gifted you two above others that you might provide leadership and inspiration to those in need. If a mountain needs to be moved, with faith you can say to the mountain move, and it will be done," Benjamin added.

"I don't know what to say. I am just a humble man," Connor said.

"David was just a lad when he faced Goliath. Daniel was just a man when he sat within the lion's den. Saul was just a man, and a very bad man, until he came to know the Lord. God does not choose the man with greatest status. He chooses instead the person for the job and provides what is needed to do the job. Rest assured that you two are where you are supposed to be for the sole purpose of doing God's work," Mordecai replied.

They spent over an hour with the two witnesses in the tent. The blankets came and soon thereafter a grocery delivery.

As they walked by the police line on the way back one of the policemen asked, "How is it that you two got along with those two?" he pointed toward the tent.

"We are from the same family, the family of God. You might want to listen to what they have to say when they start talking again. Did you know that every person who hears them does so in his native language?"

"Really. Isn't that sort of like the tower of Babel in reverse?"

"I suppose that's a good analogy, but the point I was trying to make is that they have supernatural powers that could only come from God. If you don't believe in Jesus Christ they will convince you that you should. Do you believe in Jesus?"

"I don't know what to believe. Our Bible says that a savior will come, but doesn't say when."

"He came over 2,000 years ago. We Jews were just not ready to accept Him. The New Testament is truly God's word. The disappearances was Jesus's return to take believers home. We are now in a very contentious time. The Antichrist will arise and try to establish belief in him, but it is really a belief in Satan. Those who fall for his line are doomed for eternity. You must believe in Jesus to have the eternal good life. I believe we will all have eternal life, it's just a matter of where you spend it that is the big difference. Would you rather be walking streets of gold and drinking living water, or burning in hell with no way to quench your thirst?"

"The former of course," the policeman answered.

"Then you need to commit your life to Jesus. The last book of the New Testament talks about exactly what is happening now. If you read that and are not convinced that the Bible is God's word then you are in for a very rough seven years if you live through it all," Ephraim said.

Chapter 8

They made their way back to Ephraim's church. Unbeknownst to them their arrival and departure had been recorded on cameras. The major networks had all arrived now and were jockeying for positions with best camera angles.

Not all the networks were doing live feeds, but all were recording in case anything interesting happened. The two providing the tent and later blankets and food was newsworthy and their arrival and departure had been televised. The light was not the best but Connor and Ephraim could be identified positively.

Though not a problem at the present time it would be something that would send them both into hiding when the Antichrist established a foothold.

The newsmen were not dummies and managed to confirm the identities of both of them before the morning news shows.

CNN even called Connor on his cell phone and asked to do an interview.

He put them off by saying that he was very busy at the present time but that when he got back to Washington he would contact them.

The meetings got underway again and took a bit of a different turn than Ephraim had intended.

The fact that they had been identified was going to be hard to deal with, and since the two witnesses confirmed that the two of them were in leadership roles for the remnant it was imperative that they establish some better unknown place to work from when the situation became worse.

"I believe the most pressing issue for both you and me right now is to find someplace where we can still get the word out through this entire period," Ephraim said.

"I agree, especially now that the entire world knows who we are and what we believe. I will look into that as the first order of business when I get back home."

"The most important thing right now is to get our e-mail accounts encrypted. I have a man on my staff who can provide encryption keys. I will have him get right on that and have someone deliver the encryption tables to you," Ephraim said.

"I think we should start an on-line Bible study with full time manning. I am not sure about the format but I think we need to have someone available to answer questions at any time. I will look into that when I get back and let you know how it is going to work," Connor said.

"I also believe that we should start looking for someone to fill the leadership roles in Europe and Asia," Ephraim said.

"There's so much that needs to be done it is hard to keep a clear mind. Mexico and South America are also important and I haven't given either of them a thought since the rapture," Connor said.

When Connor was taken to the airport in Tel Aviv for his return flight to Washington he was besieged by reporters. They shouted questions over each other to the point that he could not understand any question asked.

He ignored them as best he could and went through the security checkpoint to catch his flight. The return journey had him going to London, then to New York, and finally to Washington.

When he arrived in New York he called Larry Elliott and asked him to pick him up at the airport. He would be flying into Dulles and figured they would have time to talk some on the way into Washington. "Bring Norm with you if possible," he said.

As Connor made his way through customs and to the airport lobby he was again mobbed by reporters.

When he spotted Larry and Norm he made his way to them, still followed by reporters.

He motioned them to meet him outside. Some of the reporters had cameras and he didn't want to have any more of his people identified to the public in connection with his mission.

Larry gave him a sign for the way to go and he managed to slip the reporters and joined up with the two near where the car was parked.

Larry's first question was, "Were those the two witnesses spoken about in Revelation?"

"They were indeed. Their names are Mordecai and Benjamin. They are not resurrected saints but are instead part of God's inner circle would be the best way to describe them. Was all the same stuff on television here?"

"Yeah. We saw you and Ephraim meet them and erect the tent. Then when you came out later they got good footage of you two. I guess you are a celebrity now," Norm said.

"That's a double edged sword. It means that people will know who to turn to, but also that the other side knows who we are and where we stand now," Connor said.

"What was the story with the policeman who collapsed when he touched one of them?" Larry wanted to know.

"I asked that question, thinking that the same might happen to anyone who touched them. Mordecai said that when a non-believer touches them that their systems shut down immediately and they faint. It doesn't do any harm to them but renders the two witnesses invulnerable to harm."

"You were with them a long time. What transpired while you were in the tent?"

"They said that Ephraim and I were part of the remnant and that God had chosen the two of us to lead the new believers. They are dressed in the same type clothing that was worn in the time before Christ. They said they would move around Jerusalem but would not leave the city. I imagine many people will go there from all over the world to get a first-hand account of their preaching. Did you know that whoever listens to them hears their speech in their native language?"

"I wondered about that," Norm said. "I don't believe the media has picked up on that yet. The crowd near the Wailing Wall today was bigger than yesterday if that is possible."

"We are going to have to devise some way to handle our own ministry. Now that people know who I am and where I live I imagine I will be a hot item for quite some time. That's good from the point of getting access to people to tell them about Christ. The other side of that coin is that once the Antichrist in in full control we will become fugitives. We need a much larger and more secure location to work from in the future."

Norm said, "I think most of your ministry will have to be on the internet soon. You will be able to access many more people that way but you will need someplace where you will be hard to find. I imagine someplace in the mountains would be called for. I know the government has an emergency relocation site someplace in the mountains, I think in West Virginia. It is sort of an open secret, but it has been there since the days of the cold war when it was not inconceivable that the Russians might attack us."

"Start giving some thought as to what we will need in the way of electronic equipment and power to operate in that manner. I have a feeling that we are not going to have a lot of time to get it done," Connor said.

When he got back to the church there were over 200 people there. Most of them were the regulars but there were some new faces. All wanted to know about Israel.

Connor had the sound system turned on and gave them a narrative of what happened.

"The two witnesses are exactly what the Bible says they are. They will preach in Jerusalem for three and one half years. Mordecai said that they would not leave the city, so I guess people will have to come to them. Our job, on the other hand, is to go to people, either electronically or in person. Now that I have some notoriety I imagine our pews will be filled, at least for a while. Mordecai confirmed that Ephraim and I were chosen by God for the leadership roles in the new ministry, so I guess I do have an official calling. We are going to become more involved with people like ourselves around the nation, the world for that matter. Getting the word out about Christ is the most important function we will have and we must devise some way to do that when times get harder. I hate to sound like I am begging for money but what I envision is going to take a lot of it and we need to do as much as we can while we still have the freedom to act."

"I want to start an internet broadcast as soon as we can get things set up. I imagine that will eventually become the main thrust of our ministry. We are going to look for a secure location and try to get started on that as soon as possible. I am going to do an interview with CNN soon and I imagine there will be a lot of visitors who want to know what God has to say about all this. There will also be some who want to put a stop to us, so be aware of the possibility of a confrontation. Ephraim has already had protesters at his services in Israel, so we can expect the same here."

When Connor finished his talk he asked if there were any lawyers among the group. Two people indicated that they were attorneys. "Might I have a word in private with you two gentlemen?" he asked.

They joined him and he went to the regular church offices.

After the introductions he asked them if they had become believers. Both indicated that they had.

"Then you know that all the previous members of this church are now in heaven. My problem is that I don't know how to gain access to the church bank accounts. I wonder if you could enlighten me about some method to achieve that. We also need some place to deposit the money we bring in. What are your thoughts?"

Bill Collins and Darrell Hastings were the names. Bill said, "I imagine a notarized copy of a church business meeting, at which a new board of trustees will be appointed will be enough to get the bank to accept the new leadership. New signature cards will also be required. If you wish I can check with the bank and determine exactly what is needed. In the meantime you should call a meeting of all members and do everything officially so the church will have records. It is really pretty simple as long as the bank doesn't contest anything. Do you know how much money we are talking about?"

"Somewhere around 200 thousand dollars. Then there is the church property and assets. I am not so worried about the property since it will only be the next seven years we have to worry about. I will call a meeting for Sunday after the morning service. Will you two be able to attend?"

Both nodded agreement and said they would help with the paperwork.

As Connor had promised he contacted CNN and asked them when they wanted to do the interview and where.

It was set up for the following morning at the local offices of the broadcaster. They wanted to do it early enough to get the widest audience and chose 8:00 a.m. as the time. They would send a car to the church to pick him up at 7:00 a.m.

Connor didn't sleep well that night. His mind was simply overloaded with all he knew he had to do and he had no idea how to go about parts of it. He recalled the verse which said that we were not to worry but to pray to God for guidance and leave things in His hands. He did exactly that.

He asked God to give him courage and wisdom to carry out his tasks and to be with all those who had come to belief, but he prayed specifically for those who had not been reached yet and were in need of Christ in their lives.

The interview the following morning was not scripted. The newsman asked the questions and Connor answered as best he could.

The first question was, "What were you doing in Israel at that particular time?"

"I had gone over at the request of a fellow pastor who ministers to new believers in Christ in Israel," he answered.

"Could I ask your views about the disappearance of half the earth's population?"

"It was what most Christians refer to as the rapture. What happened was that Christ took all believers to heaven in the blink of an eye."

"If that's the case then why are you still here?"

"Because I wasn't a believer at that time. I had been to church enough to recognize what had happened and that alone made me become a believer."

"Why do you say all believers were taken away?"

"Because immediately after the event all the churches were empty. The only ones left were those who didn't really believe. They may have been going through the motions for the benefit of others but they didn't have a true belief, otherwise they would have been raptured with the others."

"Is there something in the Christian Bible that says this was going to happen?"

"Only in about a dozen places. The books of the Old Testament talk about it in Isaiah, Daniel, Zephaniah, Psalms, Joel, Ezekiel; they are too numerous to mention, and you must remember that I wasn't even a believer until after the rapture so I don't have a very good knowledge of all the references. The New Testament, in particular the first Book of Thessalonians, Chapter 4, verses 13-16 say that Christ will come to take his believers home in the blink of an eye. That was what happened to reduce the earth's population by about half."

"So what happens now to people like yourself who decide that God was responsible and that you now believe in Him?"

"All you have to do is read the last book of the New Testament to find out. The events from here on out are laid out in the order in which they will happen."

"What about the two mysterious people who appeared in Israel? Are they part of the predictions?"

"First, those are not predictions, they are God's factual account of what will happen from now until the end of time. The two who appeared in Israel are indeed part of the Revelation narrative. They were to appear and preach the gospel of Christ for three and one half years. They will be protected by God himself until their mission is fulfilled. If anyone attempts to do them harm they will be destroyed by fire, which comes out of the mouth of the two witnesses. If any non-believer touches them they will immediately be immobilized, just like the policeman who touched one of them on the first day of their appearance."

"You really believe that God sent these two people to Jerusalem and that He can protect them?"

"I do."

"What makes you so sure about that?"

"The Bible first and foremost. Let me ask you a question. Did you know that anyone who hears them speak hears them in their native language?"

"I had not heard this."

"Absolutely. As to the rest of it, I touched them and did not feel any ill effects, while the Israeli policeman, who was not a believer was immediately incapacitated. Everything I know about them is directly from the last book of the Bible."

"What is your role in what has to be considered a resurrected religion?"

"I am simply an instrument of God to preach the true word. The Bible says that an Antichrist will arise, and I think that is happening right now. The world will be subjected to a one religion rule and those who do not worship the one world God will be put to death. This hasn't happened yet, but is soon to come."

"And will you also have divine protection?"

"I wish! I am simply a human being and from here on out I will do what God leads me to do. The Bible says that many of the new believers will be martyred, that means killed for their beliefs, so there will be a lot of persecution during the next seven years until Christ comes back again."

"So the world is to only last for another seven years?"

"No, the tribulation is to last for seven years. Christ will then come back and claim his rightful place as the ruler of the world."

"And you seriously believe all those things?"

"I defy you to study the Bible and tell me that all the recent events are not substantiated in the scriptures," Connor said.

After they finished with Connor's interview they had a segment with Madam Gonzorov, the One World Coalition chairperson.

When asked to comment about Connor's interview she said, "Well if an Antichrist is to arise he might be a good candidate. He is certainly preaching a one world religion. I don't believe that the two men who appeared in Israel have anything to do with God or anyone else. They are simply taking advantage of the unstable situation in Israel. They can be killed just like everyone else. It won't be much longer before someone does I have no doubt."

She did all in her power to discredit Connor and refute what he had said.

Connor was taken back to the church by a driver and if anything there were more people there then than upon his return the day before.

He went inside and found the church packed. There was not even enough room for everyone to sit. He moved to the front and mounted the platform. He motioned for the sound to be turned on and when that was done he moved to the microphone.

"I am gratified to see so many people interested in the word of God. I guess we were all in the same boat when the rapture occurred. I know that many have come to faith in Jesus Christ in the recent past. More of you need to take that step. Let me warn you though that if you make a decision to follow Jesus it will not be an easy path, especially during these trying times. We are now in the first stage of the tribulation which is a seven year period of God's wrath on the world. I don't pretend to know exactly how events are going to play out with the world at large, but I do know the things that are going to happen and in what sequence by reading Revelation."

"There are many references in the Old Testament to the events that are just beginning to happen now. There are going to be wars, earthquakes, famines, droughts, and other calamities that give me chills just thinking about them. God makes provisions for his own but I don't believe those of us who have come to believe in the Lord Jesus will be immune to the physical aspects of these events. The only thing I am sure about is that a steadfast belief in Christ assures me a heavenly home after I die. The Bible says that many will be martyred during the next seven year period. Those who refuse to renounce the Lord will be killed toward the end of this period."

"The two men who appeared in Jerusalem recently are called the two witnesses in the Revelation. The Bible explains exactly what will happen. They will be immune to actions by non-believers to harm them until God declares their work done. They will destroy their enemies by flames that come out of their mouths. You probably saw on television the incident where the policeman tried to lay a hand on them and immediately collapsed. I asked Mordecai about that and he said that when a non-believer touches one of them that the person becomes immobile immediately. The experience does not do them any lasting harm. The ones who try to attack them will be killed by the fire that comes out of their mouth. I don't know how this is possible but that is precisely what the Bible says and I believe it. The Book of Revelation also says they will have the ability to bring plagues and droughts, just as happened in Old Testament days. These two are not returned prophets but are members of Gods inner council I suppose is the best way to describe them."

"After preaching for three and one half years in Jerusalem God will allow them to be killed. They will lie in the streets of Jerusalem for three days and then will be resurrected for all to see."

"Now you can wait around for that time to get the proof that the Bible is true or you can accept the word of God on faith. Faith is the essence of a belief in Christ."

"By accepting Christ you will not be making your lives easier but harder. The Bible says that the Antichrist will institute an edict that all must worship the one God that they represent, which is Satan. Those who do not profess a belief and take the mark will be killed. That sounds like a movie script right now, but it will happen just as the Bible says it will."

"If you need visual proof of the two witnesses just watch them on television. Every person listening to them hears them in their own language and the message they preach is the same as you hear right here. Without Christ you are lost. We will have a hymn and any who want to pursue a belief in Christ can come forward and talk with us."

It was a very short talk and after the prayer many of the newcomers came forward. Connor had several of the earlier members come to help deal with the new converts.

This was not even a scheduled service and more people were there than the church would hold. What would happen with the scheduled services? It was a good problem to have, Connor thought.

One of the men who came forward asked Connor if he could talk to him in private after things calmed down. Connor agreed and after a few minutes the two walked back to the pastor's office.

Once they were seated the man said, "My name is Sterling Silverstein. My parents apparently had a sense of humor when they named me. I have taken ribbing all my life about that. I was a bit like you before the rapture. I went to church occasionally but more for show than anything else. I am Jewish and was raised under Judaism. Even their teachings didn't convince me that there was really a God. I am well educated and understand about the various religious beliefs around the world. I personally thought that I was master of my own fate until the rapture. I observed that most of the missing were from Christian churches, and the way it happened could have only been through divine intervention. Belief came instantaneously. I knew right then and there that Jesus had indeed taken his believers home. I started reading the Bible to try to figure out what was necessary and what was going to happen next. Like you I determined fairly quickly that we are going to be in for a rough time in the coming years. I want to do all I can to reach others like me. To that end, I am rather wealthy and can afford to help you out financially. So what can I do?"

Connor gave the matter some thought.

"As soon as the Antichrist gets a foothold we are going to be in for a great deal of persecution. Our faith will be outlawed and we will be forced underground. The only method we will have to get the word out is through the internet and social media. I plan to start daily Bible lessons on a World Wide Web site as soon as I can get it set up. It might interest you to know that I apparently have some Jewish blood because Mordecai, one of the two witnesses told me that Ephraim and I had been chosen by God to lead the remnant. I had some doubts about becoming the self-proclaimed leader of this church but I was assured that the flock would be worldwide before much longer. What worries me most is that we need a really secure place to operate from when the Antichrist arises. And by the way, I believe   Madam Gonzorov is the Antichrist. I know she is a woman but the Antichrist is nothing more than a mouthpiece for Satan. I have asked a couple of my more capable people to search for a location that gives us some security for the coming years."

"How long do you think before you will need the new space?"

"Six months at the outside. Things are going to get gradually worse over time. We already have too many for this facility and I feel the other local churches are going to be in the same boat very shortly. We don't have a lot of opposition right now, and the events that can be substantiated by scripture is a powerful aid to our cause. The Bible says that Satan will be given power to perform miracles of his own and this will cause many to believe in him as the real God. Things are really going to get interesting at that time."

"You might be better served to search for a place in a well populated area than in the wilderness. You will be able to blend in better in a large city, and it will be easier to stay discrete. I own real estate all over the country and I can make one of the city buildings available to you if you think it will fit your needs."

"Where are the buildings located?"

"I have a couple in New York that might suit you. Another is in Dallas, Texas and one in Chicago. I also own a couple of business jets that might come in handy."

"Wow, I guess you are aptly named," Connor said with a chuckle.

"So what do you think? Shall we join forces?"

"It certainly wouldn't hurt to have a look."

"I will stay here tonight. Then tomorrow you and I can fly to New York and have a look. If you would rather be someplace else we can look at the alternatives."

"Would you like to stay with me tonight?"

"If it wouldn't be too much of a bother. My plane is at Dulles. If you want to take any of your people along that will be fine."

"Since you have a lot of money and tangible property I want to ask you what you believe is going to happen when the other side goes to the one world currency?"

"I have given that some thought. For sure the value will not be the same. I believe they will use that as a ploy to enrich their own camp as well. I just don't know how severe the problem will be. It is not going to matter after the tribulation anyway, so why worry about it."

Chapter 9

Connor asked Larry and Norm to meet him at his house when they left the church. Sterling followed him and the four met at Connor's apartment.

Connor made the introductions and said, "Sterling has offered us some possibilities for a covert place to operate when things start to get scary. He suggested that a place in a large city would be easier for us to blend in, and that sort of makes sense. What do you guys think about that?"

"It will make it easier to get the utilities we need and so forth. From that standpoint it's a no-brainer. However, we will have no way to judge others except from their profession of faith. You know that Satan will lie, cheat and steal to thwart our efforts, so I can't imagine operating in a crowded environment without being discovered. I think we still need to find a desolate location for an emergency operating site," Norm said.

"Would you two be willing to go to New York with us tomorrow to evaluate a couple of locations?" Connor asked. "Sterling has a business jet and will provide transportation for us."

Larry added, "If we have access to multiple locations that fit our needs then I think we should prepare as many as possible in case we have to move. We have time to make the modifications now, which we probably won't have later on. A couple of locations in the city and one in the country would give us options."

Norm said, "If we set up the three locations in the same way equipment wise it wouldn't be hard to switch from one site to another flawlessly. That way if one site is discovered the switch can be made instantaneously."

"What would something like that cost?" Connor asked.

"Not much more than it did to set the place up in our basement. The major costs will be in renovating the spaces. If a lot of physical things have to be changed it will cost more, but not more than a few thousand dollars," Larry said.

"Money is not a problem," Sterling said. "I will take care of that end of things. All you need to do is look the places over and decide what we need to do to make them fit your needs."

The four talked until almost midnight. When Larry and Norm left Connor told them to meet him back at the apartment at 8:00 a.m. They would all go to the airport together and plan on returning later the same day.

Sterling arranged a van to pick them up so they could all ride together.

The first site they looked at was an eighteen story building. The ground floor consisted of small retail shops and restaurants. In the central portion of the ground floor were elevators and at each side enclosed stairwells. They took the stairs to the basement and looked the space over. It was exactly the size of the outer perimeter of the building and housed a lot of the utility equipment. Electric panels, water lines, telephone junctions and the emergency sprinkler system could be seen as well as the elevator operating system.

They all looked the space over carefully. Finally, Larry said, "I don't think this will work. There's only one way to access the area and without some major cement work the area cannot be defended. Once it is discovered whoever is here at that time is history. They can either breech the area or bar access."

They looked at another building owned by Sterling. It was a much smaller affair and was near the harbor area. It was only three stories and was much older. Larry thought it might work for a backup but none of them saw it as a first choice.

"Let us go back to Washington and see what we can locate in that area," Connor said.

"If you find something there that will work out let me know how much money you need for the project and I will provide it," Sterling said. He gave each of them a business card that had his cell phone number.

He took them back to the airport and they were back in Washington before dark.

Larry and Norm contacted real estate agents the following day and asked about property for sale in the country.

They got a list of properties and directions to them and told the agent they would inspect them on their own then get back to her.

"Some of them are unoccupied. They belonged to people who disappeared and are being sold by relatives. Just let me know if anything catches your fancy," she said.

Larry knew the area of northern Virginia pretty well and thought that something out toward Leesburg and south toward Dulles airport would be ideal. There was enough traffic on Route 50 and on Route 7 to the north that they would have some choice about getting back and forth if they could find something that would meet their needs.

One of the places they looked at was once a working farm. It looked to be fifty or more acres and had a substantial two story house. Nobody was at home so they wandered around assessing the possibilities.

The place looked to be at least a hundred years old but was in a good state of repair. There was a barn and what appeared to be a storm cellar.

Larry went to the storm cellar and lifted the entry doors. He could see a pretty large space below but couldn't tell much about it. He went back to his vehicle and got a flashlight so they could have a closer look.

What he discovered was that the area was quite large and was concrete. That was unusual for a storm cellar. Usually such spaces were smaller, meant only to provide a place out of the elements in case of tornados. This was apparently used as a root cellar for storage of vegetables that were canned and would not be consumed until the winter months.

Near one corner of the space was a chimney-like flue and what looked like a gas outlet for a stove or heater of some sort.

Also against the wall toward the house was a door. They checked it out and found it went into the basement of the house. That was really strange. If the people had a basement that provided protection why would they need a large storm cellar?

Larry mentioned this to Norm.

"I think you will find that the owners are not among those who disappeared. I believe the storm cellar was used as a still to brew illegal alcohol, or moonshine since we are in the south," Norm replied.

"That's probably why this door is here. They could access the space from the house."

"I like this location," Connor said. "It is accessible from two different directions and is far enough off the main road that it will not be all that noticeable. The space is enough for a pretty large group to work and I believe we can do with it what we did to the shelter at the church. We can modify the outside opening and build a shed over it to pump fresh air inside. We could also trench the opening further into the woods and use it as an escape route if necessary. What do you guys think?"

"I agree. It is probably as good as we are going to find unless we build something from the ground up," Larry said.

"What's the asking price for it?" Connor asked.

"It's under a million, probably because of the age of the house. There has to be over 50 acres of land."

"I will check with Sterling and see if he will pay for it. If not then we will raise the money ourselves."

They didn't even bother to look at other properties but drove directly back to the church. Connor talked to

Sterling on the way back and he agreed on the spot to purchase the property.

"I think we should set up a shell corporation for the purchase. The paperwork can be done in a day for a Limited Liability Corporation. I will have my people get right on it," Sterling said.

The situation at the church was now such that there were people there all the time. Many wanted to meet Connor and see what he was all about. Others were under conviction by the Holy Spirit and wanted some direction to their lives.

Any time there appeared to be enough to warrant, Connor gave impromptu talks. He always talked about the way to Christ and about how the Biblical accounts were coming true. He baptized many and they kept the baptismal filled and heated around the clock.

He also had the clerical people continue with the background checks, just to get an idea of the lifestyle of his converts. Many were coming to the church from different locations. Washington was, after all, the nation's capital and many had to be there for government business. He had records kept of the different locations. What he had in mind was to train some people to minister to those in their local areas.

Military people, some with pretty high rank, came and those he kept on file to turn to when he eventually set up an intelligence organization. He was planning for the long term and it would be important to keep a finger on the pulse of what the Antichrist was up to. He didn't voice these thoughts to anyone but Ephraim when they were talking on the phone.

Ephraim was doing likewise in Israel. He was in a much better position than Connor to accomplish those things and had a background better suited to the task. His position with Mossad gave him access to people from all walks and surely some of the people in the spy agency had turned to Christ.

Over the next couple of months after he returned from Israel he established a loose coalition of churches in the Washington and surrounding area. He branched out a bit farther each week and all were getting good results.

Sterling made another trip to Washington and delivered the LLC papers to Connor. "You are the CEO of the LLC. There's a bank account with money in it. I am going to give you a couple of credit cards. One is in the name of the LLC and the other is a personal card of mine. Use them for as much and as often as required. I will take care of the bills when they come in. I used my business address for the LLC so you won't have to worry about any of the details. I would like to look at the property though."

They drove to the country on Route 50. When they arrived and looked the place over Larry told him, "I want to build a tunnel from the place where the outside entrance is now located into those woods back there," he said pointing about 75 yards away. "We will bring fresh air in from the woods and only use it in case of emergencies. I want to reinforce the door entering the space from the basement to make it difficult to breech."

"Who is going to do the work?"

"I am, with help from our members. I can get it done in a couple of weeks with some help."

"I think you made a good choice. This place will be much more secure than the city. It is far enough out that you shouldn't have trouble with people being followed. You need to think about where to park vehicles that people arrive in."

"I plan to convert the barn to a car park. It will hold 14 vehicles according to my calculations. If we need more space we will have to park them in the woods out back. I'm also going to set up an observation post in the hay loft. I will run a communication line from there to the hideout when I am doing the work on it. I also want to set up some remote cameras in the woods around the place."

"Sounds like you have covered all the eventualities," Sterling said.

"Something will come to light after we are finished that should have been done as a first step. It always happens that way. I still think we should find one of your buildings, maybe one in Dallas to use as a back-up though," Larry said.

"When you're ready let me know and we will go for a look."

Larry selected his work crew from church members and had a couple with trucks and trailers go shopping with him. He purchased almost $8,000 worth of building materials and arranged to rent a backhoe and grader for a couple of weeks. He rented trucks to haul them because he didn't want to take a chance on compromising the location this early in the game.

Over the next few days Larry trenched the area leading from the storm cellar location all the way into the woods. He went down six feet and the space was four feet wide. As he moved the dirt he had the crew start erecting the side walls from 2X8's. He showed them how to put the boards in place then use wedges to hold them in place until they could stabilize the cavity across the top.

When all this was done he would pour concrete over the top, reinforced with rebar. That would hold up even if heavy equipment was driven over the tunnel. He would test it himself when he used the grader to level the ground after the project was completed.

He planned to put sod over the entire back yard after they were finished so there would be no evidence of the construction at all.

Camera locations were chosen, mostly about 10 feet up in surrounding trees. He used shielded wire to keep it weatherproof. He even had the crew do a bit of maintenance to the house, just to justify their presence if anyone should notice the activity.

No strangers showed up during the entire process. The interior work was much as it had been with the bomb shelter. They simply had to run additional electric lines from the house panel to the storm cellar. All the wiring for the cameras came to the same location and Norm would eventually hook the cameras up to the television monitors. Larry planned multiple monitors because they had so many cameras. There were a dozen in all and it would take three monitors to handle all the inputs.

They would experience the same problem with sanitation that had happened at the church. Chemical toilets were again used as a solution.

Larry even had the walls painted in a light pastel to make the work easier on the eyes. The entry door was reinforced as had been the one at the church. A small structure, similar to a pump house, was erected over the area in the woods where the tunnel terminated. Larry used old lumber to construct it so it wouldn't stand out. He also transplanted some of the shrubs to block any view from the property toward the house. He rigged it so that a latch on each side of the small structure could be released and the entire thing could be lifted by a single person with leverage from the inside. A lock was placed on the outside, which would probably never be opened.

Once the physical part of the plan was completed they purchased all the electronic components that would be needed and delivered them to the room. It was going to be a tighter fit than the bomb shelter but it would suffice. He also purchased a large generator in case they needed the power to keep operating. Supplies streamed into the place each day. Food, and whatever else they thought they needed they bought with the credit card Sterling had provided.

Chapter 10

While the work had been going on with the new location the One World Coalition was also gearing up.

Madam Gonzorov was on the tube every evening talking about all the positive things the coalition had accomplished.

"The new food distribution system will go into effect this week. We now have over a million troops trained and we will start to address trouble spots in the world. As most of you know, the biggest problem the world faces at the present time is in the Middle East. We give warning that those who do not cooperate will face the consequences."

After her television appearance that evening she got together with some of her advisors. "The Christians are gathering strength. I think it is time to put a stop to their activities. I don't want it to seem as if the coalition had anything to do with it. Arrange for some protesters and have a few people with weapons among them. If you get a chance kill some of the leaders."

Because of the large crowds, and the ever present danger of lawlessness, Connor had told the ushers to carry weapons. He also kept his pistol in the holster at his back. He knew that sooner or later trouble would find them.

He didn't know if it was just a premonition, or if God, through the Holy Spirit, was giving him guidance, but he felt that something was going to happen soon.

The crowd was standing room only when he took the pulpit. He was early into his sermon when the ruckus started outside. First it was just noise and soon chants and yelling could be heard. Connor ignored it as best he could. He even brought the outside behavior into his talk as the forces of evil.

Not much later he heard the sound of gunshots and told the people to remain seated and pray. He would go out and deal with the matter. He went to the front entrance with four ushers and they walked outside.

A crowd of fifty or more was gathered just outside the entrance.

"Good evening folks. Sorry we don't have room for you inside just now, but if you give me half an hour I will have a special service for those of you who want to hear the word of God."

Someone yelled out from the middle of the crowd. "We just want you to stop preaching this garbage and get with the program. The One World Coalition is doing the right thing and you are just making it harder for them to operate."

"That's very true. The One World Coalition is just as phony as this demonstration. How much are they paying you to cause trouble?"

He obviously hit the mark because someone said, "That's none of your business what they are paying us. We are here of our own free will and if you don't stop your preaching we will burn your church down."

Another gunshot sounded and the crowd started to back away. One of the ushers had fallen to the ground. Connor saw the man in the crowd holding a pistol and took out his own. He didn't hesitate but fired directly at the man. Two more with guns were on the other side of the crowd and when the other ushers saw Connor with his weapon out they took theirs out. More shots rang out and ricochets could be heard bouncing off the brick work of the building.

Another of the ushers had been hit in the arm but was still standing. The gunmen in the crowd were all down and the crowd was disbursing quickly.

Connor saw that the situation was in hand and went to assist the usher who was on the ground. He had been hit in the side but it was not bleeding a lot. The one with the arm injury was being assisted by a couple of other people who came out of the church.

"Someone get these two to the hospital," Connor said.

"What about those," someone asked pointing to the people on the ground in front of the church.

"If their own people don't care for them then I see no reason that we should. I think we should continue the service."

He moved back inside. Most of the people at the service had taken him at his word and were in the pews in prayer.

He got back to the pulpit and picked up where he had left off.

He heard sirens just as he was about to wrap up. "I think the police will want to talk to some of us. I also think this is the opening salvo in what will be unrelenting persecution of those who know Christ as their Savior."

The police came into the church and asked what happened.

"A crowd gathered outside to protest against our services. I heard a couple of gunshots and went outside with my ushers to see what was happening. We were attacked with weapons and responded in kind. These people will bear witness to what I said.

"How come you are armed?"

"I am always armed. What should I do, stand as an unresisting target for scum like those?" Connor asked.

"There's nobody out there now."

"About ten minutes ago there were four people on the ground with gunshot wounds and two of my people have been taken to the hospital by church members."

Just as this was happening a news van pulled up to the church.

There was nothing to be seen but bloodstains on the ground and on the entry portico to the church.

Once they were set up they came looking for Connor. He answered their questions and described what had happened.

"These people attacked you without reason?" the announcer asked.

"No. Their reason is that they don't agree with our religious beliefs. That's not a valid reason, but it is a reason. The ones with guns were probably hired to cause trouble," Connor said.

"How is it that you happened to be armed?"

"We are Christians, not ducks in a shooting gallery. If we are attacked, as we were here, we will defend ourselves. We are entirely within the law by exercising our right to self-defense and protection of private property," Connor answered.

"Were these people from the neighborhood?"

"I don't believe so. I didn't recognize any of them."

"Then what reason could they have for protesting here?"

"Maybe you haven't noticed, but half the world's population disappeared recently. All those people were believers in Christ, in other words the good milk has been skimmed from the top. What's left are those who did not at that time believe in Christ. Our group is composed of people who looked at the mass disappearances and decided that God was responsible and that we were on the wrong side of the fence. These people here jumped to Christ's side. We believe it is our calling to educate others about Christ and what it means to live a Christian life. That doesn't mean that we will just raise our hands and say kill me to those who don't believe. We don't force our beliefs on anyone but lay out the facts from the Bible about what has happened and what is to come."

"And you know what is to come?" the newsman asked.

"The entire scenario is in the last book of the Bible," Connor said.

When the interview was over the newsman asked Connor if he could show him in the Bible the explanation for recent events.

Connor took him to the large print Bible at the front of the church. The book was already turned to the Book of Revelation.

Most of the members and visitors were still inside the church and Connor apologized for the interruption but took a few minutes to explain about the rapture and show the newsman the verses that dealt with that, of which there were quite a few.

He then showed him the section dealing with the two witnesses in Israel. He invited him to have a seat while he finished his sermon. The man took a seat. His cameraman was in the back of the church, unnoticed by most.

Connor moved his talk back to Revelation, partly for the benefit of the newsman. He wanted to graphically show him how events taking place were exactly what the Bible said would happen.

"Since the time of Christ more than 2,000 years ago the church has been like a live organism. There were times when believers in Christ were devout and tried very hard to adhere to Christian principles. There were also times when the church tried to bend the Bible to their own belief systems. In other words they tried to make the word of Christ fit their behavior rather than having their behavior adhere to instructions from Christ. There were seven churches in the ancient times, and here I am talking about the time Christ was among us here on earth. He uses those seven churches in the opening chapters to describe what has happened to the church over the ages. He likens each of the ancient churches to a time when believers fell away from a true belief in Christ."

"That portion of the Revelation is symbolic but is supported by other scripture from both the Old and New Testaments. What that section of the scripture does is show the justification for the actions which are to come, though Christ doesn't need any justification. The explanation is for our benefit, to help us see why God is angry enough to visit these horrendous calamities on the earth's population."

"We have gone through the period of apostasy, or false teachings, The Bible says that false Gods will arise. That has also happened. Not to throw stones at other religions, but all the ancient far-eastern religions, Buddhism, Hinduism, Confucianism, Islam: the list is too numerous to mention all of them, but anything other than a belief in Christ falls into the category of false Gods."

"The Bible talks about the rapture in several places. That is the mass disappearances that took place not too long ago. There are several things that will happen next. One of them is the ascension of a world leader who seeks to unite the world under one umbrella. That is happening as we speak. It will be accomplished peacefully but once in control the Antichrist will wage war. There is to be a seven year tribulation in which some of the worst calamities the world has ever seen will occur. We are in the early stages of that tribulation period. The Book of Revelation says that two witnesses for Christ will appear. Just last week this happened. These two are preaching in Jerusalem now. They cannot be harmed by man until they are finished with God's work. That will be three and one half years from now. That is in the Book of Revelation. These two people have special powers. No non-believer can touch them without falling into a faint. If someone tries to harm them bodily, fire will come out of their mouth and kill their enemies. Another interesting note is that whoever hears them preach hears it in their native tongue. There are what, over a hundred languages?"

"And for future reference, those who are alive three and a half years from now will witness their death, and three days later, their resurrection. That's straight from the Book of Revelation. Now that should be enough to convince even the harshest skeptics that the Bible is God's word. There are instructions throughout the New Testament about how we should respond to the teachings of Christ and how we should act toward each other. We will have a brief hymn now and those who want to seek a relationship with Christ can come forward and we will pray with each of you."

During the invitation hymn a large number of people came forward. Connor had enough help with the ushers and other members to counsel each of them.

The reporter, whose name was Darren Waite, hung around until the church started to empty. He cornered Connor and said, "Are you absolutely sure about all those things you said?"

"They were right from the Bible. This period of time was prophesied as early as 5,000 years ago. The New Testament also has Jesus own explanation of events and they coincide exactly with the Book of Revelation."

"I am going to have to dig into this a bit further. I didn't realize a lot of what you told those people was direct from the Bible."

"You might want to watch your step professionally because the Antichrist is on the rise. I suspect the leader of the One World Coalition is the Antichrist, who is nothing more than a spokesperson for Satan. You will see her tie everything together using peaceful means until such time as force is necessary to bring nations into line with the one world agenda. You will also see the institution of a one world religion, and I am not talking about Christianity."

"What do you get out of all this?"

"Ultimately, eternal life. For the present time I expect a lot of what happened earlier tonight. Christians will become targets for all kinds of causes. Non-believers have

110

no alternative but to oppose us. They don't believe in our God, but they don't have any alternative either. We are going to be in for a really rough time through the seven year tribulation period, simply because we believe in Christ."

"May I call you if I have questions?"

"Certainly. I am going to the hospital to check on my people now," Connor said and handed the reporter a business card.

Neither of the ushers were seriously injured. Any gunshot wound is serious, but theirs were not life threatening. The one who was hit in the arm had to have some minor surgery and the one hit in the gut had been lucky that the projectile didn't hit any vital organs. On the way back home Connor thought about the events at the church. He had not had any fear, and he had no remorse about defending the church. That was really out of character for him. He had always been a bit squeamish about violence, even in movies and the only way he could reconcile his attitude now was that God was responsible.

When Darren and his cameraman were on the way back to the news station the cameraman asked, "Do you believe all that stuff he was talking about?"

"He showed me in the Bible and it sort of made sense. I am going to do some more digging. If I can substantiate all the things he said then I might just become a Christian," Darren said.

"I was thinking along the same lines. I probably haven't been inside a church more than half a dozen times in my life. I always thought of it as what my gang called the Jesus Freaks. It will be funny if they end up having the last laugh," the cameraman said.

"Just from what he said after we got there I don't think they are in for a picnic, but non-believers will fare even worse," Darren responded. "Did you get any footage of his sermon?"

"Yeah, I got most of it after we got inside."

"I think we might want to delete that so as not to stir the pot any further until we can do some digging."

"Gotcha."

Darren was silent for the remainder of the trip back to the station.

What Connor said had really hit home with him. Like his cameraman he had not been inside a church very often. Most of the times were for weddings or some special family celebration. He would take a critical look at the things Connor had pointed out to satisfy his own curiosity. He had never believed in anything other than the fact that a person lived, then at some point died. To him that was the end of the line. There must be some sort of inner spirit or the human body couldn't operate as flawlessly as it did. He had experienced periods of sorrow and remorse but just figured that was the way of life. What if there really was a life after death? That was something to ponder.

Chapter 11

It was late Monday afternoon when world news stations interrupted their programs for a special report from Jerusalem. The cameras had been in place since the appearance of the two witnesses. When they moved away from the wall for any period of time the news media still followed them with other cameras. The good locations that had been staked out they held onto.

They were preaching their normal message when a sniper tried to take a shot at them from the roof of a nearby building. Nobody had any indication that anything out of the ordinary was about to happen, until Benjamin moved alongside Mordecai and whispered something. The two turned to the direction Benjamin had indicated and flames shot from both their mouths. We are not talking flame thrower type flames, rather arrows of flame that were much like the arrows from a bow, except the speed of the flames was almost too fast to follow. Everyone could see where the flames had headed but didn't see anything else.

"Let all who see bear witness. You cannot harm witnesses for God. Turn from your evil ways and embrace the one true God," Mordecai continued as if he had not been interrupted.

Several people went to the building where the flames had been directed. They found two men on the roof of the building with holes through their hearts, much like a red hot peg had been driven through them. There were singe marks around the entry wounds and in their backs.

The in-place cameras had gotten the film of the fire erupting from the mouths of the two and hand held cameras bore witness to the results. Both the men on the roof had rifles and it was apparent they intended to cut short the sermons of the two.

All that was on the news during the special report. Some of the newscasters wondered about how such a thing could happen but didn't mention it on the air. It was too unbelievable to be true and they didn't want to look bad about speculating. They did get eyewitness reports from people in the plaza when the event occurred though.

One man who was being interviewed about it said, "It was just as the Bible said it would happen. Fire came out of their mouths and killed the two would be snipers. If I had any doubts before that just about made up my mind. These two are truly witnesses for God."

Connor and his church group were holding services every night, almost like the old time tent revivals. There was such a demand to hear the word that it was hard to keep up with the crowds.

The night after the incident in Jerusalem there was another standing room only crowd. All the pews were filled and people stood along the sides and back of the sanctuary. The area around the entrance was also packed. When Connor came to the pulpit he noted Darren Waite along one of the side walls.

He talked about what Christ had to say during his time on earth and delved into the hard times the early church had. "When Christ came to earth his own people didn't believe that he was the Messiah. He was mocked, ridiculed, and eventually died on the cross for telling the truth. Fortunately there were enough who believed in Him to spread the word, especially a man named Saul, who was one of the staunchest persecutors of Christians until his conversion. Many were killed for their beliefs and the same has held true down through history. I don't have the time or knowledge about all that to enlighten you at the moment but I will dig into it for future sermons. The point I am trying to make is that Christians have been persecuted throughout history and we are no different in that sense. Where we are different is that we are living in the end times and things are going to get much worse for those of us who believe in a living God."

"Just like the Jews in Christ's time people cannot see the truth, even when it stares them in the face. Even though Jesus' life and death were prophesied hundreds of years before the event, people refused to believe. And now, with the evidence plainly before us in the Bible, people still refuse to believe that God's children were taken to heaven in the blink of an eye. People are trying to come up with alternate explanations when there are none."

"The event we saw on the news last night from Jerusalem was not trick photography. Just as the Book of Revelation states, the two witnesses took care of the would-be snipers with fire from their mouths. Now how much plainer can it be? Jesus not only tells us that they are invulnerable but how they will defend themselves! Folks, if you can't see that then there is no hope for you. God cannot be any clearer. Read the rest of the Book of Revelation from Chapter 11 to the end and see what terrible things are going to happen in the next seven years. Those of us who came to a belief in Christ after the rapture will have to endure these things just like everyone else. We may be immune to some of the things but I don't know what they are or even if that is God's plan. I just know that I believe with all my heart that a better life awaits when it is over, and no one can take that away from me, though Satan will certainly try."

"Those interested in a personal relationship with Christ come forward now as we sing our hymn of invitation."

Again most of the new people came forward. Darren waited around until most of the people had left before he approached Connor.

"I read the rest of the Revelation last night after I saw what happened in Jerusalem. It was exactly as the Bible said it would happen. I guess you would say I believe now. What do I have to do?"

"In the Book of John Jesus said, 'I am the way, the truth and the life. No man comes to the Father but through me'. What that means is that you have to believe that Jesus came to earth to die for the sins of all mankind, that he was crucified and arose from the dead."

"If you go to the first Book of Thessalonian's Chapter 4 verses 13 through 16 you will also read exactly what happened when all the people disappeared," Connor said.

"Yeah but what do I have to do?"

"The Bible says that if you confess me before men then I will confess you before my Father. That means basically that you need to let others know that Jesus is now the ruler in your life. The Holy Spirit will guide you. It isn't like he is constantly whispering in your ear, but you will start to recognize things that are not within the framework of how God wants you to live your life. Things will just seem wrong, or in some cases right, according to the truth of the Bible. Most Christians believe that you should be baptized based on the example Jesus set when he was on earth."

"I think my cameraman is leaning in your direction too."

"Don't think of it as my direction but the direction of God. Just be aware that your life will not get better in its earthly aspects. You will be persecuted constantly for your beliefs, and may even be put to death before the tribulation period is over. The tribulation is Satan's time, and God gives him free reign for the seven years. Our job is to proclaim the name of God to those who are not on God's side. Right now the job is as easy as it is going to get. Very soon we will be driven underground and have a tough time getting access to people who worship Satan, as that is exactly what it is going to come down to."

"When can I be baptized?"

"Tomorrow night. Work on your cameraman in the meantime. You two could be very important to the ministry in the coming bad times," Connor said.

"What else do I need to do?"

"There's a song that says, 'prayer is the key to heaven, but faith unlocks the door'. I believe there is no such thing as too much prayer. I try to talk to God just as if He was standing where you are. It doesn't have to be on your knees, or even in public. You just have to sincerely seek God's guidance in all you do. There's another Bible verse that says, 'faith as a grain of mustard seed can move mountains'. To me that says that all things are possible with God. We just have to sincerely believe that he is capable of anything if we have the faith in him."

As expected the One World Coalition put a different spin on the event in Jerusalem. They first ballyhooed the impossibility of what the cameras showed and wrote it off to trick photography. They had even sacrificed two of their people to deceive the world about what was really happening, they said. The Jews were trying to bring the world to their own God and would do anything to get their way.

Whether they were responsible or not was anyone's guess, but that night someone tried to burn the church. The volunteer who was sleeping in the bomb shelter heard noises and looked at the feeds from the cameras. There were several people outside with gas cans and he didn't feel competent to confront them, even with a weapon. He called Connor and let him know what was happening. Several church members showed up about the time the matches were touched to the gas. The interlopers dispersed very quickly and Connor and his people managed to put the fire out before a lot of damage was done.

Connor called the police and fire department and filed the report. He didn't even acknowledge that they had film of the attempt. What the attempt did was to convince Connor that there should be two people there after hours, one always awake. He instituted that procedure the very next day.

Another thing that they did was to purchase used furniture to fill the house in the country. It would be better if someone lived there to keep an eye on the place. They didn't know of anyone who even suspected that they now owned the place but it wouldn't hurt to err on the side of caution.

The One World Coalition deployed troops to all the major countries, ostensibly to assist in the food distribution program, but the headquarters indicated that they would help local police forces, most of which were short-handed, to enforce the laws.

Madam Gonzorov had new uniforms designed for the troops. The uniforms themselves were brown and the helmets and leggings they wore were black. She had a new crest designed which they wore on helmets and shoulders.

They had apparently simply taken over the United Nations weapons stockpile. They had also integrated the U.N. troops into their own organization.

The world leaders were all members of the governing group so there were no checks and balances to the arrangement. If the group wanted to institute some procedure they could do it with a vote at one of the meetings. Much of the coordination was done by phone.

The night after the conversation with Darren he was at the services for baptism, along with his cameraman. The baptism took a long time as there were so many.

Connor didn't take anything for granted with his new converts. He asked each person if they truly believed in God before they were immersed. In the final analysis that didn't count for much if they were lying. He had no way to discern that except to observe their actions after the fact.

God had made it plain that the Antichrist would go to any lengths to negate the effectiveness of the new believers. Lying was perhaps at the milder end of the spectrum of the things they would do over the next seven years.

They now had troops accompanying news crews, again the excuse was for their protection, but the real reason was censorship of what they reported. The people who had this job were all handpicked by the coalition leader.

Riots had broken out in some of the third world countries where food was being distributed. Nobody knew what sparked the events but all ended in bloodshed and the announcement of the One World Coalition that firmer steps would be taken to assure the safety of those distributing the food.

Connor thought it quite possible that the One World Coalition had staged the riots. A new set of rules regarding foodstuffs was publicized having to do with producers. No one would need to market their food products. They would purchase all they could produce at a fair price and then distribute the food to places where it was needed.

There was still plenty of land available for farming but the rapture had taken care of a lot more than fifty percent of the farmers. The problem was that there was not many people who knew anything about farming and those who did didn't want the back breaking work associated with the endeavor.

The latest announcement hinted that a one world currency was being considered to more equitably compensate those who were now growing the food.

Connor called Sterling and said, "I think the one world currency is just around the corner. Maybe as soon as a month away."

"Yeah, I heard the news tonight. If you need anything that is going to cost a lot of money now might be a good time to make the purchases with the credit cards," Sterling responded.

So far Connor had not come up with a third location in case both locations they were now using were compromised. For sure the church would not be available to them much longer once the Antichrist started having her way.

The place in the country seemed to be their ace in the hole for now. Larry suggested that they erect a sturdy gate at the entrance and try to find a back way in so there would not be evidence of a lot of cars coming and going at the farm.

He used the satellite maps found on the internet to look the area over. He found what appeared to be a game trail not more than a mile to the north of the farm. He and Norm drove out in a 4 X 4 and had a look. The initial move off the highway was the hardest part and once they were into the woods they followed the trail until it passed close to the farm. They then made their own path through the trees until they were within a short distance from the fake pump house.

"I think this will work," Larry said. "We can leave the cars in the woods and won't have to worry about parking."

Connor rode out with them the following morning and looked the area over where they would have to leave the paved road. The earth was hard packed and even a modest amount of traffic exiting would not be that noticeable unless someone knew what they were looking for. They could use that ploy until the area started to become an obvious turn-off then switch to the regular road to the farm.

They had more than a thousand names on the church rolls now and Connor needed to have three services on Sundays to accommodate everyone. Still new members were gained each day.

Since Norm had worked with the National Security Agency he had a rudimentary idea about intelligence collection and Connor asked him to try to come up with a blueprint for what they needed once they had to operate undercover.

Norm worked on the project for a couple of days and came to Connor with his ideas. "The first thing we need to do is make the farm legitimate. If we can find someone to actually farm it, it will draw attention away from what is really going on there. The Coalition will know that it is a working farm and will come by routinely to check on it. We can squirrel away some of the vegetables to help feed our own as well."

"I don't believe we will be getting the whole story from the news outlets about anything the One World Coalition does so we need someone who can get the information to keep us informed. I think Darren would be a good candidate for that. I have encrypted all our computers and that shouldn't be a problem. It is going to have to be a matter of reacting to what they do rather than setting up a hard and fast organization."

"We also need to make sure all the GPS functions are disengaged in cell phones."

"It would be a good idea to plant some motion detectors outside the house. If there are a lot of large animals around there will be some false alarms but I would rather have to deal with that than to be surprised by someone sneaking up on us," Norm said.

Most of the Senators and Congressmen had been appointed by the different states and the government was fully staffed again. That didn't make a lot of difference in the long run. The President was part of the One World Coalition governing body and most of the edicts that came out of New York were rubber stamped as U.S. laws.

Gonzorov was fully in command now. Connor wondered if she might have some powers to deal with the group that he didn't know about. It was certainly not beyond the realm of possibility.

Darren told Connor that there was a lot more violence now but they kept most of it hushed up. People who opposed the Coalition for their own reasons were lashing out at the troops and police on a regular basis. They were not even reporting the deaths that resulted from the confrontations.

The cameras detailing the activities of the two witnesses had been taken down and there was little or no news about them on the television networks.

Ephraim had called several times and Connor knew through him that there had been several incidents of people confronting them. "The fire we saw the first time was peanuts compared to what they do when someone in the crowd attacks them. It is almost like a flame thrower when the assailant is close by," he said.

"Are the crowds still large?"

"Growing every day. You can't find a hotel room anywhere in the city."

"Would it be possible for someone in your organization to tape some of the talks by the two witnesses? If you can do that and send them in an encrypted e-mail we will put them on social media here. We get very little news about what is really happening over there now," Connor said.

"I may be able to do it but don't expect the pictures to be high quality," Ephraim said.

Connor mentioned that the church needed someone who was familiar with farming to set up a program to grow some of the food they would need. "We have one place now and are looking to find another. Anyone interested see me after the service.

He was pleasantly surprised to find four couples willing to farm the land. He figured two couples at the place they already had plus another close by if he could find something else for sale in the area.

His group started looking the next day and they found a place within three miles. Prices were stagnant since the rapture and they offered $200,000 for the property that would have been worth over a million just a short time before. The offer was accepted and a lot of the church members pitched in to make the new place livable and even helped clear the land for planting.

While they still had the money available Connor bought new mechanized equipment for both farms. He had the farmers do the shopping to get exactly what they would need to care for the crops.

He purchased the new place in the names of the couple who would be responsible for the crop production.

Very quietly Connor checked the names on his rolls for anyone who worked with any law enforcement agency and found three people who might be able to feed the group news about what was going on in their respective areas.

He was trying to set the intelligence section up so that only those who really needed to know were aware of their functions.

Both the bomb shelter at the church and the place in the country were fully staffed now, as well as the regular church office.

The people who were operating the place in the country were primarily responsible for feeding everything of any importance to the Israeli's and postings on social media. Only those directly involved in the operation knew about the location. When they had to vacate the shelter at the church they would obviously bring more in on the secret but for now Connor wanted to play it very close to the vest.

Norm was in his element with the intelligence section and had taken over a corner of the room at the farm to keep people informed.

The fields at both the farms were plowed and many people helped with the planting. The only drawback with either of the farms was that there was no irrigation. Farmers in that area depended on the rain, which did not always come when needed.

As both Connor and Sterling thought, the one world currency came into being soon after they had talked about it.

Sterling had been to the farm several times and decided that when they had to go underground he would like to help out there if Connor would have him.

It also became apparent that the church was under constant surveillance now. Things were going to start to go downhill very rapidly any day now.

As expected the value of the dollar was worth less than half what it had been before the change.

Chapter 12

Connor kept in touch with the other churches in the area on an almost daily basis. All their rolls had increased dramatically since he had made contact with them and he was trying to coordinate the activities, such as would have been done by local associations in the past.

While Connor was talking to Norm about their lack of intelligence concerning what the One World Coalition was up to he suggested that they try to get someone inside the organization. The task would be much easier now than when Madam Gonzorov consolidated her power.

"I can go to New York and see what I can find out. Maybe Sterling can help us out some. He has to be in touch with other believers in that area," Norm said.

Norm placed a call to Sterling and told him what they planned to do and asked when it would be convenient to come to New York for a couple of days.

"You can come any time. I will put you up at my apartment and we can discuss ways to accomplish what you have in mind. Let me know when you are coming and I will have someone meet you at the airport," he said.

Norm left the following day.

Connor was planning a series of sermons on the references in the Old Testament to the end times and was doing a lot of research. He was at his desk in the office when one of the ladies from the 'other' office in the bomb shelter came into the office.

"Have you heard the latest?" she asked.

Connor looked up and shook his head negative.

"There has been a change in leadership at the One World Coalition. Madam Gonzorov has yielded her position to the President of Turkey. Her reason was that a man could do a better job than a woman, especially in dealing with the Muslim countries. The change is effective immediately. What does that do to your theory of her being the Antichrist?"

"Blows it out of the water, obviously, but I believe she was playing a scripted part in any case. The Turk is now at the top of the list as the Antichrist, but I would bet a lot of money that she stays on as his assistant, that is assuming I was a betting man. She has followed the script in the Bible too closely not to be involved," Connor said.

Connor turned his office television on to get the firsthand account of the event.

The announcer was saying, "And to recap, Ahmet Demir, president of Turkey is assuming the position as Chairman of the One World Coalition. Madam Gonzorov will stay on as his deputy. Mr. Demir will continue in his position as President of Turkey. He has said that he would continue the policies already in place and try to improve the conditions in undeveloped countries worldwide."

It wasn't long before Connor's cell phone rang. It was Ephraim from Israel. "I believe Madam Gonzorov and Mr. Demir are a team," he said.

"It sure looks that way. Isn't it amazing that we can be misled even when we know what is coming?" Connor replied.

"That's the way Satan works. He lulls us into a false sense of knowledge and we tend to believe what we have been conditioned to accept. He was probably testing the waters with Madam Gonzorov and odds are they are on the same team," Ephraim said.

"That makes a lot of sense. What do you see happening next?"

"If I interpret Revelation correctly there will be wars. The first thing he will do will be to sign a peace treaty with Israel, which officially initiates the tribulation. I imagine they will pit the One World Coalition against whoever resists the changes he wants to make. He will want to rid the world of weapons of mass destruction, mainly nuclear weapons. That's going to be a tough nut to crack, especially with Israel, and probably the Chinese as well," Ephraim said.

"I don't think America will give hers up without some resistance either, although our President can probably be talked into anything," Connor replied.

"I believe what he will do is try to get rid of the more lethal stuff by compromise. Once he has all that off the table he will then send his troops in with superior firepower and subdue those who resist," Ephraim said.

"Have there been any more incidents with Mordecai and Benjamin?"

"Yes. Every time they move to a different location someone seems to try to impede their progress. Many have tried to physically assault them but with the same result as the cop had the first day they appeared. Only one other assassination attempt has been made and the results were about what you would expect. They have banned the news media from transmitting any video, though there has been some still photographs taken."

"Are your believers still getting a lot of opposition?"

"Yes. We have protesters almost constantly at our church. Some of them don't even know what they are protesting. There have been some awkward moments but the police do not appear to be taking sides yet."

"We still have people watching the church but no more overt opposition since the shooting incident," Connor said.

"I have a feeling that will change within the next few weeks."

"We are trying to get someone into the One World Coalition camp so we can get better intelligence about what they are planning."

"If you have any luck don't forget to pass the information on to me."

"Will do," Connor said, ending the conversation.

Connor went back to what he was doing, which was trying to reconcile the fact that the implication of the first four seals had been fulfilled prior to the rapture. He wasn't sure about how that played out in the current situation. He knew that there had been wars since the beginning of time, and that there had been a lot of people who filled the role of false Christs. There had also been a lot of famine in the world down through the ages.

As to the pestilence, the black plague in the middle ages, the rise of diseases such as smallpox, and certainly the current widespread AIDS epidemic filled the bill for that one.

To Connor's way of thinking the rapture, and the subsequent beginning of the tribulation period would not have commenced without the fulfillment of the first four parts of the prophesy having occurred. Of that Connor was certain.

He was attempting to build a model which would show without doubt that God was behind all that was happening. Faith was important but he felt that a graphic illustration of the things which had occurred over the last two thousand years would help people to reach that faith. This he knew was not a new religious tactic as ministers had done this since the time of Christ.

The most important part of the argument was something he could point to that everyone would understand in the rapture, but he felt it was important to lay the groundwork to get to that point.

Now that he was researching things that would lead others to faith he was amazed at how blind he had been to God's word for the better part of his life. In his own case he knew that it had been his ego, or pride; call it what you will, but the bottom line was that he considered himself to be intelligent enough to decide his own path in life. He idly wondered how many others had been like him. Apparently a lot because he still had a lot of people to convince to change sides, or put away their pride and look at what the Bible said with an open mind.

Once he built the case with factual information related to history it would be a lot easier for the people he would be talking to, make that preaching too, (he had finally recognized what he was doing for what it was) to realize that God was in control and that times were not going to be easy no matter which side of the fence they were on.

Connor did not know what was happening in the rest of the United States but assumed that other areas were much like his own. He made a note to try to get a handle on that through their web site if possible. The new believers needed to stand together insofar as possible in opposing the Antichrist.

The Sunday services were now to the point that they had to have them almost continuously to accommodate all those who wanted to attend. They were doing three sessions in the morning and two in the afternoon and all saw the sanctuary filled to capacity.

One of the first things that happened to give Connor some indication of what the opposition would do came the week after Demir became head of the One World Coalition.

As the first service was starting on Sunday a fire Marshall came and informed Connor that the church held more people than the building was designed for and he would have to either cancel the service or reduce the number to the official capacity level.

The Marshall had to be operating under someone's orders and the likely one would be the Fire Chief or the Mayor, or possibly both.

It took almost 15 minutes to get enough people to leave to reduce the number to what was required, which was 280.

That wasn't the end of it. At each service there was a Fire Marshall at the church to assure that fire regulations were strictly adhered to.

The good side of that is that the Fire Marshalls had to listen to the sermons and the church gained a couple of more converts in that fashion. That in turn meant that Connor learned that it was the Mayor who had insisted upon the actions the Fire Department had taken.

With so many converts it was inevitable that some would be musicians and that aspect of the service took on new life. A choir was formed and a small orchestra, though it only had eight instruments. Connor didn't even know when or where they practiced but the music they produced was appropriate and very well performed.

They didn't do an offertory but had collection plates in the foyer under the supervision of ushers to accept any donations attendees wanted to contribute.

Hardly a week went by that they didn't receive donations in the thousands.

The church rolls had risen to more than 2,000 and it was just not possible to accommodate that many people with what they had. As most ministers would tell you, that is a good problem to have.

Sterling was the one who came up with the best solution. Before he talked to Connor about it he purchased a large tract of land, actually three adjacent lots that a building contractor had been working on when the rapture occurred. That blew a hole in the demand for new housing and the construction came to a halt.

Sterling knew of the situation and that the builder was nearly bankrupt when the One World currency was issued. He purchased the land, which was only a couple of miles from the church and approached Connor with his proposal.

"Do you remember how they used to have the tent revivals in the early to middle part of the 20th century?" he asked.

"Yes, though I never attended," Connor said.

"What would you think about doing that here to get around what the mayor is trying to do?"

"How would we find a place, and what's to stop the Mayor from shutting us down for some fabricated reason?"

"I have the land, about two miles from here in a housing tract that went belly up. We will need to comply with fire department regulations but they will not have much to say about that in an open gathering. The sticker might be permits for a public gathering, although we might be able to get around that because it is private property. Unless the housing association has some prohibition against it, which I don't think they will because it has not been formed yet, we should be okay. I will have a tent set up that will accommodate somewhere around 1,000 and we can give it a shot."

"I like the idea, but I must say in all truth that I don't believe it will last more than a couple of weeks before they find some way to shut us down again," Connor said.

"One step at a time. We can be looking at other alternatives while they are devising their method of shutting us down," Sterling said.

"Run with it. I will have the secretaries notify all our members by e-mail and they can pass the word verbally to anyone they invite. When can we look at the property?"

"Right now if you want. The weather is warm enough that we can dispense with the necessity to heat or cool the tent, which is really huge. The only major drawback is going to be parking space."

"We can ask people to car pool. If necessary we can then have the drivers come back here and bus them to the location," Connor said.

Connor located Larry Elliott and the three went to the location to have a look. Two of the lots were unimproved, that is to say were still covered with trees and other vegetation, while the third had been cleared and preparations started for digging the foundation of a house.

"It won't take very long to clear the lots," Larry observed. "The lot that is already cleared can be used for parking. The lots are at least two acres each and that is a lot of real estate."

"When do you think you will be ready for the tent?" Sterling asked.

"Figure about three days to clear and level the lot. It will be expensive but it can be done rather quickly if we don't worry about making the timber ready for use. I can negotiate with the people who haul it off that they can have the timber at no cost," Larry said.

"I know who to contact about the tent. I can have it erected the same day if you let me know early enough," Sterling said.

"What about sound equipment and a stage?" Connor asked.

"No problem," Larry said. "When they start erecting the tent I can find out where to locate the stage and have the lumber ready the minute they finish getting the tent up."

"Are you sure we don't need permits for this?" Connor asked.

"Since it is on private property and nothing will be bought or sold it can be called a private outing. I'm sure they will try to close that loophole as soon as they possibly can, but until they do we will continue. I think it would be a good idea to have some press, and private photographers as well, attend the first service," Sterling said.

The land clearing started the next morning. As soon as the staff put out the word to the congregation a steady stream of people came to the lot offering help.

Sterling had gotten the huge tent from a circus and hired their crew to erect it. They could do the job in less than three hours in normal circumstances and these circumstances were hardly normal. They drafted some of the people who came to offer assistance and stationed a couple of them at each of the poles. What was normally done in increments of work suddenly was done instantaneously.

The lumber for the stage was ferried into the tent by willing hands and Larry had more help than he really needed. Fortunately some of the new members had building experience and could help with the supervision. By the end of the day the stage was erected inside the tent and lighting wires run for the spot lights and other needed electrical functions.

The music group had a top notch sound guy and instead of moving the equipment from the church Connor told them to purchase new components.

Within two days the installation was complete, including a semi-truck loaded with folding chairs that Sterling had purchased from three different stores because none of them had the quantity needed.

Some of the people who lived in the houses already completed came to see what all the activity was about. Some of them had become believers after the rapture and offered their driveways for parking.

Twelve dump trucks of wood chips had been delivered and spread around the area to keep dust and mud to a minimum.

The church had a bus that had a capacity of 26 and that was not going to be large enough to ferry the people back and forth. Sterling solved the problem by purchasing two used school buses from the school district. Since the rapture the student population had fallen to the point where half the buses sat empty and they were glad to unload them.

Connor decided that they would hold the services for the coming Sunday at the church so as to get the word of the new location to everyone.

Connor used the sermon he had been working on when the news arrived that Ahmet Demir had assumed leadership of the One World Coalition.

He used the examples he had extracted from the history books, supplemented by Bible prophecy from both the Old and New Testaments.

"What I am attempting to do is show you that the sequence of events portrayed in Revelation are precisely as history says they have occurred. The first four Seals spoken of in the Revelation deal with false prophets, war, famine and finally pestilence," he said.

"The descriptions of the ancient churches helps to explain some of that. Those descriptions are symbolic. In other words the Revelation is not talking about the old churches at all but is using them as examples to us that help us to understand what is really being said. The churches actually represent the different activities of the Christian religion down through two thousand plus years."

"All the cities mentioned, where the churches were located, are in Asia Minor, or to be more accurate, what is now southern Turkey. All are described as having their own set of unique problems, but most of that you can learn by reading the letters of Paul to the different churches. I don't believe God felt it necessary to reinforce Paul's admonitions to the churches in his letters. So if we take the initial chapters of Revelation as symbolic we can see that the first four seals opened by Christ beginning in chapter six represent things that occurred since Christ was here on earth."

"First false prophets. That has been happening for two thousand years. All the different religions and sects that came about since Christ was on earth represent a barrier to true believers. When someone didn't like what the church taught they simply started their own group of worshipers. The only problem with that was that they were not teaching the true word of God, but bending scripture to meet their own interpretations. This was a problem in almost every segment of the earth's population. Confucius, Buddha, the Hindu God(s), were made objects of worship.

Even our own Protestants and Catholics strayed from the truth. All of that fulfills the prophesy of false prophets arising. To illustrate that point I direct your attention to the people like us who remain on earth. Only about half the population disappeared. If not for the false prophets don't you think a lot more would have disappeared? Now my view is that God was not necessarily talking about some person or idol becoming an object of worship, though that is certainly a large part of the problem. I am talking about things like loving a sinful life, our own vanity, or even a Godlike worship of the dollar, or franc, or drachma, or any other currency. I could go on in this vein but I am trying to illustrate to you that the first four seals actions have already occurred."

"The second seal dealt with war. Look down through the ages and I defy you to prove to me that there was any time in the last two thousand years when a war was not going on. Back in early times they used bows, swords, lances, and whatever else would best do in their enemies. Just to mention a few of those who helped to fulfill this part of the prophesy, Attila the Hun comes to mind, as does Napoleon, and several others of the same ilk. Lest we should forget, there were the Holy Crusades, which were nothing more than a license for the church to purify and eliminate those they didn't like in the Middle East. If we take that to the current time, in the last century there have been almost constant wars, each more terrible that the forerunner. The Nazi's and the Communists did terrible things as well."

"The third seal deals with famine. There have been famines that we know about from the Middle Ages to now. When was the last time any of you watched television without seeing an advertisement soliciting funds to quote, feed the hungry, unquote."

"The fourth seal deals with pestilence. That simply means disease. In Christ's time leprosy was one of the more noticeable diseases. As time went on and people moved about the earth's surface more freely things such as cholera, smallpox, the plague, which incidentally wiped out more than half the population of Europe and the Middle East. Take that a bit further and we have things like Ebola and AIDS. So I submit to you that the things I just enumerated have fulfilled prophesy of the first four seals."

"That brings us the fifth item on God's agenda, Tribulation. That began the day Jesus called his children home, but according to Daniel is not officially ushered in until the peace treaty is signed between the Antichrist and Israel. We are now in the early days of that seven year period in which events too terrible to mention will occur. The tribulation is mentioned more than thirty times in the Bible, apart from Revelation, and none of it is good."

"The Antichrist will arise, and I think he is already there in the person of Ahmet Demir. The seven years of the tribulation will be unlike anything the earth has ever experienced. Those who believe in a risen savior will be persecuted, and many killed for their beliefs. The first thing that happened was the formation of a one world government. That would be the One World Coalition. From this point on it is downhill for those who believe in Christ. We will be ridiculed, and opposed at every step. Eventually those who refuse to take the mark of the Antichrist will be killed outright. Israel will be conquered by the forces of evil and this will eventually lead to what most people call the battle of Armageddon. This will be the last gasp for the forces of Satan as they try to take on the forces of God. No surprise there as to who comes out on top."

"There are a bunch of other things that will happen during this period but we don't have time to get into all of them. Instead I would suggest that you read the Book of Revelation and consult our web site for references to other books of the Bible that will help you to understand them better. Now we will have our hymn of invitation. Those who wish to learn more or have decided that God is the answer, please come forward and we will talk with you."

At the close of the hymn some 25 people had come forward.

While everyone was waiting for the closing prayer Connor elucidated a bit more about the new facility. "Since we have outgrown this building we will hold services like they did a hundred years ago, in a large tent. The address is in the bulletin. Because we have so little parking there I would ask folks to come here and car pool to the other facility. Then the drivers will be picked up here by bus and brought back to the tent. We should be able to seat around 1,000 so tell your friends and neighbors to come have a listen."

Chapter 13

The work on the tent had only taken a week and they had not been bothered during the process. Connor attributed this to the fact that the authorities didn't know what they were doing. Now that the announcement had been made and the address published in the church bulletin there was no way they would not be found out in short order. The only unknown was how the Antichrist would react.

With so many people to accommodate they still had to have a service in the morning and one in the afternoon on the first Sunday they used the facility.

At the morning service the tent was packed and people were standing outside to hear the sermon.

Some of the people he had detailed as security forces reported that some of the watchers from the church had shown up and had several people inside the tent. The ushers were all armed, though not obviously so. Since the incident earlier with the protesters nobody had objected to the procedure.

The security staff had set up a watch rotation to have at least three people at the site at all times. It would be a simple matter for someone to try to torch the tent during the night and while that would not be a catastrophe it would set them back replacing the tent.

They had detected people riding by the site during the late hours but had not had any trouble. Some of those driving by might have been trying to confirm the location to come to church during services but the wee hours of the morning was not the most opportune time to do that sort of reconnaissance.

They went through three weeks of using the tent before they had any trouble.

When the early arrivals showed up on the fourth weekend city officials were already at the site. The police chief and the fire chief both were present, along with several police officers.

They said nothing to anyone until Connor arrived. They then went to him and presented him with an eviction notice. He looked the paper over and handed it back. "I'm sorry but I can't comply with this until you can show me what laws I have broken," he said.

"You can't have a public gathering of this sort without getting a permit," the police chief said.

"This is not a public gathering. You are standing on private land and all the people here are part of the same family. We don't charge admission and we don't serve food, so what regulation are we violating?" Connor asked.

"You are telling me that all these people are related to you?" the police chief asked incredulously.

"That's correct. We are all part of the family of God," Connor replied with a straight face.

"You haven't heard the last of this," the police chief said as he stomped away.

Both services went off without further incident that day. They had a total of almost 3,000 people at both services.

Instead of the sermon he had intended to preach Connor told everyone about the visit from city officials. "Now this is only my opinion but I believe they were directed to shut us down by others. I imagine the word came from the Mayor, who heard it from someone in the government, who heard it from someone in the One World Coalition. You all know who runs that. I imagine we will witness a complete rewriting of the city's regulations concerning public gatherings in the very near future. This is but one manifestation of what the Bible says will happen in our times."

He then went into Revelation and read the applicable portion of the prophecy that talked about the Antichrist and the one world religion. "The peaceful takeover has already occurred and now things will start to get worse as the Antichrist solidifies his position. Don't be surprised if you hear of him working miracles either. I don't know what form they will take but the Bible says God gives Satan the power to perform miracles until the tribulation comes to an end. Those of us around when that happens will see Satan get his comeuppance as they say in the old western movies."

Connor had been right about the changes in city regulations. When they went for the service the following Sunday Connor was presented with a sheet of rewritten ordinances. It stated that any gathering of more than 100 people, whether held on private or public land required a permit from the city. There was a lot of jawing among the people who had planned to attend the service but Connor didn't want a showdown with city officials at this point. He knew the direction didn't actually come from the city but from the One World Coalition.

Neither Connor, nor anyone else in his group knew what to do at this point. They could go back to using the church and holding multiple services but they would still need to get a permit according to the new city regulations.

Of course the first thing that came to mind was prayer for guidance from God and Connor did that, as did many in the church. Sterling was staying in the Washington area almost full time now. He called Connor on Monday after the new city regulations were delivered and asked him to meet him at an address not familiar to him. The address was in Fairfax, which is adjacent to Washington and is fairly spread out.

Connor agreed to meet and drove to the address. He didn't know what to expect but was surprised when he discovered who Sterling had with him. He recognized the Mayor of Fairfax and wondered what this was all about.

When he parked and went to the two Sterling explained the situation.

"Mayor Freeburg received a call from the D.C. mayor about our camp meeting and decided to see what it was all about firsthand. He attended the services yesterday and learned about what had happened. Not only is he not in the other camp but because of your sermon decided that you were right and the other guys were wrong. He accepted Christ during the service though he didn't come forward. He thought he might better be able to help if he kept a low profile. He suggested that we might move the tent to this location. He owns the land and is willing to either sell it to us or donate it for our use."

Connor shook hands and said, "You realize that you will be pressured by the One World Coalition to shut us down?"

"I figured as much but I can at least stall them for a while. It's funny you know. I am Jewish and never gave any thought to religion of any sort. I figured I knew more about how to live my life than some God I couldn't see. Even after all the disappearances I still didn't put it together until I heard you talk about the things that were happening in fulfillment of Bible Prophesy. I looked up some of the references you gave after I got home and the entire situation became as plain as the nose on my face, and that takes up a lot of space."

Connor laughed at the quip. Freeburg did have a very prominent nose.

"I am Jewish and you would think I knew more about my ancestor's beliefs but the reverse is true. I probably, make that certainly, know less about the Bible than most of those you were preaching to yesterday. Now that I can see the reason for what is happening I don't want to miss the next train," he said.

"You mean when Christ comes again you want to be ready?" Connor asked.

"Exactly. I'm a little slow I guess but with your help I saw the light. I now need to know what I have to do to make sure I am doing what God wants me to do."

"The Bible says that once we receive Christ though faith that we are indwelt by the Holy Spirit, which is another manifestation of the Godhead. You can't see the Holy Spirit either, but you can certainly feel him. I think that is what most people think about as a conscience. When you start to do something that isn't according to God's plan you will have a guilty feeling. The opposite is also true. If you are doing what God wants you to do you have a good feeling about it. Lest you should feel alone in your unbelief read Revelation again. I believe it is in the chapter 7 where the part about the 144,000 from the Jewish tribes is mentioned. All these were non-believers before the rapture so you are far from alone among the Hebrews. As a matter of fact, Mordecai, one of the two witnesses in Jerusalem now told me that I was also part of that number and I didn't even know I had any Jewish ancestors."

"There hasn't been much on television about those two lately," Freeburg said.

"That's because the One World Coalition has banned reporters from reporting about them. I have a friend who leads the new Jewish believers and he keeps me posted. Those two are part of the prophesy and were sent by God to preach to the Jews. They will preach for three and one half years and then God will allow them to be killed. Their bodies will lie in the streets of Jerusalem for three days and then God will resurrect them."

"I wondered about that when I read about it in Revelation. Does fire really come out of their mouths?"

"Yes, and when anyone who isn't a believer tries to touch them they immediately collapse. Ephraim and I both hugged them without any adverse results. What I can tell you is that they felt as warm as if they had been sitting around a fire, and it was winter time in the open air.

142

Another thing you should know is that you are bringing a pile of trouble down on yourself by believing. The next seven, or six and a half years now, are not going to be a picnic. We will be persecuted, ridiculed, physically attacked and once the Antichrist decides to implement his one world religion, killed if we don't worship his likeness. The Bible also says that those who refuse to take his mark will be slain. After the trumpet judgements and plagues talked about in Revelation start to come about many of the earth's population will be killed. Only about a tenth of the population will make it to the time when Christ returns. Those aren't very good odds, but I would much rather be doing what God Wants me to do than what the Devil demands. I also don't believe new believers will be immune to some of the things that are going to happen. God might be planning otherwise, but I just don't know, and I don't think the answer to that question is in the Bible. It does say that we are not meant to understand the mystery of God's ways. If it sounds like I am trying to change your mind I apologize. That is not my intention. I just think you should be aware of the consequences of your belief."

"I appreciate your forthrightness, but I believe seven years of misery in exchange for eternal life is a good bargain, and you know we Jews are always looking for bargains," Freeburg said with a chuckle.

"So what is your suggestion for this land Sterling?"

"Do the same thing we did at the other location. It will take a couple of days to clear the land and another day to move the tent, but that should buy us another three or four weeks. I will start to look for land in other locales where they don't have regulations about public gatherings and we will just continue to move about until things start to get out of hand."

"I wish there was some way to fight it but as the saying goes, 'you can't fight city hall'."

"One thing we can do is make sure it makes the news. Remember we have someone in that business and he might be able to slip something into his newscasts to further our cause," Sterling said.

"If we start on this today can we have it ready for Sunday?" Connor asked.

"I think so. Get Larry out here as soon as possible and he can organize some labor to help with the clearing. I will arrange to have the tent taken down and moved out here."

Connor called Larry from there and asked him to come out. It took thirty minutes and he brought a couple of others who were in the building trades.

"How much land is yours?" Connor asked Freeburg.

"I have over a hundred acres. Clear whatever you need for parking too. Just to be on the safe side I will file for a building permit for a temporary structure in your name and send someone out to point out any requirements of the city. I know the electric and sewer will have to be inspected but since everything else is temporary you should be okay. I suggest you use portable johns and locate them in pods at different areas around the property."

Larry nodded his acceptance. "I can get started on it today. You wouldn't believe how many people want to help. I can have a crew tear down the stage at the other place and re-erect it here."

When they got back to the church Connor called Darren Waite and asked him if he could work something into the news about what the city had done.

"I don't know if I can or not. You realize that I am just a reporter who runs down stories. I don't do any of the studio reporting so the only way I will be able to do anything is to insert a comment while reporting on some other story," he said.

"Just do what you can without getting into trouble," Connor said.

Strangely enough Connor need not have worried about Darren mentioning the situation. The local news that night told the story from the political side of the question. The news reporter had some film during the services on Sunday and used that as a lead-in to his story.

"What you are looking at is an illegal meeting held by one of the local churches. They erected a large tent on some housing lots to hold their meetings. As you can see a lot of people came to the meeting. City officials went to the site and requested that the meeting be broken up since they didn't have a permit for a public gathering. The pastor told the police and fire chiefs that everyone there was part of his family. When the chief's expressed their disbelief they were told that all the people were part of the family of God," the announcer said trying to hide a laugh and not succeeding.

"After consulting with others in leadership positions within the city the regulations were rewritten to prevent things like this from happening in the future. The regulations state that any public gathering of more than 100 people requires a permit from the city and that city officials have to approve the site before meetings of this type can be held. These are the people who say God was responsible for the mass disappearances some months ago. Now to other news..."

Connor was delighted with the newscaster's story but would have bet money that he would be looking for a new job soon.

There was a spike in the number of people accessing their web site after the story, and the phones were busy for the rest of the night. Most of the inquiries were about where the church group would meet now. Connor instructed the secretaries to tell people to call back on Friday and they would be given the address of the new facility.

The next day's newspaper headlines indicated that the Antichrist was starting to become more brazen. It read,

Coalition forces put down rebellion in Iran.

The story related that the Muslim population of the Middle Eastern countries was advocating an overthrow of the One World Coalition and they had sent troops to monitor the situation.

A car bomb had been detonated near the troops and several were killed. When the troops went to the mosque and demanded to have the persons who were responsible handed over they met armed resistance and acted accordingly. Some sources said that as many as 5,000 Iranians were killed. No word yet on the number of Coalition casualties.

Connor had not given much thought to how other religious groups would fare during the tribulation, such as the Muslims. The Antichrist was apparently going to have to wage war on several fronts to consolidate his leadership. The Muslim reaction was probably what would happen in India, China, Japan, and other countries who worshiped a different deity.

He tried to look at the entire population from the standpoint of the Antichrist. Christians were going to be harder to deal with than the pseudo religions who worshiped other Gods and Satan would know that. Therefore getting those people under his thumb before getting serious about dealing with the new flock of Christians would be a higher priority.

It appeared that the new location would be ready for Sunday services and they published the address in the web site and started giving it to callers.

When Sunday arrived Connor was astounded at the number of people who showed up. His church rolls were over 3,000 now and the tent would accommodate probably 1,500 if they packed them in. The first service at 10:00

Sunday morning saw the tent completely full a good 15 minutes before the service started.

Some of the church members had carpooled but the parking area they had prepared was filled. Some people anticipating a large crowd had brought lawn chairs and set up along the edges of the tent on the outside.

Connor consulted with Larry and they decided to open the tent flaps to allow the sound to be heard outside and accommodate those who could not get inside. The weather was warm and the opening of the tent flaps would allow the breeze to help the situation a bit.

There were nearly 4,000 at the first service and the second one in the afternoon was almost as well attended.

For his part Connor stuck with the basics. First was the way to Christ and second was the commitment required. He always had a segment on Revelation because he thought it was very important for the people to understand that they were very close to the end times and that they could expect a rough road ahead. Still many people came during the invitation.

They didn't have any trouble from the city as the Mayor had made sure that everything was done according to city regulations. Freeburg called Connor on Tuesday and told him that he had received a call from the One World Coalition requesting that he have the meetings canceled but he refused on the grounds that they weren't violating any city ordinances.

On the second Sunday that they used the site they again opened the flaps to accommodate more people and make it a bit more comfortable for those inside.

Connor had just mounted the podium and was ready to begin his sermon. As he opened his Bible his marker fell to the floor. He bent to retrieve it and heard one of the choir members behind him yell out in pain. A second later he heard the report of a rifle. Instead of getting to his feet he rolled to the back of the stage and onto the ground four feet below. There was pandemonium in the tent as people sought cover.

Connor moved to the side of the stage and peered around it from a lower angle. He knew where the shot had to come from by the person in the choir who was struck. He had been pulled from the stage and several people were treating him using the stage as cover.

The area from which the shot had come was a slight rise in the terrain. One would not call it a hill, but it provided enough elevation for a clear shot with the sides of the tent rolled up. Connor could see several cars moving from the parking lot in that direction and four or five others moving on foot toward the area. He thought that might be a foolhardy move but nothing happened during the next few minutes.

He had come to the conclusion that the rifleman had made his getaway when he heard several shots fired. People were starting to get to their feet and the flurry of gunfire caused many of them to hit the deck again.

Soon the group who had gone in pursuit returned and told Connor that the shooter was dead. "There was only one individual and he apparently had made his way to the location through the woods because no car was found."

Mayor Freeburg was present at the service and placed a call to the police and reported the incident. Those who had killed the sniper left his body where it had fallen.

Connor mounted the stage again and picked up with his sermon.

When the police showed up a couple of the ushers took them to the location where the body lay and Connor didn't even interrupt the service.

Afterwards he got together with Sterling and Mayor Freeburg. "I don't know if they will be able to connect the shooter to anyone in particular but it really doesn't matter. Whether it was some disgruntled individual or he was ordered to make the attempt by someone else it is all the same. What's the status of the choir member who was hit?"

"He has been taken to the hospital. I don't know how serious the wound was. He was hit in the upper chest, but on the right side," he was told.

When Connor got to the hospital he was told that the victim was in surgery but was expected to pull through.

Connor called Ephraim later in the day and told him what had happened.

"I see God's hand in that," Ephraim said.

"I hadn't thought about it in those terms but of course you are right. I just happened to bend down when the shot was fired."

"I guess God isn't through with you yet."

"That would appear to be the case," Connor replied.

Chapter 14

Over the course of the next two weeks the news was filled with accounts of attacks on religious locations worldwide. More Islamic mosques were bombed, Buddhist temples were attacked and India was in a state of civil war between Muslim's and Hindu's. The One World Coalition sent troops to those areas, ostensibly as peace keepers.

Instead of dying down the troubles seemed to get worse.

There were isolated attacks against Christians in places like England and Greece, even in Finland and Sweden, but very low key. From what was on the news Connor surmised that the leaders of Christian churches were the main targets.

It was in the seventh month of the Tribulation when all television stations interrupted their programming for a special report. A nuclear explosion had been detected in one of India's larger cities. Within an hour another news bulletin reported that another nuclear explosion had been detected in Karachi, Pakistan.

No surprise there since India and Pakistan were bitter enemies. The Indians apparently blamed the Pakistani's and retaliated.

Ahmet Demir was on the news immediately after the second report and said that additional troops would be deployed to the two countries involved and that he was hoping to get a ban on nuclear weapons. "The world peace is simply too fragile to allow situations such as this to make matters worse."

Within a month the One World Coalition had drafted a resolution whereby all nations would destroy all their nuclear weapons. The resolution wasn't unanimous but there were only a few holdouts. Israel, the United States and Russia were the detractors to the resolution and Demir reported that he would be visiting each of those countries for individual talks with their leaders.

Even before Demir could embark on his mission two more nuclear detonations were detected. One was in Moscow and another in Beijing, China. The public thought that the additional explosions were orchestrated by one country against the other but no evidence of a delivery system for the weapons had been detected by any of the nations with satellite surveillance of the two areas in question.

A journalist for one of the higher profile networks postulated that the rash of nuclear detonations might be an intentional act by some entity trying to push for a ban of nuclear weapons. He was immediately taken off the air and no more was said about that subject.

While it was certainly possible that the journalist had been right on the money, the One World Coalition, to whom he was obviously referring in his remarks had no nuclear capability that the public knew about. The United Nations, the predecessor organization certainly didn't.

That Demir could get weapons from countries who did possess them the born again Christians had no doubt.

Since it appeared that Demir could not get all countries with nukes on board he proposed an alternative. Since Russia, the United States and China had existing storage facilities for such weapons the three locations would become the depository for all nuclear weapons in their respective areas. A fourth area in the Middle East, in Turkey, would store the weapons from the Middle Eastern Countries.

According to his proposal all weapons would be identified as to country and if the weapons were needed in case of a world war or to defend their home countries the weapons would be returned.

Connor thought that proposal was so ludicrous that no one would accept such circumstances.

That just goes to show why Connor was not a politician. Demir structured the plan so that members of each country's Nuclear control boards would provide troops to man the storage site for ready access to the weapons should they be needed.

The scheme was just crazy enough that it worked. Russia, China and the United States would end up storing only their own weapons, which they would do in any case. That took care of the opposition from those countries. The Israeli's were the only hold-outs. They did not want their weapons to go anyplace unless they sent them on the nose cone of a rocket.

Demir visited Israel and talked with the Prime Minister and his cabinet. An under the table deal was made with the Israeli's allowing them to keep half a dozen nukes while storing the remainder in Turkey.

The measure passed the One World Coalition's vote and was implemented within 60 days.

The violence continued in India and most of the Middle Eastern countries. News coverage was minimal considering the huge number of casualties and the manner in which the One World Coalition was going about 'keeping the peace'.

It seemed that new government leaders for a majority of the countries arose almost overnight. India had a new Premier since the incumbent had been killed in the fighting. Iran also had a new head of government, as did Afghanistan, France and Germany. In the Far East some of the lesser known countries had changed governments two or three times in little less than a year.

The Russian Premier was under fire for agreeing to the nuclear ban, though the opposition was quickly squelched. In almost all cases the new leaders were more closely aligned with the One World Coalition.

Religious wars were still going on all over the world and no one had even guessed at the number of casualties.

Still the Christian segment had not come under any harsh resistance and this bothered Connor and Ephraim considerably.

Connor was still having to move the meeting location every month or so to avoid clashes with city or county governments.

Demir announced plans to build a new governing complex in Babylon. His reasoning was that it was more centrally located to the areas in most need and historically had been one of the most successful centers of commerce of all times. The Iraqi's agreed to provide barracks for the peace keeping forces and the new headquarters would house the administrative staff.

Connor wasn't sure about how this move related to his understanding of Revelation. He spent more time reading what others had said about the sequence of events before the rapture. The only things he was absolutely certain about was that the rapture had occurred, the Antichrist had arisen, and the two witnesses had appeared.

He assumed that the wars going on at the current time were part and parcel of the second horseman. The next thing to happen would be famine but who was to say that more than one of the events couldn't happen simultaneously? The move of the one world religious leader to Babylon was prophesied and that couldn't happen overnight. They would first have to have some place from which to operate.

Demir had predicted that the complex could be completed in a year, so other things would be happening while the construction was taking place.

The single thing that amazed him most was that the Christian populace had not been subjected to the kind of things he expected. His assumption that Demir wanted to get the rest of the population under control before he devoted a lot of time and effort to his major opposition seemed to be a fact and he wondered when the hammer would fall.

All the services his church held were standing room only, even when the people didn't know from week to week where they would be meeting.

He had kept the number of people who knew where the farm hideout was located to a bare minimum. The original group, under 200, were the only ones who knew about it and he urged them not to talk about it outside their small group.

Sterling had been like a man possessed keeping ahead of the authorities with places to set up for their services. He and Larry had become almost inseparable the job was so daunting.

Connor continued to sound the warning that things were going to get much worse. Every sermon he preached emphasized that the tribulation was the time when Satan would be most powerful and that things would go his way until the end.

"All we can do is maintain our faith no matter how dark the situation becomes. God has assured us of a heavenly home when all this is over and nothing can take that away from us as long as we continue to believe in Him."

The news was obviously being censored because they heard very little about what was going on in the areas where war was raging. They also heard very little about what was going on in Israel, though Ephraim kept Connor updated almost daily.

Ephraim's group had grown to the point that he did most of his sermons on the internet and several locations broadcast them at normal church times. He too was worried that they had not been subjected to any really rough stuff from Demir and his lackeys.

Demir had started his own church services. He televised his services worldwide and espoused his belief that God had given him powers beyond mortal men. He was like the faith healers who used the tent revivals in the 20th century. While some of the healings he supposedly performed were fake, others had the ring of sincerity. The Bible said that God would give him the power to perform miracles and it could be that this was the manner in which he chose to promote himself as the deity.

Through a combination of showmanship and his real powers it became readily apparent that he was something more than a mortal man. He had, through some miracle, proved that he could heal. A man had been brought to him during one of his services who had been attacked by detractors outside his meeting place. He had been severely cut across his abdomen. He was literally holding his intestines in with his hands.

Demir lifted his hands and prayed for healing. He then placed his hands over the man's hands and within seconds the incision had healed and there was no evidence of the wound.

The man sang his praises and bowed down to him. The cameras caught the entire sequence and the man was interviewed afterward. "He is truly God. I know how badly I was hurt and after he touched me it was as if it had not happened."

Other less dramatic events seemed to prove that he had healing powers and it was not long before leaders in almost every country proclaimed him the one true God. He did nothing to discount the accolades and his stature grew by the day.

All that tracked with Connor's view of what was to happen. He expected the wars to gradually die down with the rise of Demir to God-like status. He would unite the world under his own religious rule and the evidence shown on the media would go a long way toward settling the religious differences between the various world religions.

If Connor understood what was to happen next, and he thought he did, then famine would immediately follow the many wars that were raging around the planet. Also, if Demir was the religious leader, someone would have to be the political front man.

Not only did the wars, mostly of the civil variety, hamper food production but there was a pretty severe drought all over the planet. Even the state of Virginia, where Connor lived, was well below normal for rainfall. They only got about half what was normal and many of the farms had stunted crops if they managed to keep anything alive.

The farm that his group operated had a creek running though it and someone suggested pumping water from the creek to irrigate. Since the farm was not overly large they simply pumped the water into tanks on the back of pickup trucks and hauled it to the rows of crops and pumped it out onto the ground along the rows of vegetation.

One of Larry's friends was a plumber and he rigged a two inch line from the pump to the fields that was moveable. That way they simply pumped directly to the fields. It was a bit labor intensive but kept the crops thriving.

Other parts of the North American continent were very dry based on normal rainfall and with the smaller number of farmers after the rapture they produced less than a forth of what was usually available.

Europe also experienced drought and parts of Asia, where mostly rice was grown, had the same problems.

The Bible said that the two witnesses would have the ability to bring drought and pestilence and Connor suspected that they might be responsible for the conditions. He thought this because the insects were more voracious than normal as well. Much of the crops that were growing were eaten by locusts, grasshoppers, crickets and other worms that normally fed on thriving plants.

Even very early in the growing season it became apparent that the world was going to be in for a rough year.

Connor made another trip to Israel and consulted with Ephraim. Together they went to visit the two at the Wailing Wall and Connor asked about the coming calamities.

All they would say was that whatever happened was what God wanted to happen.

The farm made a lot of money that year. With the dearth of crops anything worth eating brought a good price, even with the One World Coalition making the purchases. In addition they squirreled enough away to help take care of their fellow church members.

There still had not been much opposition to the new Christians. There were isolated incidents of violence but nothing like what Connor thought should be happening by now.

Within eight months of starting the construction on the facility in the location of ancient Babylon, it was marginally ready to move into.

Demir even lobbied to have the name changed back to Babylon. "After all," he said, "was it not Babylon in ancient times?"

Nobody could argue with that, and frankly the Iraqi's didn't much care what it was called. They looked at the One World Coalition as a provider of commerce to make their lives a bit more tolerable.

Right on the heels of that move Demir decreed that there was simply too many religious beliefs in the world and that worshiping one God would make things better for everyone. He had one of his higher profile minions suggest that since Demir had Godlike abilities it made sense for him to be the object of worship.

A few more miracles were performed that made the news before Demir 'reluctantly' agreed that he was indeed immortal, along with the other powers he had. "We will let everyone make his own choice for now, but all churches, mosques, temples, and other areas where people congregate to worship will be called Church of the Divine One."

The One World Currency was changed to show an image of Demir and it was ordered that a lifelike statue of Demir should be produced for each house of worship as soon as possible. Since the project was already well along, without the general public's knowledge, it went rather quickly.

As the famine got worse around the world it got more attention than any other news item. Rationing was instituted and food was very tightly controlled.

Many deaths occurred in backwater areas that were not easy to access. Many of the areas were not strangers to famine and accepted the death toll stoically.

Nobody seemed to know for sure how many casualties resulted from the famine but food theft became the most common crime for which thieves were prosecuted. And on top of that the penalty for stealing food was death. Jewelry and electronics were the most popular items stolen prior to that time but fencing stolen food became more profitable.

The reasoning behind the death penalty for stealing food was that if they incarcerated the thieves they would waste more food keeping them alive and they were in fact responsible for deaths by stealing food from others.

The procedure was readily accepted as the best manner in which to deal with thieves.

The Christian communities decided they could live with the designation of the 'Church of the Divine One'. After all, God was the Divine One to them. They still worshiped their own God and they had a better than average percentage of survivors through the famine than the population at large. That was due in part to the Christian principle of sharing with others in need. Most people lost a few pounds during the period and the percentage of overweight people dropped dramatically.

Within eighteen months Demir was firmly in control of almost every segment of society worldwide. Connor surmised that he used some mind control technique to achieve the cooperation of some of his opponents, but no one really knew.

When Madam Gonzorov was assassinated and brought back to life by Demir he decreed that he be the object of worship for the entire world population.

This was the point at which the Christians came under heavy fire.

Connor had continued to warn everyone that hard times were coming but he was not sure he was believed by everyone, especially the newer converts.

With the entire planet under his control Demir pulled off the gloves. He instructed his security forces to go to every location where the Christians were holding services and insure they had his stature on prominent display and if any refused they were to be executed on the spot.

Most of the locations were known through surveillance during the previous 18 months and the forces started to gather in the areas where churches were located.

The gathering of troops did not escape the attention of the Christians and they quickly passed the word to their leaders.

Connor decided to take a drastic step which would make him even more of a fugitive of the One World Coalition. He passed the word to the Christians to come to church on Sunday armed.

He fully expected troops to show up and try to enforce the edict that the image of Demir be worshipped and there was no way on God's green earth that he would do that himself or have the people he led do it.

When the first service started on Sunday there were more than two thousand in attendance. Most had gotten the word to come armed and about two thirds had done so, both men and women. He noticed women carrying purses that he had never seen with them before.

When the service got underway they had the tent flaps open for better ventilation, but also for a better view of what was going on around them. The tent was set up in Loudoun County, just west of Fairfax and a bit to the north. It was only the second week thay had used the location and they so far had not been bothered.

Connor had just completed the opening prayer. The statue of Demir mandated was nowhere in sight. As a matter of fact, the church didn't have one. When Connor looked up after his prayer he noticed the tent was almost entirely encircled by One World Coalition troops. A small group was marching toward the entrance to the tent. Silence fell on the worshipers like a curtain.

The leader of the group entered the tent and asked where their stature of Demir was.

Connor looked directly at him and said, "We don't worship Demir. We worship the true God."

The man already had a pistol in his hand and raised it and shot Connor, at least he thought he did. Connor, however, remained standing.

The shot had galvanized his parishioners though and within seconds a full scale battle was underway. The troops inside the tent fell immediately to multiple gunshots. The troops outside the tent reacted quickly and started spraying gunfire into the tent.

Connor did not know why he was still alive. He had seen the weapon pointed directly at him and from the distance a miss was highly unlikely.

The training Connor insisted on for his people paid off and they returned fire like veterans. Because the troops were badly outnumbered the battle was over rather quickly. The aftermath was another matter entirely.

More than 200 people inside the tent were dead or wounded. They couldn't take them to hospitals because they would be found by the Coalition forces and killed in their beds.

The only viable option Connor could see was to transport them to the hideout in the country and try to care for them on their own. They had several doctors and the limiting factor would be a lack of medical equipment and supplies.

Connor organized the teams to transport the wounded and others to gather the dead. The Coalition forces he didn't worry about, other than to instruct someone to pick up the weapons and ammunition to add to their stock. The action was so sudden that he didn't believe any of the troops had time to report what was happening by radio.

"You folks who are not involved in the transport of the wounded go ahead home and pray for all of us. This has to be the beginning of the hard times and they will try to do us in quickly. We will continue to broadcast on the internet so keep an eye on the website. Don't talk about any of this to your neighbors or it will lead the Antichrist directly to you. Remember, seek God's guidance in all you do, and try to keep a low profile."

Before everyone departed Connor said a prayer for those who were killed and asked for God's mercy on those wounded. Several people volunteered to move the dead and bury them.

Chapter 15

Connor had started to keep a suitcase in his car at all times a few weeks previously and couldn't think of any reason he should go by his house. It was possible that it was being watched and he didn't want to take the chance of leading someone to the place in the country.

As he drove he replayed the scene in the tent. He was absolutely certain that the gun fired at him had been well aimed. Why he wasn't struck could only be God's intervention. Maybe he had interpreted the section of Revelation wrong about the 144,000 being sealed by God. Perhaps it meant that they could not be killed as some seemed to think. He had interpreted 'sealed by God' to mean that their faith would be unshakeable, but since on at least two occasions he had been spared when he could have certainly been killed might mean that the 144,000 were under God's protection. He would have to discuss it with Ephraim.

When he arrived in the woods behind the house it was packed with vehicles. There had been over 100 wounded and it was going to stress the facility to handle all of them. He would need to get together with Larry and Sterling to come up with a plan to deal with the situation.

Many of those who had transported the wounded were not part of the original group and the circle of knowledge about the hideout became much wider. It was only a matter of time before Coalition forces would come calling. They needed another back-up plan immediately.

Once they got the wounded into the facility and treatment was started, he got all the newcomers together and gave them a short lecture about security and the fact that they should not reveal the location to anyone outside the group there now.

More of the wounded died during the night, simply because they did not have the equipment necessary to treat the severity of the wounds.

Cots had been moved into the farm house and more than 20 were being cared for there. About a dozen with less life threatening wounds were moved to the farm house down the road.

When Connor had dealt with the immediate problems he called Ephraim.

"You won't believe what happened here," he said. "Coalition forces showed up during our worship services and demanded to see the statue of Demir. I told them we didn't have one that we worshiped the True God. The leader had his pistol in his hand and was no more than about 25 feet from me. I saw the bore of the pistol as he tried to shoot me. He didn't hit me, though I don't see how he could have missed. That is the second time I should be dead. I am wondering if I misinterpreted the part about being sealed. What are your thoughts?"

"Well, Revelation 7:3 says, hurt not the earth, neither the sea, nor the trees, till we have sealed the servants of our God in their foreheads. The next verse goes on to talk about who is to be sealed and that is the 144,000 from the tribes of Israel. I am not sure at what point this is to occur but modern thought is that it will occur at the same time Satan seals his believers."

"The scripture says that the task will be performed by an angel of God but doesn't mention where the event takes place in the sequence of events. I am leaning toward the belief that we were sealed from the beginning. I know that we were not aware of any physical action, but it could be like the indwelling of the Holy Spirit. It simply happens when we become believers. Maybe the sealing was like that," Connor said.

"What you say certainly makes sense. I have been working with many I know to be part of the 144,000 and I don't recall hearing of any of them being killed, though many believers have already been killed," Ephraim said.

"Maybe it is not visible to us but is intended for God's angels to know who to protect."

"That is also a distinct possibility. How many were hurt in the attack on your congregation?"

"We had over 100 killed and about the same number wounded. We took the wounded to the hideout and our doctors cared for them as best they could. Several more died. I don't know what the final count is going to be. I guess we really go underground now."

"I don't expect to hear anything about it on the news. What happened to the troops?"

"They all died in the attack. My people were all armed and returned fire after the first shot was fired at me. They really made me glad that I insisted on the firearms training," Connor said.

"Not a single one escaped?"

"Not a one. And I don't think they had time to even relay the word to their headquarters about what went down. It should be interesting to see how this plays out in the news."

"For sure it means that the rough stuff is now underway."

As they talked someone ran inside shouting, "Come outside and look at this!"

Connor said, "Got something happening. I will get back to you."

He hung up and followed the man outside.

The clouds were boiling and turning black. The sky was alive with lightening. Large raindrops started to fall. Soon the rain turned to hail, not just small pellets, but some as large as baseballs.

The group who had been watching retreated under shelter very quickly. The hailstones grew larger with every passing minute.

Connor grabbed a trashcan and put it over his head. He then made his way to the house to see if the roof was holding up to the onslaught. As he crossed the open space he glanced at the fields and to his amazement noticed that the hail was not falling on the crops.

He mentally reviewed his understanding of Revelation and decided that this had to be the start of the trumpet judgements. The first was supposed to be hail and fire mixed with blood. This was by far the worst hail he had ever witnessed.

He got inside the house and asked if the roof was holding up, to which the answer was yes. There didn't appear to be any damage other than a few dents.

Connor told those in the house that he believed this was the beginning of the trumpet judgements and that they could expect fire and blood as part of the judgement.

The hail continued to fall until the trees were stripped of leaves and small branches. The ground could not be seen in any direction except the fields where the crops were growing. Before much longer there was at least three feet of hail on the ground.

The hail gradually ceased and the rain recommenced, though it was not like any rain any of them had ever seen. The droplets were aflame, like burning gasoline. As the burning rain fell the hail started to melt and the trees caught fire. That went on for almost half an hour before the burning rain changed again. This time the day was as dark as night. The blood blocked what light from the sun had been coming through. The only light was from the burning trees, and that was prevalent as far as the eye could see. The cars they had parked in the woods were now nothing but burning hulks. The only transportation remaining to them was the cars parked in the barn.

Connor's cell phone was ringing and he sought someplace out of the way to answer. It was Ephraim. "Are

165

you getting the hail and burning rain?" he asked without preamble.

"And the blood, although I believe the reference in Revelation was as much about the death to be caused by the events as the raining of blood," Connor replied.

"The news here is starting to report about the strange events. They say there are casualties in the thousands but no hard and fast numbers. Many houses and cars caught fire when the rain turned to fire, and a lot were destroyed by the hail which preceded it."

"You want to hear something really amazing? Our crops on the farms were not damaged by either the hail or the fire."

"I wonder if that is true of other Christian farms."

"I don't know but I am going to check as soon as possible. Maybe you can see what happened to the Christian farmers in your area," Connor said.

The two were on the phone back and forth for most of the evening and night. In between calls to Ephraim, Connor called some of the other church pastors and inquired about the crops. Most had no idea but a couple were farmers and reported their crops were spared.

As Connor carried this thought through he realized that the Antichrist would now know who the Christians were, since they would be the only ones with any surviving crops. That was going to make it even harder to keep a low profile.

Connor finally found enough time to have the video crew tape a segment for airing the next day. He explained what had occurred at the church and gave casualty figures. He then explained that the first trumpet judgement had just occurred and quoted Revelation 8:7.

"According to the Bible a third of the earth's trees and grass was burned up. The hail caused extensive damage and though no figures have been broadcast by the One World Coalition about casualties I have confirmed that the phenomenon was worldwide and that the hail alone caused casualties in the thousands. Every car that was on the road when the hail came is now junk. The phenomenon brought on by God as part of His wrath against a sinning humanity has been foretold for more than 6,000 years. What just happened is only the beginning of God's wrath. I can't tell you when it will happen, but the next item on God's agenda is to turn the seas to blood. The Book of Revelation says that one third of all sea life will be killed. The events that just happened should be enough to convince anyone with half a brain that God is in control and wants all sinners to repent and turn to Him. Don't take my word for it. Read the Book of Revelation and you will find that recent events are chronicled in the exact order in which they occurred. Demir is no God. He is Satan's right hand man. The recent attack on my church indicates that he will now go all out in his persecution of Christians. He will kill many for their beliefs but we can all rest assured that if we truly believe in God, and that Jesus is His Son who came to earth to die for our sins then he cannot touch our promise of eternal life with God the Father. If you have not accepted Christ as your savior, now is the time. Get down on your knees right where you are and ask for forgiveness through Jesus Christ and your fate for eternity is sealed. Your physical body might be taken away, but your spirit will live with Christ for eternity."

"To all those churches in the United States with whom I have had contact, please call and let me know your situations. I will attempt to update the materials at least every other day and more often if circumstances permit. On another note, the crops of Christian farmers were spared from destruction during the first trumpet judgement. This means that if you still have crops that fact identifies you as a Christian. I don't know how to instruct you to react if confronted by coalition forces, but it is my belief that God does not intend for us to allow ourselves to be led meekly to the slaughter. I will fight to the death and have recommended to those under my charge to do the same. In the final analysis, dead is dead, whether you submit like sheep, or make them hunt you like wolves. We are all in for a great deal more calamity, just less than five years by my calculations, before this is over and Jesus returns for his Millennial Kingdom, so get tough and keep trusting in Christ."

He closed the segment with a prayer that God would provide guidance and care for all who believed in Him and that He would grant peace to those already martyred.

The website was inundated with hits from all over the world. The servers could not keep up with the volume and the system had to be reset numerous times, sometimes in as few as twenty minutes. The response was overwhelming. Most of the queries could be handled by the FAQ section of the program and professions of faith were not in the thousands, but in the hundreds of thousands.

Ephraim called again and told Connor that he had watched his latest webcast and wanted to use it on his own site. "It is better than anything I could do and lays out the true facts. I will do a lead in and introduce you as part of the Jewish Remnant working in America if you have no objections."

"It has to be true since the two witnesses told us. Now that it is apparent that other Christians can be killed easily by the Coalition forces my belief that the remnant is protected by God seems to be more valid," Connor said.

"While I agree with you, I have no intention of making myself a target for the Coalition to test the theory."

"I don't think you will get a direct attack by Coalition forces in Jerusalem until after the treaty is broken at the half way point in the tribulation. You will have opposition from other sources, and probably Coalition forces incognito will be a part of that, but a direct attack on you is not likely until after the two witnesses are allowed to be killed," Connor said.

Connor had not slept for almost 24 hours and after he finished the call he found a vacant cot and literally crashed.

Larry and Sterling kept others at bay by answering the questions they had and let him catch a few hours of sleep. They too had been awake the same length of time and once the need for sleep became too much to deal with they crashed as well.

Chapter 16

When the news finally got around to the confrontation at Connor's church several days had passed. The hail, fire and blood took up most of the coverage for three days. There was no way the Coalition could cover up those things since everyone on the planet had witnessed them.

The casualty figures, which may or may not have been accurate, were placed in the millions. The more populated and industrialized nations suffered the greater numbers simply because of the circumstances. Many people were on the roads in their vehicles when the hail commenced and that alone caused more accidents than could be documented. When the hail changed to flaming rain many of the people whose cars had been disabled who had remained with the cars for protection from the hail were now trapped.

The change to fire set many of the vehicles on fire and even those who exited their cars were set aflame by the fire droplets. The blood rain mixed with that of the victims and the streets literally flowed with blood.

At first all the news stations were doing was reporting on the terrible results of the events. That changed within 12 hours of the culmination of the events.

A spokesman for the One World Coalition held a press conference and attributed the spectacular events to very unusual weather patterns and the simultaneous eruption of several volcanos in different parts of the world.

"While it was a calamity of great proportions the only logical explanation is that natural events just conspired to cause great damage almost worldwide. Africa was not as hard hit as were Europe, Asia and the American continents. The El Nino' played an important role in the heavy casualties in the America's and the eruption of volcano's in Iceland and Sicily seemed to have had a very adverse impact on the weather in Europe and northern Asia. We will continue to keep you informed as new information comes to light."

After the initial twelve hours of coverage of the same scenes from all over the world the grisly scenes almost totally disappeared from the news media.

The news of the attack on Connor's church was reported on the third day after the first trumpet judgement. The report was nowhere close to the truth. According to the One World Coalition spokesman the contingent of OWC forces were on routine patrol in the area where the church was located. That area was only a small portion of the area they were patrolling. "It is not clear exactly when the attack on our forces occurred but they were out of radio contact for more than twenty four hours before their massacred remains were discovered. It appeared that they were taken by surprise as none had fired their weapons. The attack is believed to have been orchestrated by the pastor of the church, who was in contact with the two strange preachers in Jerusalem early after they appeared," he said.

"Is there any tie-in with the two in Jerusalem?" one of the reporters asked.

"We are not sure at this time, though it is likely. Connor Frederick, the local preacher in question, is thought to be the leader of the Christian movement in North America and as such is a fugitive from justice. Anyone who knows the whereabouts of Mr. Frederick is encouraged to contact coalition forces. A substantial reward is being offered for information leading to his arrest. Any information provided will be kept strictly confidential."

"How many coalition forces were killed?" another reporter asked.

"More than sixty. Their trucks were found three blocks from the location of the massacre. Apparently they were making a surreptitious approach and were taken by surprise. All their weapons were taken, as well as ammunition."

"Then how do you know they didn't fire the weapons?" asked one of the braver, or more foolhardy, reporters.

"All the bodies were close together, as if they had been herded into one location and executed. There was no evidence of resistance, and there were no other bodies in the area, which would not seem to have been the case if a battle in fact occurred. None of the area hospitals reported treating any gunshot victims during that period, so we assume that there were no casualties other than our own," he said as he gathered his papers and started to leave the podium.

"One more question, if I might?" said the same reporter who had asked the previous question.

"Yes," said the OWC spokesman.

"Did you question any of the people who lived in the area about the situation?"

"Of course. That was one of the first things we did after discovering the bodies. No one seemed to remember hearing any gunfire, so we assume silenced weapons were used."

While he was still facing the camera the reporter asked, "Do you suppose the Christians might be fighting back against the one religion edict?"

"While I don't think that is a likely scenario, it is possible that some of the religious groups have become militant, though with weapons bans they will not be very well equipped to do battle with trained forces. The outcome is a foregone conclusion when you look at all the factors. I think it more likely that this is just a militant group, possibly not even of the Christian faith, who are nothing more than hooligans. Besides, anyone who cannot look at Demir's capabilities and see that he is the one true God is lacking mentally. He has the power to heal, he is the glue that holds together the entire world, and he has brought people back from the dead. No other God can do that! The Christians are not so large in number that they pose any valid threat to Mr. Demir, my God. The group as a whole displeased their God and he punished them to the last person two years ago. Have they forgotten so soon? Demir is the one hope for the entire world."

With that he turned and left the stage.

Shortly thereafter Ephraim called. "Looks like you are a wanted man now," he started the conversation.

"No surprise there. I am just glad he waited this long to start in on us. One thing it will do is increase our reader base on the web site. Still no mention about the Christian farmers crops being spared during the calamity, and strangely enough the OWC troops haven't harassed any of the farmers. I suspect that what the Christians are growing is all that will abate a total famine and Demir knows that. If he starts to requisition the crops others will learn about it and destroy what they have left," Connor said.

"I imagine most of the world's population will tire very quickly of seafood, that is, until the next trumpet judgement. I see a progression in God's coming actions," Ephraim said.

"Well he decreased the earth's population very dramatically with the hail and fire. How about the crops in Israel? Did the same thing happen with the Christian farmers there?" Connor asked. "I haven't heard from a lot of our people yet but I assume the same thing happened all over the world."

"The farmers among our congregation reported no damage to their crops so that must be the case."

"Have you talked with Benjamin and Mordecai lately?" Connor asked.

"Not in more than a week. When I get the word that they are moving to a new location I try to talk with them someplace enroute for a few minutes. I seem to get the information on their moves through the Holy Spirit, either that or telepathy. In any case I always know when they are planning a move and what route they will take."

"Have you been in contact with any of the other 144,000 in Europe and Asia?"

"Yes, quite a few actually. Most are leading small churches but have been extremely successful in converting those they have a chance to preach to. They all watch my web site and yours. They are really surprised that an American is so successful until I tell them that you are really Jewish," Ephraim said.

"I am thinking about doing some travel all over the United States and Canada. It might be a good time to do that to shore up the confidence of those in lesser populated areas. I will ask Sterling and Larry to go along, primarily so we can use Sterling's plane," Connor said with a chuckle.

"Are you going to plan an itinerary or just take them as they come?"

"Probably the latter. I will get an idea where the greatest need is from the other churches and with a private plane it will be easier to make up an itinerary as we go along," Connor replied.

"Keep me in the loop," Ephraim said.

"Will do," Connor said and hung up.

Connor was still staying at the hideout at the farm. Some of the lesser critically wounded had been sent home with folks appointed to live with them and provide care. The wounds were still very serious but once they had been stabilized it would be a matter of time before they were healthy again. They managed to decrease the number of full time patients to thirty at the facility, which was manageable. A couple of the doctors had colluded with other Christians at the hospitals where they worked and sent car loads of medical supplies to the farm. Others had purchased medical first aid supplies now that they knew there was a definite need for them. It was kind of like the weapons. Some were opposed until after the first attack, then did a quick turnabout.

Sterling was still spending part of his time in New York, taking care of business, though he knew that when the Millennial Kingdom arrived he would no longer have need of the huge amount of money. The primary motivation now was to provide as much help to Connor's efforts as he could.

Connor placed a call to him and asked if he could come down within the next couple of days, to which he agreed.

The video casts were all saved, in the event that they came upon hard times and couldn't get a new one prepared for the upcoming schedule. Since the message was basically the same they could get by for a few days if they had to really lie low.

In the lull after the attack Connor was trying to get ahead with his sermons. He wanted at least seven that had not previously been shown as a ready supply. He was in the process of videotaping one when his cell phone rang. He signaled a cut to the cameraman and looked at the caller ID on his phone. The ID was blocked so he expected some sort of mischief when he answered it. "Hello," he said.

"Do I have the pleasure of speaking to Connor Frederick?" the voice asked.

"I expect you already know the answer to that question. What can I do for you, and who are you?"

"Not one expecting to earn the two million dollar reward for information about your whereabouts," the caller replied with a laugh.

"I somehow don't get the joke, if that was a joke," Connor said.

"There actually is a two million dollar reward out for you, but that wasn't the reason I called. I got your number from a friend of a friend. I have been following your sermons on your web site and I am impressed with not only your Biblical knowledge but with your charisma."

"That still doesn't tell me who you are, or what you want for that matter."

"I want to become a Christian. Let me rephrase that. I already became a Christian because of your preaching, and my rather sound and logical mind. I researched all the Biblical passages you quoted and looked at what has been happening in the world and concluded that you know what you are talking about. Ergo, the other side is a big sham and I am on the wrong side of the fence. I accepted Christ and genuinely feel that I am now a child of God. I realize that puts me in a very untenable position and I have to do something about it. I wonder if there is any chance that we could meet face-to-face to discuss the matter."

"While your testimony is music to my ears, I have not survived this long since the Rapture to walk into something like that blindly. I am willing to meet with any Christian who has a legitimate spiritual need, but unless I know who you are I will be very circumspect."

"I can't blame you for that. I am in precisely the same predicament. If anyone should even suspect that I have become a Christian not only my livelihood, but my very life may be forfeit."

"Then you are not much different from the millions of other new Christians around the world. It won't be too much longer before Demir insists that all his followers take his mark. Christians are not allowed to do so and many will be killed for refusing the mark. In the meantime he is trying to thin the ranks as much as possible," Connor said.

"I realize all that from hearing your sermons, but I am in a pretty difficult position right now." He took a deep breath. "My name is Edward Hawthorne and I am a Congressman from Texas. I am also the Speaker of House and have full time government protection. That means that I can't go anyplace alone and that every move I make is observed. You tell me how we could get together and we will discuss it," he said.

"Well, first, congratulations on jumping from the frying pan into the fire. It was the right decision, no matter what happens between now and Christ's return. As to a way to get together, let me put you off for a day. I have someone coming to visit tomorrow that might be able to come up with a plausible plan. Is there a number where I can reach you, or would you feel better calling me back?"

"I will call you back tomorrow evening between six and seven if possible. If you don't hear from me don't write me off. It may be that I am just in a situation where I can't make an unobserved phone call."

"Due to your position I assume you know how easy it is for the government to monitor phone calls," Connor said.

"That's one reason I was reluctant to give you my name. Let's just hope they let this call drop through the cracks, or that God directs them into other endeavors. I really feel it is important for us to talk, so I will make every effort to call you tomorrow evening."

When he hung up the cameraman looked at him questioningly.

"That as you might have guessed was someone who might be able to do us some good. He is an elected official and has accepted Christ. He is now between a rock and a hard place with regard to his actions and wants to meet to try to devise some strategy. The only problem is that he has government protection, probably secret service, and will have trouble getting free of them long enough to meet. Any suggestions?" Connor asked. He had long realized that those in unimportant positions had brains as well as everyone else and was not surprised when the cameraman answered.

"I assumed it was something like that from your side of the conversation. It won't be easy to slip the protective detail unless he goes to some desolate place where they will not be as concerned. Something like a fishing trip, assuming he is a fisherman, which is not a sure thing, or someplace inside a government building where they would not be as vigilant. Maybe even the Senate office building."

"I'm not sure I like the latter. There's a two million dollar price on my head now," Connor replied. "I guess I will wait until tomorrow and talk to Sterling about it."

"Two million dollars, huh. I could probably live on that for the next five years," he replied, referencing the Millennial Kingdom.

"Let's finish this one up. I think I need about fifteen more minutes."

They did so and Connor wandered outside to think about all he had to do. He was still concerned that the word on their location would leak to OWC forces and he had no back-up plan. That he thought was the most pressing issue at the present time. Next was the churches in North America, and now the Congressman.

Since the Bible says not to worry, but place your concerns with the master, that is what he did. He was near the rows of crops and he stopped and prayed for guidance and wisdom to do the right thing. When he finished he felt much better.

Sterling made his appearance the following day at noon. He and Connor took a walk through the woods and Connor briefed him about the call from Hawthorne. "He was reluctant to give me his name, for very good reason. He wants to meet someplace private if possible and see if we can come up with some way to use his influence."

"It will be hard finding some way to meet in private because of his security," Sterling said.

"I wanted to know if you will be willing to use your plane to fly me around to visit the churches in North America. I don't see any way to plan an itinerary, but we can make short hops from one location to another based on what we learn. That might be a way to get together with Hawthorne if we can choose a meeting place in his home state. I wouldn't think the security troops would be so strict in his home area."

"That's about the most logical solution. Even if we can't arrange anything in Texas we can find out where he believes the most likely location is that he could slip away," Sterling said.

"He's supposed to call back this evening between six and seven if he can arrange to be alone at that time."

"Suggest that to him and see if he can come up with a likely location. It should pose no problem for the two of us to get there with the plane at our disposal."

"Another problem that is really important now is that we find an alternate location in case this one is compromised. With satellites at their disposal I can't imagine the other side not using them to scout out possible locations for us."

"We have not looked at the buildings I own in Dallas yet. Maybe we could do that during our travels," Sterling said.

"What I would really like to find is some place remote that is similar to the place we are using now. If we plan it as a really secure facility we might be able to keep the location a secret except from the very essential people to keep the ministry going," Connor said.

"Do you have any place in mind?"

"Somewhere in the mountains. I don't necessarily mean the local mountains. Even the Rockies or Ozarks would be good. We will need an airport nearby, or at least a place to land your plane, and adequate cover for vehicles."

"An abandoned mine would be my recommendation to deal with those factors. There are coal mines in the Appalachians, gold and silver mines throughout the southwest, even some natural caverns in all those locations. I will see what I can do about locating geological maps to find out what is available. I know of a couple of areas in the

Ozarks that might possibly come close to what you are talking about," Sterling said.

"So what do we tell Hawthorne?"

"Tell him to pick a location and give us a couple of days' notice so we can get there. Give him my number and have him call me so that he is not in frequent contact with you. The reward will be too tempting for a lot of people to pass up if they get a line on you. You might also want to think about a disguise of some sort for our travels."

"I can grow a beard and maybe take to wearing a cap or hat," Connor said.

"That's a start, though you might want to do a bit more than that when we know we are going to be out in public."

When Hawthorne called back that evening Connor related what Sterling had said.

"The only place I might be able to slip away is on my ranch in Texas. It is a working cattle ranch and when I go home I ride a lot. The Secret Service bunch are not avid horsemen and the place is pretty desolate. Let me look at the schedule for Senate votes. We are nothing more than a rubber stamp for OWC anyway and it won't make a lot of difference if I miss a few days of meetings."

"Let me give you Sterling's number and the two of you can do the coordination. That way you are not tied to me."

"I will call him when I can make arrangements."

After the call from Hawthorne, Connor contacted one of the pastors from his previous trips to North Carolina to see about paying a visit. He was enthusiastically invited and they agreed on the day after the next.

Sterling acquired the geological maps the day after the call from Hawthorne and he and Connor spent a lot of time going over them. They found a large number of likely spots but a closer examination would be necessary to see how well suited they were to their purposes.

One was an abandoned Sulphur mine near Harper's Ferry, Virginia. The only major problem was accessibility. It was something to keep in the back of their minds if nothing else worked out better.

The most promising areas were in Arizona and Nevada. There were enough mountains that a lot of mining had been done in both states since the middle of the nineteenth century and in those days when the ore played out the mines were simply abandoned. Copper, silver and gold were the major sources of mining and there were several abandoned mines in southeastern Arizona, north central Arizona, north western Arizona, and all along the Sierra Nevada range in western Nevada.

One area that showed great promise was near the town of Jerome. It was a major copper mining town around the turn of the twentieth century. The town is located on the side of a mountain and the population approached ten thousand during the heyday of the mines. Now the place was billed as a ghost town and tourist attraction.

Connor had visited the town several years earlier and remembered the abandoned mine about two miles south of the town. He didn't know how accessible it was but he remembered seeing a road leading to the closed off mine entrance. It was definitely a place they wanted to look over in person. There was an airport in Prescott, just over the mountain range, some 25 miles distant. Sedona and Cottonwood were even closer and might be able to handle the small jet. That would be something to check into.

The visit to North Carolina drew a capacity crowd to the church. Lookouts were posted at strategic locations to alert the local pastor to any coalition forces sited. The church service only got one day's notice but that was enough to draw the largest crowd they had ever had. Connor talked about the attack on his church in Virginia and the fact that more than 100 were killed and even more wounded.

"The news didn't get word of that. We managed to kill all the troops before they could notify anyone that anything was amiss. We had time to bury our dead and transport our wounded to a hideout that was designed for that purpose. I want to stress that you folks will need to have plans for when the attack comes on your church. It is not a matter of if it will come, but when. The troops who visited us were specifically looking to make sure we had the likeness of Demir on display, which of course we didn't. The leader of the troops was about 25 feet from me with his pistol in his hand. When I told him that we only worshiped one God, our God, he raised the pistol and shot at me. I was looking directly down the bore of his pistol and I still don't see how he missed. All I can attribute it to is God's protection."

"When he fired all of our congregation took on the troops who were arrayed around the tent where we were holding services. If we had not been armed they would have killed almost two thousand people. I know that some of you might be against the use of firearms but self-preservation demands that we be prepared for the worst."

"Demir is trying to thin our ranks now that he has the other religions under control. It will not be much longer before he institutes the order to have his mark on everyone. Once he does that you will not be able to access any government service, buy food, or engage in commerce of any type without the mark. Those found without the mark after that time will be summarily executed. What happened with the hail and fire was the first trumpet judgement. It killed millions of people. The second trumpet judgement will be the turning of the oceans and seas to blood. The Bible says that more than 1/3 of the marine life will die as a result of this. That is going to make the famine even worse. I don't know anything about when it will occur, but that is the next major event according to the Book of Revelation."

"You may have noticed that the Christian farms contained the only plant life to escape the hail and fire.

182

That obviously is by God's design. It is also noteworthy that Demir has not harassed any of the Christian farmers. He knows that they will be providing the only source of food, other than seafood, and he doesn't want to take the chance that Christians will destroy what they are growing if he goes on the offensive over the issue. That is the only source of grown food to combat what is already a major famine. Livestock provides some of the needs but not nearly enough."

"If you haven't already done so, I suggest that you find a location as a rally point in case of hard times. Your very survival could well depend on it."

As the choir sang the hymn of invitation many people came. Between Connor, the local pastor and some help from lay people they baptized all the newcomers.

From there Connor set up visits to churches in South Carolina and Georgia.

He repeated the process in those two locations and set up additional visits to Alabama, Louisiana, Mississippi and Arkansas.

They had been on the road for over a week when Hawthorne called and told them that he would be visiting his ranch for a week starting the following Friday. That would give them enough time to complete the schedule they had already set up.

"You can land in Odessa and I will have a trusted ranch hand meet you at the airport. He will take you to a line shack on the ranch that the hands use to stay overnight or to get out of bad weather. Bring enough food to last for a couple of days. Once you are safely there I will be notified and get to you as soon thereafter as possible. I will bring a couple of ranch hands with me to allay the concerns of the protective detail about being out on the range alone."

By this time Connor's beard had grown enough that he was pretty much unrecognizable from the pictures the OWC had of him.

Connor had kept in touch with Ephraim at least every other day and things were beginning to get more violent against his church in Jerusalem, though OWC did not provide any overt support to the protesters.

During one of his sermons when the protests had grown rather louder than normal Ephraim went outside his church and preached to the protesters with a portable speaker system.

"What are you protesting my friends? That I choose to worship the living God? Why are you so concerned if you are so sure that Demir is the true God? If that is true then he should be able to vanquish the God I worship at any time of his choosing. Is he so concerned that my God is more powerful? I certainly believe that is true, and the Bible supports everything I have told the world. If you will consult the last book in the Christian Bible you will find that every event from the great disappearance to now has been foretold. If you can prove otherwise I will fold my tent and steal quietly away." The crowd had quieted when he came outside and some of the protesters were raptly listening to him speak."

"Why do you choose to protest what others than you believe? If you are right then what does it matter to you what others believe? When judgement day comes they will not be a bother to you. If you choose to put forth your views, then you should do as we do and have regular services to educate the people about what you believe. But in our Bible, Jesus said, 'I am the way, the truth and the life. No man comes to the Father but through me.' The major disappearance of all Christians was what we call the Rapture. All God's believers were taken to Heaven as one. Everything that has happened since is foretold in the Bible. Not just in Revelation, but in all the prophetic books of the Old Testament. I challenge you to read the Bible and then decide if protesting our beliefs is in your best interest."

The people inside could still hear what was being said and many of them wandered outside to better hear what was going on.

The protesters broke up and some of them stayed to get further information from Ephraim about Christ.

Connor and Sterling were met at the Odessa airport by a real life cowboy. He wore blue jeans covered by chaps, a chambray shirt with a bandana tied around his neck, and a large brimmed hat. He had a huge pistol strapped to his right hip in a holster belt with cartridges filling the holes made for them. His skin was like leather and his handshake revealed hands as rough as either Connor or Sterling had ever encountered.

He introduced himself as Zeke and led them to a pickup truck parked nearby.

Sterling told the pilot to take care of the plane's necessities and that he would call him later in the day to give him an idea about the schedule.

With that the pickup left the airport and headed south.

Chapter 17

Connor had placed the supply of food in the back of the pickup truck. Both he and Sterling were armed with pistols and a couple of rifles were in the storage compartment of the plane. It contained mostly canned goods and bottled water.

None of the group said much as they left town and headed out into the countryside. They drove for almost half an hour before the truck took a barely discernible dirt road off the county road they were traveling. Another 45 minutes brought them to a ramshackle building with a flue rising out of the roof slanted at a 45 degree angle. The place was not much larger than a storage shed found in most back yards of tract houses, but it had a substantial door and a window with one pane covered by plywood where the pane had obviously been broken.

"Be it ever so humble, etc., etc.", Zeke said.

The three climbed out of the truck and went inside.

The cabin was actually quite cozy. Bunk beds were stacked along both sides of the walls, barely allowing room for a small stove between them and a cupboard with tin cups and a couple of metal plates and a frying pan. An old fashioned glazed coffee pot sat atop the cabinet.

"It's not much, but when a storm blows in it gets us out of the weather. The winds are predominately from the southwest so we have a small shelter for a couple of horses on the northeast side of the shack," Zeke continued. "Ed will be here as soon as he can. I expect it will be a couple of hours at least. I can put on a pot of coffee if you like."

Both declined the offer.

"Are you a Christian?" Connor asked.

"Never had much reason to be anything, rather than a cowboy," he answered.

"Well, while we are waiting let me convert you. You obviously know about the disappearances and the events that have happened since?" Connor asked.

"Yep, heard about all that."

"And what did you make of it?"

Zeke visibly gave the matter some thought. "Didn't affect me an awful lot so I guess I didn't give it much thought one way or the other."

"All of the events that have happened in the last year or so were foretold in the Bible more than 6,000 years ago," Connor said.

"How's that possible?" Zeke asked.

"All things are possible with God."

"Yeah, but how do you know what happened was known that long ago?"

Connor took out his Bible and turned to the Book of Daniel. He read the portion about Daniel's dream of the seventy and seven years.

"How do you know that refers to the time we are living in?"

Connor next turned to Revelation and started from the beginning. He explained how the seven churches referred to the ages of the church since Jesus was alive. When he got to the meat of the story he explained about the rapture and turned to 1 Thessalonians and read the section dealing with the rapture.

"That was what happened when all the people suddenly disappeared," Connor explained.

"Then how are you still here?"

"I wasn't a believer when it happened. I am what you would call a convert. The rapture itself was what woke me up. I had been to church enough to know what Christians believed would happen but couldn't make myself take the leap of faith."

"So you became a Christian after the others disappeared?"

"That's about the size of it. Let me show you why I truly believe in Christ now."

Connor read the description of the judgements and the two witnesses appearing in Jerusalem.

"The hail that happened not long ago took millions of lives and killed all the crops on the earth, with the exception of those being grown by Christian farmers. Even the burning rain did not touch these crops. Now, listen to the description of the first trumpet judgement, which was written by the Apostle John 2,000 years ago."

He read the appropriate passage and then asked, "Is that not exactly what happened?"

"Seems to be the case," Zeke said.

"Now, the two witnesses in Israel," Connor continued and read the passage from Revelation about them.

"The Bible says they cannot be harmed until God allows them to be killed in three and one half years, exactly half the tribulation period. If they are attacked fire comes out of their mouths and kills their attackers. I know that to be factual and can show you a very low quality video of it."

Connor manipulated his phone and called up the pictures Ephraim had sent him of the attack on the two from close quarters.

Zeke looked at the video and handed the phone back.

"Another thing about the two," Connor continued, "anyone who hears them speak hears them in their native languages."

"Okay, so I am convinced that what you say is true. What does it mean?"

"It means that if you believe that all these things were directly related to what the Bible says then the rest of the Bible must be true as well. Does that make sense?"

"I guess so."

Connor next turned to the passage that says the only way to God is through Christ. "God says that there is life after this life on earth is finished. Each person has the

188

individual responsibility to choose his or her own path. A belief in God, through Christ, leads to eternal life in heaven. A disbelief leads to eternal life in a place to awful to even contemplate. So the choice is yours. Life eternal in heaven, or life eternal in hell."

"Any sane person would choose the good eternal life," Zeke said.

"Then you must confess a belief in the fact that Christ is God's son, who came to earth to die for our sins. It's as simple as that. That belief alone assures you of eternal life with God. You will still be subjected to all kinds of horror on this earth until you draw your final breath, but after you die you will go to a much better place where there is no suffering or hardship, no hatred, no jealousy, none of the things that make this life so hard. Do you believe that Jesus Christ is the son of God?"

"Yes."

"Then you are now a Christian."

"Just like that?"

"Just like that!"

"What do I do now?"

"Read the Bible and try to live according its instructions."

"I guess I can do that, but I don't read too well," Zeke said.

"That's not an insurmountable problem. Download an audio Bible and you can listen to it while you are out riding," Connor said.

"I will do that," Zeke replied.

Not long thereafter they heard the beat of hooves. Zeke quickly opened the door and stepped outside. It was Hawthorne and a couple of others. They all climbed down and Hawthorne asked Zeke to keep an eye on their back trail to assure that the security people had not defied his order to stay at the ranch house.

Hawthorne shook hands with Connor and Sterling. "I hate to have to drag you way out here, but I thought this was the safest way to meet. The beard really helps to disguise your identity. I don't think I would have recognized you on the street," Hawthorne said.

"Are these two going to stay?" Connor asked.

"Yes. I think I have them converted, but you might want to reinforce a bit of biblical scripture."

"What's the story with Zeke?" Connor asked.

"He's a bit slow mentally and doesn't talk much, but he is very reliable and has been around the ranch since I was a small lad. I hope you got along all right."

"You might want to get him a decent phone so he can listen to the Bible from an audio file. I have him converted but he says he doesn't read very well," Connor said.

"He doesn't. I will do as you suggest. I am surprised you were able to get through to him with the complexity of the Bible."

"It wasn't hard. I just asked him to recall all the events that have happened over the last year and read him the descriptions from the Bible and told him when the words were written. He seemed to put it together rather well. I really think I got through to him, though I didn't realize that he was mentally challenged," Connor said.

"Maybe we should hear what you told him," one of the others said. "If you can get through to him we might be able to grasp the significance as well."

Connor very quickly recapped all that had happened from the rapture and read the applicable portion of scripture to support each event. When he was finished both said that they thought the evidence was irrefutable.

"Then if you believe that you must accept that the remainder of the Bible is God's word. He says that the only way to Him is through Christ, His son. A belief in Christ, that he lived on earth, died for our sins, and rose again is the foundation of Christianity. If you believe that, then you are Christians. You then need to confess that belief to others."

"You truly are a gifted preacher. These two will help Zeke along the proper path," Hawthorne said. "To get to the reason for this meeting, I need to know what will benefit you in your ministry that I can help with."

"I'm not sure there's much you can do in that regard. We have our webcast going out constantly, with updated material at least daily. Ephraim, my counterpart in Israel, is doing the same. We cross over to each other's files if something seems compelling. We also use secure communications by computer to keep each other up to date. My biggest worry now is that our hideout will be compromised and we will be back to square one. I want to find another secure location, hopefully one more suited to our needs and more defensible before they get a line on the place we are using now," Connor said.

"Are the computers you use secure?"

"We have a guy who is pretty smart. Used to work for the CIA. We go through multiple IP addresses and change them quite often. I think it is about the best we can do. It won't hurt if they learn the IP that originates the material. That will allow them to shut it down, but we are prepared for such an eventuality and have others on standby to make an immediate switch if it becomes necessary. What we want to mask is the physical location," Connor replied.

"Do you get any firsthand information about the OWC?" Sterling asked.

"Not much. What we usually get is directions on how to vote on issues, and that comes second hand, usually through the President, who seems to be totally brain washed," Hawthorne replied.

"Funny you should mention that," Connor said. "Just a couple of days ago I got the thought that Demir might be using some sort of mind altering technique on the leaders. I have no idea what I am talking about here, but I wouldn't rule out some form of hypnosis or even supernatural ability to bend that group to his will."

"I can certainly keep an eye out for anything out of the ordinary in that regard," Hawthorne said.

"I think your most advantageous use to the ministry will be the provision of intelligence about what they are planning," Connor said.

"I will do what I can but don't expect too much. I am pretty much tied to one location and will only be able to pick up what others let slip."

"The mid-point in the tribulation is going to be decision time for you. The two witnesses will be killed, Israel will be attacked, and the Antichrist will insist upon his mark being applied to every living human being. Those who refuse will be summarily executed, so plan accordingly," Connor said.

They talked for another half hour but not much was accomplished. Hawthorne was simply not in a position to do much for the ministry.

Zeke took them back to Odessa and they boarded the plane and headed west.

Connor had not made any additional plans for what happened after the meeting with Hawthorne. He now said to Sterling, "What would you think about a trip to Jerome?"

"Sounds good to me. Where do we want to land?"

"I think we should try either Cottonwood or Sedona. I know the airport at Prescott can handle the jet, but I am not so sure about those two. Ask the pilot what he thinks."

As it turned out they landed at Sedona. It was a good half hour or more to Jerome and they rented a four wheel drive SUV, just in case they needed the capability.

Connor drove and somewhat slowly. Both he and Sterling studied the countryside during the trip. They came to a church, which had cars in the parking lot, so Connor turned into the driveway. They got out and approached the church.

The doors were unlocked and they went inside. There were at least 20 people sitting in the pews and a man was at the front with an open Bible on a stand in front of him.

"Good day to you brothers. Would you care to join us?"

"Is this a regular service, or did these folks stop by because they saw cars in the parking lot like we did?" Connor asked as he walked toward the front of the church.

"We try to have someone on hand to deal with tourists who decide to stop and see what we are about. Who are you gentlemen?"

"My name is Connor Frederick and this is Sterling Silverstein," Connor said.

"You did say Connor Frederick? The Connor Frederick?"

"Guilty. We were driving by and saw the cars and decided to stop and see what was going on."

"My name is Manny Rodriguez. I'm not a Bible scholar or anything, but I watch your webcasts at least daily and use most of what you have to say to try to explain to people what happened and why. Some of these folks are regulars and others just stopped by like you did. We probably have 50 or more every day that does that so we decided to take advantage of the opportunities."

Most of the regulars knew who Connor was but the newcomers just sat in silence.

"You want to say a few words?"

"I will be happy to."

Connor replaced Manny at the front of the group and he started an impromptu sermon.

"Most of you who watch the webcast know that my church was attacked by OWC forces just prior to the first trumpet judgement, though it didn't make the news until three days later. The Antichrist had too much to deal with because of the hail, fire and blood. At any rate we were having services under a circus tent in a large area we had cleared for the purpose. There were upward of 2,000 people at the service when about 60 to 80 OWC troops showed up and surrounded the tent. They asked us to show them the image of Demir, which of course we didn't have. I told him that we worshipped the one true God and that wasn't Demir. He took out a pistol and shot at me. At that point my congregation pulled out their weapons and returned fire at the troops ringing the tent. All the OWC troops were killed and over 200 of my people were either killed or wounded."

"I tell you that to alert you that we are now in a shooting war with Demir's forces worldwide. He is systematically trying to wipe out as many Christians as possible before he institutes the edict for taking his mark, which he apparently feels certain will annihilate the remainder when they are unable to buy food or other essential items without the mark. Many will be executed on the spot when they refuse to take the mark."

"I know I am over the heads of some of you newcomers, but that's the background of where the Christian population stands today. I have a bounty of 2,000,000 on my head by the OWC."

"Now why all the fuss and violence you might ask? To begin, the disappearance of millions of people not too long ago was what Christians referred to as the rapture. Jesus came in a cloud and took all believers to heaven instantaneously. The rest of the world has been trying to explain the event away as anything but what it really was. How do we know it was the rapture?"

"The only people who disappeared were Christians. That's why the churches have been so empty since the event. Now I know you are curious about why I didn't disappear as well! The simple truth of the matter is that I was not a believer when it happened, though I had been exposed to enough of the truth that is should have sunk in. Many others were like me. They had been exposed to God's word but thought they knew better what to do with their lives than some entity that resides somewhere out there," he said in an all-encompassing arm wave.

"Personally, I knew enough to recognize what had happened in an instant and prayed right there in my car, which had stopped of its own volition in the fast lane of an interstate highway. When I glanced around and saw that many of the other cars which had stopped just as suddenly had no occupants I put two and two together and concluded, 'rapture'. I truly did believe right then and there that there was a God, and that he had just relieved the world of about half its population. That alone proved that he was much smarter than me, and had been all along. I decided that whatever days I had left were going to be devoted to Him."

"I had no idea how to go about that but reasoned that the first step was to learn as much as I possibly could about what had happened and why. I started that very evening by reading the Book of Revelation through at least twice, cross referencing to the Old Testament prophetical books where necessary to get a context for what I was reading."

"I very quickly learned that the rapture was the beginning of the most horrifying seven years the earth will ever know. Let me take you through what has happened so far, then I will touch on what is to come."

Four additional people entered the church and looked around.

"Have a seat and enjoy the sermon folks," Manny said.

The newcomers found seats and Connor continued.

"The rapture was the signal to the true end times. God took his believers out of the world to spare them from the terrible events that are now happening. In the New Testament, the Book of 1st Thessalonians, Chapter 4, verses 13-16 tell the story. Verse 13 starts out, 'I would not have you be ignorant brethren concerning those who are asleep...'. "The writer is referring to those who have died in

Christ, meaning that they were believers. The passage continues to say that those asleep in Christ will rise first then those who are alive and believe in Christ will rise with him into the clouds and to heaven. That is exactly what happened on that day that will never be forgotten."

"The final book of the New Testament, Revelation gives you a blow-by-blow account of events that will occur during the period of the tribulation. The first five chapters talk about the seven ancient churches that were established during Christ's first time on earth. The descriptions are symbolic and according to all I could find represent the different eras from the time of Christ to now. The church, which is Christ's body, has splintered, grown and contracted during the 2,000 year period, and many false religions have come into being. Individual churches, instead of trying to adhere to God's word, tried to bend the scriptures to suit their own life styles."

"Not to get too deeply into that, but by definition any religion which does not have Christ as the person of worship is a false religion. I know that isn't a politically correct statement but it is the absolute truth. Revelation, from chapter 6 on deals with the events that are to happen in the seven year period between the rapture and the second coming of Christ."

"All the people who are alive and believe in Christ right now are new believers. That means they came to belief after the rapture, at which all believers were taken to heaven."

"The first four seals from the Book of Revelation are commonly referred to as the Four Horsemen of the Apocalypse. They represent false prophets, war, famine, and pestilence. The false prophet has arisen in the person of Ahmet Demir. Since he became leader of the OWC there has been constant war, though you probably didn't hear a lot about it on the news. He has systematically wiped out the Hindu, Muslim and Buddhist believers before turning to new Christian believers. If you think the nuclear detonations were carried out by India, Pakistan, China and Russia, then you are sadly mistaken. I don't know how he managed the feat, but Demir was responsible for all that."

"A famine is underway as I speak, brought on by God, or possibly the two witnesses in Jerusalem. More about them in a moment. The pestilence will arrive on the tails of the famine. Now, more solid proof that events are being orchestrated by God, according to His word. Revelation tells about the appearance of the two witnesses in Jerusalem to preach the word of God. They are invulnerable to harm from the Antichrist for three and one half years. If anyone attacks them they will be devoured by fire which comes out of the mouths of the two witnesses. I have met them personally and witnessed their defenses. The Bible is correct in every respect. After the time God has allotted for them to preach he will allow the Antichrist to kill them. Their bodies will lie in the streets of Jerusalem for three days and then they will be resurrected. If you still need proof at that point in time that event will confirm the truth of the Bible."

"The hail, fire rain, and blood that happened recently is foretold as the first trumpet judgement in Revelation. God told us exactly what was going to happen. Something that leads further credence to this being God's work is the fact that all farms being tended by Christians did not receive any damage from the hail and fire. Now if that doesn't convince you the next judgment will be that the world's oceans will turn to blood. One third of all sea life will be killed. It only gets worse from there."

"If you are convinced that God is at work here then you are half way to salvation. The second half is to accept that Jesus Christ came to earth as the Son of God and Died for the sins of all humanity. If you truly believe that in your heart, then you are assured of a home in heaven when all this is over, or when you die, which if you accept Christ might very well come first. Every sermon I preach trying to reach unbelievers I stress the fact that accepting Christ is not taking the easy way out. You will be ridiculed, persecuted, and many, in fact most, believers will be killed by forces of the Antichrist. On that note if there are any among you who want to take the next step, come forward and we will pray with you."

Every single person in the church came forward.

Between Manny, Connor and Sterling they counseled them, determining who was local and who was from other parts of the country. All were advised to find a functioning church and ally themselves with a congregation.

"You need to do that not only for your spiritual well-being, but as a means of protecting yourselves from what is to come," Connor told them.

After the tourists had left Connor called Manny aside and asked him how well he knew the area.

"Like the back of my hand. I was born and raised right here and I have worked everywhere from Camp Verde to Prescott," he replied.

"How well do you know the mines around this area?"

"I used to play in some of them when I was a kid. That was before they boarded them up. Why do you ask?"

"We are looking for someplace to continue the ministry when things get a lot tougher. The place we are using now was once a moonshine still in the countryside of Virginia. I don't know how long it will escape the attention of the OWC since there is a huge reward offered for my scalp. We need someplace that can accommodate a large number of people, is secure, and is defensible. It would be a plus if there was more than one way in and out. It would also be nice if the route to and from the entrance was hidden from view. I visited Jerome several years ago and remember the mine headed up the mountain on the other side of town. I know it was sealed off but I remember there being a road to the entrance."

"You're right about that. The mine inside is huge. There are a lot of tunnels that branch off from the main entrance. I have been inside and explored some of them. One leads to the outside about 50 feet above the main tunnel and almost a quarter of a mile away. I can show you, but you are going to need a lot of line, lights, weapons and some food. You can't do the job in a day, maybe not even in two or three. If you want I will lead you there and help you explore. I quit my job, figuring I only have another few years to worry about and God's work is more important than anything else."

"We can compensate you. Sterling has more money than he will ever need. We are going to need some people to help do the work necessary to make the place fit our needs if it looks promising. I plan to move our whole broadcasting effort and all the people to run the ministry. There will be between 50 and 100 people that will have to be housed, fed and otherwise cared for."

"A lot of the people from Jerome have become Christians and will be willing to help," Manny said.

"What's the population of Jerome now?" Sterling asked.

"There were only about 250 full time residents before the rapture and that took about 100 of them. Some of the others moved on since tourism has dropped off to nearly nothing. You might be able to entice some of the non-believers to leave with a substantial offer for their property," Manny added.

"When can you make time to go with us?" Connor asked.

"Right now is a good time. We will need to go shopping first and by the time we get that done it will be too late to accomplish much. I suggest we go get what we need and you guys can bunk with me tonight, unless you'd prefer a hotel."

"Bunking with you sounds fine if you have the room."

"Nothing but room since the wife and kids disappeared."

"A familiar story all over the world," Connor said.

"You know about hindsight since we are all in the same boat," Manny offered philosophically.

Manny went back to the group and asked one of his people to take over for a few days. "I will be back, but I am not sure when," he said.

Manny directed them to a hardware store and the three went inside. They all got carts and Manny started filling them with items that would be needed. "What's the budget?" he asked.

"There is no budget. Get everything we need. Err on the side of redundancy," Sterling said.

"What's that mean?" Manny asked.

"Get everything you know we need, plus what you even think we might need," Sterling replied.

Manny took him at his word. Three shovels, a couple of pick axes, regular axes, several five gallon buckets, a roll of screen wire, several packages of steel stakes, a ten foot tent. The list went on and they had to get additional carts. When they were ready to check out the cashier asked Manny what he needed all the gear for.

"I have become a guide. These gents want to know what is in these hills and have hired me to show them," he replied, not lying but not giving much information about the real reason either.

Most of the purchases were packed inside the SUV and the tent was tied on top. They drove to Manny's house and he suggested they pull into the garage and leave the stuff in the car overnight.

Sterling called the pilot and told him they were going to be in the area for a few days and to take some time off, after making sure the plane was secure, of course.

Chapter 18

The road through Jerome led to and across Mingus Mountain, coming out in the town of Prescott Valley. From there one could go in any direction on relatively good roads. The airport at Prescott was only about ten miles from the intersection with highway 89 and 89-A, the one coming down off the mountain.

Manny led them around the foothills near Jerome to the road leading to the blocked off mine. The road was in good enough shape that they didn't need the four wheel drive feature of the SUV.

When they arrived at the mine entrance Connor noted the road above that he had traveled on when he had been here before. From the road above the blocked area looked like concrete but a closer inspection revealed regular lumber blocking the entrance with only concrete road dividers blocking vehicle entry to the mouth of the cavern.

Manny showed them an open area away from the road side and said, "This was one of the main entrances when it was a working mine. Ore was brought from here by wagons to the smelter, which was in the flatlands a few miles back toward Cottonwood. Materials needed at the mine were also delivered here. The flat area around the entrance is manmade. They must have had a really tough time hauling enough fill in here with wagons."

"I noticed the land is posted," Connor said. "Does that keep people out, or is it just there to take care of any legal liability of the owners?"

"I don't know about the legal aspects, but it does keep tourists from messing around here," he replied.

Manny led them to the door and moved it frame and all out of the way. It had a padlock but it was only for show. Those who knew about the easy movement didn't even bother with the padlock, even if they were on official business.

They stepped inside and used flashlights to look around at the size of the cavern. It was nor very wide, but extended as far back as the light would shine.

"Better watch out for rattlesnakes in this part. They sometimes come inside but they give you warning before they strike."

As they moved farther into the mine they encountered branches off the main tunnel. Manny had brought a couple of rolls of line and he tied one end to a boulder, playing out the line as they moved farther into the mine.

It was obvious right away that this was exactly what they needed, assuming they could get power to the place. It was about half a mile from Jerome on a straight line. They could run the power underground and nobody would even know the place was occupied.

Sterling said, "If we can entice the non-Christians to sell their property and create a town of all Christians it will make it a lot easier to operate. If everyone is in the know we will all work together and will only have tourists to worry about."

"The other option is to convert the non-Christians," Connor said.

"We can start on that chore this evening if you want. I sometimes come up here and hold services unannounced. I am sure you will be more successful than I have been," Manny said.

"I like the idea," Connor replied. "It will give us a chance to get some numbers and evaluate the possibility of housing our people out in the open."

"We might also want to check into the ownership of the mine, just in case we encounter problems," Sterling said.

"There's another mine entrance much closer to town, on the west side. They use it to show tourists how mining was done in the old days. I believe that shaft joins up with the one we are in, though I don't know that for certain."

"All the more reason to attempt to own the town," Sterling said.

"I was thinking about our electrical needs and had concluded that underground would be the way to get the power to this place, unless we can run it through the mine," Connor said.

"Either way that will not be a major hurdle," Sterling said.

Manny chimed in. "You can use heavy conduit and run it above ground. Nobody will know the difference and there's no kids to worry about electrocuting."

"Though a lot of children will be born between now and the Millennial Kingdom, they will not be old enough to be out exploring on their own before the end comes," Connor said.

They spent four hours walking around the various tunnels. Manny remembered the way to the other exit he had mentioned earlier and took them to it. It opened directly onto the hillside and was covered over by low scrub growth. Manny pointed in the direction of the road from where they stood. It could be seen, but just barely.

Wildlife trails could be seen from the location in the lower reaches of the valley below. The hillside was not extremely steep and even a novice hiker could manage the decent easily. If one wanted to travel away from the road the going would be a bit tougher but was still manageable.

"I like it," Sterling said. "I don't believe we will find any place better suited. We have access to air and road travel, a certain degree of security, and if we can button the town up for our use it will give us a legitimate reason for people being here."

"I agree," Connor said. "We are going to need a satellite dish and there are a lot of options for locating it in a secure place. We could even disguise it as a television dish and have it right out in the open on one of the houses in town."

"Is there any law enforcement in town?" Sterling asked.

"Just a couple of constables. If they need to address anything dangerous they call the County Sherriff," Manny replied.

"Let's unload the supplies and leave them in the mine. We can then go to town and assess the situation there," Connor suggested.

As they drove back to the main road and into Jerome there were not many cars on the road. Connor thought that Jerome was truly a ghost town.

"Many of the cars got squashed by the hail and burned by the fire rain. Not all the people living here now have automobiles, though there are an abundance left over from the rapture. They have no place to go so they car pool for grocery shopping and that's the main reason they leave town."

Manny was driving and found a parking place near one of the few restaurants still open in the town. The three got out and went inside. There were only four customers and all appeared to be locals.

Seems everyone knew Manny and he introduced Sterling. He then looked at Connor and said, "Do you want to use your real name?"

This brought wary looks from others in the establishment.

"You might as well, since I plan to preach anyway."

"This gentleman is Connor Frederick. He's the guy who heads up the Christian element in the entire country," Manny said proudly.

Even those sitting eating got up to shake hands.

"I see why Manny asked. I heard the OWC is offering a hefty reward for information about you, even if it doesn't lead to your capture. If they can verify the validity of the information they will pay anyway. They want you really bad. What did you do to rile them up so much, other than preaching the gospel, of course," the waitress asked.

"They harassed us quite a bit back on the east coast and ultimately sent about 60 troops to one of our services. We had almost 2,000 people in and around an open air tent, sort of like a circus tent. The leader came within about 25 feet of me and pointed his pistol and demanded that he be shown the statue of Demir as mandated by the OWC. I had to tell him we didn't have one because Demir was not who we worshipped. He then shot at me, whereupon I took out my own pistol and shot him. The troops had ringed the tent and they started firing into the crowd. Fortunately most of my people were armed and all the troops were killed. Sadly more than 100 of my people were killed and about that many more wounded. That took place the day before the Hail and Fire rain."

"Wow, they are really getting serious about stamping out other religions," she said. "We don't even have a functioning church here. Manny comes over at times and talks to those who will listen. I think most of us left believe that God was responsible for what has taken place lately but we really don't have a good grasp on events. Would you really be willing to preach to those of us who are left?"

"Absolutely. My mission in life is to bring others to Christ. I was told by the two witnesses in Jerusalem that I am part of the remnant, or the 144,000 mentioned in the Book of Revelation."

"I am not familiar with all that but I will round up everyone in town and get them here. I think the restaurant will hold everyone."

"The weather's nice. How about the area up by the fire station," Manny said.

"That will work too. Let me get on the phone and get some help rounding people up."

The three had a sandwich and coffee while the people were gathering.

When they walked to the area where the crowd had gathered there didn't seem to be more than forty or fifty. "Is this all that's left of the town population?" Connor asked.

"Well first, let me introduce myself. I'm Connor Frederick. Some of you might have heard of me since I am a fugitive from OWC justice. I have a $2,000,000 dollar price tag on my head. All that came about because I became a Christian right after the rapture. I don't mean hours or days later, but right at the moment I realized what had happened. You see I had been to church enough to realize that the empty cars around me could only mean one thing, that Jesus had fulfilled his promise to take his believers home in the blink of an eye."

"I prayed right there in my car for forgiveness and vowed to do all in my power to obey the call of God for the rest of my life, which if you don't know is now a bit less than six years. We are now in what the Bible calls the great tribulation and it will end with God's defeating the forces of Satan and the establishment of a Millennial Kingdom on earth, reigned over by Jesus Christ Himself. Now how do I know these things?"

"Realizing that all Christians were gone and that there would not be anyone to educate those of us who turned to Christ a bit late, other than ourselves, I seemed better suited to the task than anyone else in our group who came together the next day. I studied, prayed, and tried to assist others in any way I could. The others seemed to accept my leadership and it snowballed from there."

"You all know about the rapture. The events since that time have been as follows: apostasy on a large scale, war, famine, and pestilence. Those are the first four seals mentioned in Revelation. The rise of the Antichrist, which is Demir, as the world leader. Then comes his edict to worship him as the only God. Soon he will decree that everyone bear his mark either on their hand or forehead. This will be required in order to buy anything from food to gas or anything else that you can now walk into any store and purchase with simple money."

"Now what has God done about that? First of all he tells us what is going to happen and when in the Bible. We are now in the timeframe of the trumpet judgements. The first was the Hail and fire and blood. It killed millions of people worldwide but didn't harm the crops of Christian farmers. Every other crop was wiped out. Next is going to be the turning of the seas into blood. One third of all marine life will be killed when that happens."

"Most of you have surely heard of the two witnesses who magically appeared in Jerusalem to preach the gospel. What you might not know, unless you have studied the Book of Revelation is that they cannot be harmed for three and one half years. If they are attacked they destroy their enemies with fire which issues from their mouth. Now I know that sounds strange, but it is absolutely true. I have witnessed that personally. I have also been in contact with them and they told me that I am part of the 144,000 mentioned in Revelation as being sealed by God to preach the gospel to those remaining after the rapture. If I am sounding egotistical I apologize, but those are the facts. He confirmed that there is Jewish blood in my ancestry and that Ephraim Ellsberg and I were chosen by God for leadership roles in the tribulation ministry."

"I thought that the term 'Sealed by God' meant that we would have unshakeable faith, but I now believe there is more to it than that. At least two attempts have been made on my life, both while I was preaching. The first was a long range sniper. I had just mounted the pulpit when I dropped the marker out of my Bible. I reached to pick it up just as the shot was fired, missing me and hitting one of my choir members. Our ushers ran him down and killed him."

"The second time was when we were confronted by about 60 OWC troops. The leader had his pistol pointed at me from about 25 feet and when I told him that we refused to worship the image of Demir he shot at me. I could see the bore of the weapon pointed right at my heart but somehow he missed. There were about 2,000 people in the open air tent and over 100 were killed. We killed the troops and left them where they lay."

"One of the first things I did was insist that all my church members be trained in the use of firearms, and that they have one handy at all times. Had that not been the case over 2,000 people would have been massacred. 100 was bad enough, but it drove home the necessity to be prepared to defend ourselves at all times."

"I am straying from the subject, but I want you to know the Christian life is no picnic. If you accept Jesus Christ as your Savior you will be hounded by the OWC, persecuted at every turn, and many will be killed for their beliefs. So what's in it for you? How about eternal life? Everyone will have eternal life, but on judgement day those in Christ will enter a paradise too beautiful to comprehend. Those left will go the other way, to Satan and an eternity of what the old preachers called fire and brimstone. I don't claim to know exactly what it will be like, but it will not be pleasant."

"The Old Testament Prophetic Books foretold what is happening now more than 5,000 years ago. They had visions and wrote them down. The Books of Daniel, Isaiah, Zephaniah, Jeremiah, Ezekiel, and others all tell the same story, and the Book of Revelation lays it out in chronological order. There can be no doubt that we are now in the end times. So what do you do as an individual? You turn to Christ. The Bible says that the only way to the Father, that's God, is through the son, that's Jesus. So if you are convinced that all that is happening now is according to God's plan, then you must accept that Jesus Christ is God's son, and that he lived and died for your sins. It's as simple as that. You must have faith that what God says is true and that a heavenly home awaits you after this life is over. Now, questions?"

"What do we actually need to do, I mean other than believe what you say is true?"

"First let me clarify who says it is true. I am just the mouthpiece. God says it is true. As to what you have to do, read the Bible. Try to understand how God wants us to live our lives. The New Testament is all about Jesus, and the reason he came into the world. He says that we should love one another as ourselves. He also says go forth and make disciples. If you study the word it becomes so exciting that you can't help but talk about it to others. Most believe that to seal the bargain with Christ you should be baptized. I don't think baptism is necessary to get you to heaven, but I do believe it is an outward sign to others that you have turned your life over to the master."

"Can those of us who want to be baptized now?"

"Absolutely. We don't need a church, just enough water to dunk you," Connor said with a chuckle.

Every single person there wanted to be baptized.

"Let's drive up to Mingus Lake and do it there. It's only about twenty minutes," one of them said.

The restaurant and other business establishments were locked and the group caravanned to Mingus Lake. It was a government lake and was for public use.

When they arrived people simply emptied their pockets and marched into the water. Connor had done enough by now that he had the appropriate verses memorized. He said, "Before we start, allow me to say a prayer for what has happened here today. It was God's plan, as you will understand when I tell you more in the coming days. I thank you God for how awesome you are and for how you work in all our lives, even in these troubled times." He went on to pray for all those in peril and for those who had been martyred in the service of God.

The baptism's took half an hour and they lounged around the lake a while to dry out before starting back to town.

"Is this the entirety of the town's population now?" Connor asked.

"There are a few others who own property but they have moved away with the drop in tourism. Not much way to make a living without the tourist dollars," the waitress said.

"Do you think they might be willing to sell their properties?" Sterling asked.

"Most of them will take even less than market value probably. They certainly have no plans to return."

"Can you get me a list of all the properties that are owned by absentees?" he asked.

"Probably from the town records. They aren't official, but most folks know everyone else. We can probably do it by committee and get all of them," she replied. "What do you have in mind?"

"I want to make this a totally Christian town. I will purchase all the properties not owned by those of us here and that will assure that we are not bothered until the OWC gets down to the bottom of the barrel. They will have more high profile geese to cook before they get to small towns like this. I didn't see any churches in town. Are there any?"

"Most of us who went drove down the hill. There's a church on the right about three or four miles down toward Cottonwood and more churches in the town itself," she replied.

"Then let's head back to town and start on the project. We will explain a bit more about what we have in mind while we are there."

The group went back to the restaurant and all went inside. It was a tight fit but they had room for everyone.

Lisa, the waitress, got a lined pad and sat on one of the stools near the counter. "Okay, someone start off. Let's work from the south to the north and try to remember all the property owners for each place."

One of the men started the process and they worked their way through the town. There were thirty seven properties unoccupied and owned by absentee owners. None of the group had any idea where to find any of them.

"Are we pretty sure the list is complete?" Connor asked.

The list was passed around and most had a second look to make sure they had not inadvertently left anyone off the list.

When it got back to Lisa she said, "I think that's it but you can check it against the county records to be sure. You will need to go to Prescott to do that though."

Connor glanced at Sterling to see if he had any reservations about revealing their plans. Sterling nodded slightly signifying that he had no objections if Connor thought it was the right thing to do.

"Now that you are all Christians I am going to confide in you with the assurance that God will help you keep your mouths shut about what we are about to tell you. We operate a website that is the primary means of preaching to the entire world. It has more than a million viewers every day. We are now operating from a location that I believe will be compromised soon. We need to find someplace secure for our people to continue to operate the site. It is pretty labor intensive. More than 50 people are needed to keep up with the needs. Sterling and I got to talking and decided that an abandoned mine site or a cavern someplace would be the best option. The mine site here is ideal. If we can assure only Christians inhabit Jerome, then we can live fairly normal lives here and move the entire operation to the mine, especially if Sterling purchases all the now vacant properties."

"That's going to cost a bundle," one of the men said.

"I have a bundle," Sterling replied to laughter.

"So what do you think of the idea?" Connor asked.

Most nodded, and some started talking among themselves. Connor just stood silent for a few minutes to let the conversations play out.

"What role will we have in this?" another asked.

"You are more than welcome to work with us in whatever capacity you have any expertise. We are going to worry a lot about security so I want to establish our own police force, only not in uniform, to watch the area and identify any strangers with an undue interest. We will need to keep the tourist shops open and if there are not enough sales to live on we will supplement your wages. It will have to be a total team effort. Some of the people I will be bringing to run the place have a little money and we should be able to contribute to the overall community. If there are needs that we can't meet Sterling will pick up any expenses beyond our means. Money comes in from the website constantly but we use on-line sources for that. Once OWC catches on to what we are doing we might have to change things, but for the moment we are totally solvent. Before you agree to jump in with both feet you must consider the danger involved. You know there's a price on my head and anyone who thinks they recognize me from the other side of the fence will try to collect. That's for starters. Demir has got to be going bonkers trying to shut us down. Ephraim in Israel is doing the same thing we are. He uses some of my sermons on his webcast and I use some of his material. We have a pretty good cyber-security guy who routes the signal through multiple websites and IP addresses. He says it is not foolproof but will make them work very hard to figure it out. Once the do they can shut us down but we have a backup plan that kicks in automatically if that happens."

"It takes a full time staff of about twenty just to answer computer queries or phone calls. We list a cell phone number and change it almost daily. We disable the GPS function in our cell phones so they can't locate us through them and if you are agreeable to all I propose here I want to go to satellite broadcast. We will need to mount a dish antenna someplace where it can't be spotted and we want to fortify the mine against attack so that we have time to get out if OWC attacks."

"You're treating this like a war," one lady said.

"That's exactly what it is. Christians against the OWC. All my people are armed at all times and know how to use the weapons. I hope I am not placing any of you in undue danger but I don't think God means us to stand helplessly by and allow OWC forces to annihilate us, which is exactly what they are doing."

"We've been out of the mainstream out here in the middle of nowhere but I can see your reasoning based on what the Bible says about it. I'm all in for the duration."

Several others nodded and the rest looked at each other.

Lisa finally said, "This has to be all or none. If we don't want to help out with this to the last person, then I suggest that Mr. Frederick find another location that suits his purposes. As for myself, I see the need, and I also see the risk. Having said that, I don't think the risk is any more severe than just living our daily lives wondering when the OWC will issue the edict to take the mark of Demir. I only just got the guarantee of eternal life in heaven and I am not about to forfeit that for a couple of more years of life on this planet. Now are there any opposed to what Connor has suggested?"

There was no more opposition.

"The first item of business is to stock up on guns, food, and ammunition. Everyone who is not otherwise occupied make the rounds to stores within driving distance and see what you can acquire. I know there's a ban on gun sales but you might find pawn shops or gun shows with weapons for sale. They will ask much more than the market price just months ago, but pay whatever is required to acquire weapons. Even purchase from any private stocks you might know about. Remember there's a world famine going on and foodstuffs are not going to be readily available either. When my people come from the other location we will truck everything we can to help the situation. Sterling has credit cards but I suggest he go to a bank that won't ask too many questions and get enough cash to spread $10,000 among the shoppers for starters. Those of you who have any knowledge of the mine can help us determine what we need and how we are going to get it there."

Sterling said, "If someone will accompany me to the banks I will see about getting some cash."

Connor said, "If possible, first thing tomorrow morning someone should go to the county registrar's office and check the property records against the information we compiled today. Try to get contact information for the property owners if possible."

"Mary and I can do that," Lisa said.

When Sterling left with a driver to visit the local banks Connor, Manny and three others who had some knowledge of the mine went back to the entrance.

"This is the only way you are going to be able to get equipment or supplies of any quantity inside. We can remove some of the wood and back the trucks right up to the entrance then wheel the stuff inside on dollies. I think before you think about bringing anything in you should get some electricity into the place for lighting at least."

"That is item number one on my list," Connor said.

He took out his cell phone and called Larry, who answered on the first ring.

"I was wondering when I would hear from you," he said by way of greeting.

"Things going smoothly?"

"No problems that I know about. What's happening, and where are you?"

"Out west. How soon can you catch a flight to Phoenix, Arizona?"

"As soon as one leaves," he replied.

"Make a reservation on the next flight available and call me with the flight information. I will have our pilot meet you there and bring you to where we are. It's the same pilot that flew us for the last trip if you remember what he looks like. I will have him meet you just outside the security checkpoint. Bring Norm with you."

"I'm on it. Anything in particular I need to bring?"

"Just enough clothing for a few days."

"I will call you when I have the reservations."

When he hung up one of the men from the local area asked, "You guys have your own plane?"

"Sterling is probably one of the richest men in America, even with the devalued currency brought about by the OWC changeover. He has a small jet we use at times when we want to remain totally off the radar of OWC informants. Larry, with whom I just spoke, is my construction foreman and has a lot of experience. I want him to get some of your men to help him run the electricity. We will let him look the situation over and suggest the best method to do that. We are a democracy and if you see a better way to do it than what he suggests then speak up. He won't get his feelings hurt and we want the most secure and practical way to do this."

"The mine runs straight back into the mountain for a good ways. There's sort of a staging area about a quarter of a mile down the main tunnel. It might be the best place to set up the operation," Mike, one of the locals said.

Manny said, "I remember that one of the side tunnels leads to an opening in the hillside. It's not much but will suffice for an emergency exit. Either of you know the one I am talking about?"

"Yeah. It's the fourth tunnel to the right. It goes straight to the opening."

"I think we might want to wait until we get some electricity to the place to explore much more. We know enough to determine that the mine will serve our purpose and that is all that is necessary for the moment," Connor said.

They went back to the restaurant and talked about what they would need. "We know we will need a lot of office equipment, desks, chairs and office supplies. We might want to start buying that stuff if we have someplace to store it," Connor suggested.

"We will have time to do that while getting the mine ready," Mike said.

"That makes more sense. I just have a feeling that we are not going to have much time and I want to get this done just as soon as possible," Connor said.

Sterling came back with the two ladies who had accompanied him on the round of banks. He had managed to acquire $5,000 from each of three banks and had opened a joint account with one of his companions and placed $20,000 into it by wire transfer.

Connor told him that he had talked to Larry and that he and Norm were on the way to Phoenix. "When Larry calls with the flight information we need to send the plane down there to pick them up."

"I'll go ahead and alert the pilot to be on his way. We can give him the rendezvous information after we hear from Larry," Sterling said.

Chapter 19

The next three days were very busy ones.

Lisa had gotten the list of absentee property owners in Jerome and contact information for most of them.

Larry and Norm arrived the day after Connor called and the weapon and ammunition buyers had pretty good luck. Most of the residents already had weapons, mostly rifles, for their own use and they had managed to acquire 40 odd pistols and rifles from the surrounding areas. They had the best luck in Prescott Valley, which had several pawn shops, and as luck would have it there was a gun show there as well at the old county fairgrounds.

As suspected, the prices were a lot higher than normal, but as Sterling said, money was not a problem.

Ammunition could be obtained relatively simply and they stocked up on that commodity as well.

Larry had a quick look at the mine entrance and just inside, then started to search for the best way to get the electricity to the mine. "We are going to need a lot of power and I believe the best method is to put the lines in conduit and run it overland once we get across the road on the side of the mine. It's going to take at least a mile of conduit and twice that amount of wiring. I will put a breaker panel in the mine someplace. Send someone shopping to start gathering materials. Don't forget to buy as many lightbulbs as they can find. We're also going to need a lot of timbers to shore up weak areas, especially in the work areas."

"Make a list and we will send the shoppers on their way. Sterling, what would you think about purchasing a pretty large flatbed truck to haul this stuff. We will most likely have need of it later and it makes sense to get it now to avoid any suspicious purchases later," Larry continued.

Connor was busy with Lisa working on the list of property owners. She knew many of the people and gave

Connor background before he talked to them. With some she did the negotiations and told them that the proper paperwork, along with a check for the purchase price would be mailed to them within a couple of days.

Larry called Thelma in Virginia and got the full names and social security numbers of thirty of the people he planned to bring to Jerome and told her that he was going to purchase a house in each of their names to allay suspicion by having one person's name on all the deeds, or even having a corporation own all of them.

At the end of the day there were only four people they had not reached and all the ones they talked to agreed to sell for a very fair price.

Additional research the following day led them to believe that the four in question had been Christians, so they looked for relatives of those four. Two they got in touch with that day and the other two the following day. None of them wanted to live in Jerome and agreed to sell right away. That locked the town up tight.

The power lines were to be joined to the transformer nearest the location where they planned to run the lines and they used two inch PVC pipe. All the work was done by hand and, where possible, they ran the pipe under bushes and covered it where the land was flat enough to hold the soil. The earth dislodged by the men laying the line was more noticeable than the conduit. They had the line run in a single day and Larry started working on the lighting system.

He had someone acquire a generator and brought a couple of flood lights into the mine to better be able to work. He ran lights all the way down the main tunnel tying four lights to each switch along the wall of the tunnel. Once he had the light strung to the large open area he installed a breaker panel and hooked the line to the transformer. From that point on the work went quicker.

One of the local people, Herb, had worked in the mines during his younger days, though not in this particular mine, and he surveyed the condition of the tunnel walls and ceiling for weak areas. Some of the roof of the tunnel had support beams that looked their age, which was at least 100 years old, but seemed to be in good shape. Not much had to be done in that regard, but Larry insisted that the entire ceiling of the major work area, which was about 200 square feet, be shored. He didn't want to take a chance that they would come under attack and have the entire mountain fall down on them before they had a chance to get out.

There were nearly 40 men in the group, counting Larry, Norm, Sterling and Connor and they all pitched in to get the work done. A flatbed truck had been purchased by Manny, using Sterling's money, and it was constantly shuttling materials to the mine entrance.

Connor wanted to wall most of the entrance with concrete to provide better protection against concerted heavy weapon attacks that he was sure would come before the tribulation period was over.

Larry left an opening large enough to get a truck through and formed up the remainder for a three foot thick wall of concrete. They even put rebar in it to further strengthen it.

One of the locals knew someone who owned a cement truck and made arrangements to rent if for a week for $5,000 dollars, which was more than the owner could make hauling cement on his own. It took six truck loads to fill the forms but all agreed that it was worth the effort.

Norm had disabled the GPS function in all the cell phones used by the local residents, as well as Manny's. He had then talked to Connor about what he had in mind for the satellite system so he could start locating what would be needed.

Norm was a bit out of his element with the satellite data and suggested that Ephraim be consulted about that.

His reasoning was that Ephraim worked for MOSSAD and he could get access to the kind of information they needed. "It might be a good idea to chart the location of other satellites in case we have to switch. I would really feel better if we had someone who knows more about satellite operations than I do."

"Find us someone, and I agree that it is a good idea to consult Ephraim," Connor said.

Without realizing it, Connor exercised very good leadership principles. He decided what needed to be done, assigned someone to do it, and then got out of the way.

Once he was sure that Larry had a handle on what needed to be done with the mine, and all the property transfers had been effected, he talked to Sterling about going back east to prepare that part of the operation.

They had been in Arizona almost three weeks, and the time they spent on the road before that made it a full month they had been absent from the site. The website was doing reruns of Connor's sermons and they were glad to have him back.

He got all the people together, including those running the farms, and explained what was going on, though he didn't reveal the actual location of the new digs.

"The place we have found is more isolated than this one, is defensible, and allows us more freedom to move about. We have secured the entire town. By that I mean that every single soul in the town is a Christian and will be intimately involved with the running of the ministry. Many of you are now homeowners in a different location. The property is deeded in your names. If there are those who don't want to make the move and continue to be a part of this there will be no hard feelings. I have purposely not told you the new location in case anyone wants out. So if you want to remain here raise your hands."

Tears almost came to Connor's eyes. Not a single person opted to stay there.

"Okay, now that the issue is settled, the new site is an abandoned mine in the town of Jerome, Arizona. It is near the town of Cottonwood to the north, and to the south is Prescott Valley. That's about 15 miles away and across a mountain range with very curvy roads. We now need to tape some new sermons and keep this place running until the other site is ready. I estimate it will take another month for that to happen. Since we will be somewhat isolated, we will take all our weapons, ammunition, food, and operational equipment. I suggest we harvest the rest of the crops and take the food along as well. If we have half a dozen semi drivers, with the proper licenses we will be good to go. If not, get them trained up as quickly as possible. We won't need a lot in the way of automobiles there. Probably one for every two people will suffice, so those who want to drive your cars and see some of the country, join up with a traveling companion and start making plans. Those who want to fly can fly into Phoenix and we will arrange transport from there."

"On another note, does anyone know a person who is familiar with satellite operations, and who is a Christian?" Connor asked.

It appeared that no one did since nobody spoke up.

"I want to go to a satellite if possible. We will still use the same method here as a back-up, but I believe the satellite feed will reach a wider audience."

Connor spent the next three days taping sermons. He did three each day in between other coordination chores. Sterling had flown back to New York to take care of business. He acquired pre-paid debit cards for all the people in Jerome, just to spread the purchases they would need to make over a wider range. He got them for $500 each and called Lisa and told her they would be coming by express mail and should arrive within a few days. He instructed her to tell everyone to use them for whatever was needed.

Connor contacted other pastors in the area and asked if anyone knew of someone familiar with satellite operations. One of the churches in Maryland had a member who worked for the National Photographic Interpretation Center, or NPIC, which is a government organization that studies satellite photographs and imagery. Connor asked the pastor to set up a meeting with him and he did that the next evening.

When they met Connor told him what he needed and asked if the man was interested in working with his group.

His name was Alfred Tennyson, like the poet, and he asked where he would have to go.

Connor said, "I don't want to reveal that right now. If you should fall into the wrong hands and reveal the location it will set us back to the Stone Age, not to mention getting a lot of us killed. I will say that it is far from here and the living accommodations are not bad. All your needs will be supplied and you will be doing a great service for God."

"Can I bring my wife along?" he asked.

"Of course, as long as she is a Christian," Connor replied.

"She is the main reason I am now a Christian. I suspected what had happened with the rapture but I didn't know what to do about it. She did, and convinced me to study the Bible with her until we found the church where we could get other interpretations of events."

"Can you quit your job without drawing any undue attention?"

"Sure. That's a piece of cake. I will tell them we are going to live with my wife's mother."

"When can you leave?"

"I want to talk to my wife first, but what we are doing at NPIC now is of no consequence to anyone but the OWC, and most of that is just busy work. They won't even miss me. I can probably leave within a couple of days if my wife agrees to the move."

"Do you mind if I go with you to meet your wife?" Connor asked.

"Why do you want to do that?"

"Because there's a $2,000,000 price tag on my head and I am responsible for an untold number of lives of people who are working with me. I somehow get a sense of people's sincerity when I meet them, probably with a bit of an assist from God. What we are doing is of the utmost importance to God's plan and I don't want to blow the task," Connor said.

"You don't look anything like the pictures they have been showing of you," Alfred said.

"That's by design. We go to great lengths to keep the location from which we are broadcasting secret. That's one reason I need someone like you so badly."

"You want to do that right now?"

"If it suits your schedule," Connor replied.

They drove to Alfred's house, which was only a couple of miles from where they were meeting.

His wife was a real beauty. She was perhaps thirty years of age with light brown hair and blue eyes. She had a shapely figure and a ready smile.

When they walked in Alfred went to her and kissed her lightly. "Honey, this is a fellow Christian who has a proposal for us. This is my wife Linda."

"Does this fellow Christian have a name?" she asked with a smile.

"Yes but I don't know if he wants to reveal it to you. I will let him tell you about it," Alfred said.

She turned to Connor and raised an eyebrow in question.

"My name is Connor Frederick. The OWC has a price on my head and I operate what I guess you would call the North American Christian ministry from a secret location. I am part of the Jewish remnant mentioned in the Book of Revelation, though I didn't know this until the two witnesses in Jerusalem told me. My group has need of Alfred's talents and I offered him the opportunity for new employment which requires a move. I wonder if you will be willing to make the move to the new location we are developing to replace the one we are using, which the OWC will probably discover soon."

"I am really happy to meet you. I watch your webcasts whenever I can and I was impressed right from the start. You tell it like it is and I look up all your references in the Bible. We would be honored to do our part for God's purpose."

"Okay, Alfred is going to tender his resignation tomorrow to look after your aging mother. You do have an aging mother?"

"Yes but she is in heaven already, where we should be but for chasing the mighty dollar. I was so tied up in my modeling career that I failed to grasp what she always tried to tell us about the Bible. After the rapture it became crystal clear."

"Well you can chase the dollar again. Where we are going is a tourist area and we own the entire town. Only Christians will be living there, but we have to keep the tourist shops open to maintain the fiction."

"When do we leave and how do we travel?"

"I want Alfred there as soon as possible. I need him to help set things up. You on the other hand can fly, or drive if you'd prefer. I can introduce you to some ladies who will be making the trip by car. If you want to drive your own vehicle someone will ride with you."

"I would like that. Count us in."

"I will have someone meet you here in the morning and bring you to the place we are using now. I don't believe you will need much in the way of personal belongings other than clothing and such. The places we will be staying are furnished and there's shopping nearby to get anything you might need," Connor said.

To Alfred he said, "I will also have someone meet you tomorrow evening at around 7:00 pm here. Pack a bag with some rough work clothing if you have any, otherwise we will buy you some when we get to where we are going."

On the way back to the Virginia site he called Sterling and told him he had a satellite guy he needed to get to the other place and suggested a late evening flight out of Dulles. Sterling was amenable and said he would have the plane there sometime after 7:00.

Connor wished he had thought to shave the beard before he taped the sermons, but it was too late now, unless he wanted to do them over. It had taken three pretty grueling days and he didn't want to lose the time it would take to do them again. He would have to come up with some other disguise later.

When he got back to the farm he sat down with Thelma and started to make up a rough schedule for the move. The weapons and ammunition would be packed and loaded on one of the trucks, along with some furniture in the rear area to make it appear as a household shipment if they should happen to be checked along the way.

The foodstuff would be packed in another truck and would be making a food delivery to the west. All the computer equipment could be packed in a smaller truck, something like a moving van people used when they moved their own goods.

All the church records and anything incriminating would be packed in another truck, probably another small one. The four trucks should be enough to get the job done Thelma thought.

Larry called and told him that the project was coming along just fine and that he was going to have Norm start buying computer equipment. "We will duplicate what's back there as near as we can remember. We will need to have it up and running before we tear the other stuff down."

"Alfred will be there by day after tomorrow. Hopefully he will be able to tell you how to hook the stuff up for satellite operation. Start looking for a place for a couple of satellite dishes. They need open sky but still need to be hidden as well as possible. Camouflage netting comes to mind," Connor said.

"Do you want to figure on any sleeping quarters in the mine?"

"I think we are going to need some, but not nearly the number we have back here. The town is close enough that we can live there until things get rough, or we are under siege. If the latter happens I don't think we will have our minds on sleep. However, if we get into a situation where we can't get relief crews to man the equipment the people there will have to stay until things clear up, so maybe 20 bunks. I will have the ones here brought out in one of the trucks. Just prepare a place where they can be set up in the mine."

Connor picked Alfred up the next evening and the two of them were driven to Dulles airport. Sterling had told Connor where the plane would be and a Christian security guard allowed them entrance to the airport. They went straight to the plane and within half an hour were in the air.

They stopped in Oklahoma City and refueled then flew direct to the Sedona airport. They were in Jerome before daybreak.

Connor asked someone to locate Manny and Norm and have them meet him at the restaurant. When they showed up he introduced them to Alfred and said, "Go with him to get what is needed. I don't know where he will find it, but take enough credit cards to handle the expense of whatever he needs."

Alfred spoke up. "If all you need is to send a signal to a satellite I can make do with something like the Dish or Direct TV dishes. The dish only directs the signal to the proper place. The equipment that sends the signal to the dish is the important part of the lash-up. I can get most of what I need at any good electronics store."

"If we go to Prescott, it will take about an hour to get there. There's a Best Buy and Radio Shack, plus both the major satellite providers have offices there," Manny offered.

"Then let's go there."

They took the flatbed, which was a bit crowded in the cab but not too uncomfortable. Alfred was enthralled with the scenery and commented about how beautiful the rock formations were.

There didn't appear to be a lot of traffic going their way but they passed a lot more cars than Alfred would have thought going the other way. He asked about it.

"The county jail and municipal court is in Camp Verde, near the interstate. People who live in Prescott, Prescott Valley and other locations on this side of the mountains use the shorter route for the commute to work when the weather is good. This is about as busy as you will see the road these days with half the population gone," Manny said.

"Why would they put the jail there when the majority of the people live on the other side of the mountains?" Alfred asked.

"Probably because the county is so large. Also, the jail used to be in downtown Prescott and they didn't have any room for expansion, which was desperately needed over the last few years. I guess the cheap cost of land and nearness to the interstate figured into the move as well."

"Was there a lot of crime here before the rapture?"

"Not any more than in most places. Things are kind of spread out and other than drugs the main offenses were assault and murder. People around here all have weapons and know how to use them. It takes a pretty dumb thief to try to break into an occupied house in this part of the country."

"Our people will feel right at home then. They all have weapons and know how to use them. They even have experience defending themselves," Norm said.

"What do you mean?" Alfred asked.

"You didn't hear about the group of OWC forces who attacked our church services?" Norm asked incredulously.

"No. When did that happen?"

"Just the day before the first trumpet judgement. They surrounded the tent, which held about 2,000 people and asked to see our statue of Demir. When the pastor told them we worshiped God the leader tried to shoot him while he was standing on the stage. The shot galvanized everyone else and a battle between about 60 troops and our people ensued. We had over a hundred killed and about the same number wounded. All the OWC forces were killed before they could call for reinforcements. They didn't even report it on the local news until three day later, and they made it appear that the troops were executed by unknown parties. Connor insisted that every church member be armed at all times and know how to use the weapons. There were some doubters until the last incident. Now most of our members would sooner go without their trousers than without their gun," Norm said.

"He sure doesn't scare easy, does he?"

"No, he is rock steady. He was also chosen by God to lead the Christians in this part of the world. The two witnesses in Jerusalem told him that God had chosen him and Ephraim, the leader in Israel, to lead the 144,000 who will preach during the tribulation. I don't know if he has divine protection or not, but at least two attempts have been made to kill him and by all rights both should have succeeded, but he didn't even get a scratch. And boy, you talk about steady under pressure, he is unshakable."

"He's also a very likeable guy," Manny offered.

The conversation turned to what equipment they would need to set up the broadcast from Arizona. They were in Prescott and Prescott Valley the entire day. They had to buy a tarp to keep the purchases in place on the flatbed.

It took almost a week to get all the equipment set up and tested. Larry had found a location among the rocks not too far from the back opening and led Alfred to the location.

"I will need to get some satellite locations and see if we can get the right azimuth to send the signal but it looks good. The only drawback is that it will be visible from above. I know it is very small, but I worked in photo interpretation and if they know with any degree of accuracy where the target is they can photograph the entire area from satellites and the dish can be located. It will be labor intensive, but it can be done, and I think the OWC is going to become more serious about stamping us out in the future," Alfred said.

Larry suggested locating one of the dishes on a rooftop in town like it was a regular satellite television dish and running cable from there to the mine. It would require a lot of cable but expense was not a factor so they did that. As with everything else, the men in town did most of the work and it only took a day to get the dish working.

The problem now was the software the group back in Virginia was using. They needed copies of it before they could initialize their system. The link had been tested to make sure the signal got to the satellite, and that it was rebroadcast so the software was the final issue.

"I know a couple of cyber security guys who work at Fort Meade who have turned to the Lord. Do you think it would be worthwhile to have them join our team?" Alfred asked.

"Man, when Connor hears that he will weep for joy. We have been searching for someone like that from the beginning without any luck. We have some amateurs, but they are just hackers who learned on their own. These guys must know most of the tricks to be working for NSA," Norm said.

When Connor was told he immediately asked Alfred to call them and see if they would be willing to meet with someone from the organization. The call was made and both parties, one male and one female, were reluctant to meet with someone unknown.

"You know my wife. She will be with the person who is to meet you. Between the two of them they will explain the situation and see if you want to get involved," Alfred said.

Connor thought Thelma would be the best person for the errand. She knew all about the set-up and what was needed. She was not an expert, but had a level head and knew what to reveal and what not to reveal until the proper time. He called her and asked her to get in touch with Linda and the two of them would meet the prospective new members of the group.

When they met the following evening and received the pitch they were both enthusiastic and agreed to come along. Not only that but they knew at least three other Christians in their organization who were very worried about what was going to happen when the decree was made to take the mark of the Antichrist. They were contacted and agreed to meet the group that same evening.

When the evening was concluded they had five cyber security experts ready to join the force.

Thelma said, "I don't think we want to mess around with the niceties of giving notice and all that. You guys have any reservations about getting on a plane tonight and leaving this place behind?"

"You mean like right now?"

"Don't even go home to change clothes or pack a bag. You can get what you need when you get to where you are going. I have a feeling that they are keeping an eye on all the people who work in that organization, and I mean OWC covert surveillance. It wouldn't surprise me if they are aware that you are here right now," she said.

The five looked from one to another and almost as one shrugged. "In for a penny in for a pound, as the saying goes," the older of the group replied.

Thelma took out her phone and called Connor. "I have five recruits ready to catch a plane if you can arrange it. I think it is imperative that we get them out of the area just as soon as possible."

"Call Sterling and ask him about a plane. If he thinks security will be more lax at someplace like BWI, or even Philadelphia, then have them go to whatever location he chooses. You can do some recognition stuff so they will be able to recognize the right people."

When Thelma called Sterling and relayed the needs he suggested that the group go to BWI and purchase tickets to New York or even Pittsburgh. All the tickets were for was to get them through security at the airport. They would be met somewhere in the secure area of the terminal and taken to the plane surreptitiously.

They had all heard her end of the conversation and after she hung up she filled them in on the rest. "Go to BWI and purchase tickets for a flight to someplace close. That's just to get you past security. You will be met inside the terminal and taken to a private plane and be on your way within half an hour. The guy meeting you will be in a pilot's uniform and will look for a group of six just past the check-point. If you encounter any problem meeting him call me and I will coordinate it through the plane's owner. He will probably be flying from New York, so give him about an hour, maybe a bit more to be on the safe side."

"I am embarrassed, but I don't have enough money to even buy a ticket to New York," one of the females said.

Thelma took out a bunch of banded credit cards and handed one to each of them. "These are prepaid credit cards. Each has $500 on it. Use them for the tickets and for

231

whatever else you need along the way. Money is not a problem with our organization. We have several sources and the plane that is picking you up is one of them. Linda, why don't you go along with them? If you need anything from your house I will bring it when we all pick up stakes."

"Deal," she said.

Thelma thought that was a real stroke of luck, but she would caution Connor that she wasn't sure about their convictions. He seemed to have his own methods of evaluating people's sincerity, no doubt a God given talent.

The plane flew through the night, stopping for fuel along the way. All the group knew, other than Linda, was that they were flying west. She was wise enough to keep the destination to herself. She had only been around Connor for a short meeting but she quickly picked up on his penchant for secrecy until all the players had been confirmed as on the same team.

It was dark when the plane landed and Connor was at the terminal. The plane taxied to a hangar that Sterling had rented and Connor met them there. He went aboard the craft and Linda made introductions, not revealing Connor's name.

He looked the group over and said, "I understand that you are all Christians."

They all nodded affirmatively.

"Does that mean that you simply identify with the Christian movement, or that you truly believe Jesus came to earth, died for your sins, and was resurrected?"

All nodded.

"Do you also believe that God was responsible for the disappearance of all those people, that it was the rapture?"

Again all nodded.

"And do you believe that Demir is the Antichrist mentioned in the Book of Revelation, and that he will not stop until he has tried to kill every Christian alive today and those who come to belief from this point forward."

Again all nodded.

Nobody had uttered a single word since Linda introduced them.

"Would it surprise you if I told you that one of you is not telling the truth?"

They looked around at each other, not knowing what this was leading to.

"I sense that one of you is being untruthful. I don't know if it is simply because you want to fit in with our group, or if you are agents of the Antichrist, but I simply cannot take the chance that you are working for the other side. I now give you an opportunity to explain the situation for all our benefits," Connor said.

For what seemed a long time no one said a word. As the silence drew out one of the female members of the group finally broke down sobbing.

Nobody said anything. Connor allowed her time to get it under control. "Your name was Nancy?" he asked.

Again she nodded.

"Tell us about it, and why you are here."

"I do believe in God. I also believe that Demir has supernatural powers. I went to one of the local churches to try to learn more and was approached by someone who was apparently watching the churches. When he found out where I worked he offered me a regular salary in addition to what I was making at the agency to let them know about anything to do with Christian meetings, and especially anything about you. You are Connor Frederick, aren't you?"

"Yes I am. And you agreed to do this knowing that the Antichrist will eventually fall to God's forces?"

"I don't know what is going to happen. I don't understand all that stuff in Revelation and the offer seemed to imply that I would not get into trouble for keeping them informed."

"You would not get into trouble with them, but you are certainly in trouble with us. Did you get enough from the Bible to truly understanding what is taking place now?"

"I just know that a lot of strange things have happened, and that the OWC blames the Christians. I know that there is supposedly a bunch of stuff that God is going to do but Demir has assured everyone that he is the true God and will not allow them to happen."

"Demir is nothing more than a flunky for Satan. You do know enough about the Bible to know who Satan is."

"Yes, he's the devil," she replied.

"Satan was one of God's original angels. At some point he got the idea that he could run things better than God and enlisted the help of a few other angels and they planned a coup. They were going to do away with God and run things their own way, to put it into terms that are familiar to you. Well, since God is omniscient, the element of surprise was not there. I suppose God could have just destroyed him then and there, but he instead banished him to what we call hell. It isn't a very nice place, and old Satan has been trying to escape the eternal fire and he still fights a battle against God. God allows him to play at his little game. You see when God created man he gave him the free will to make his own choices about most things in this earthly life. The one exception is that God is the only one who decides when your time is up, or if you prefer, die."

"God's chosen people are the Israelites. If you have read any of the Old Testament you will have some idea about what God went through with his chosen people from the beginning. He wanted them to be happy, so when they grumbled that they didn't have a king he set them up with a king. The Bible tells all about how that failed and how the Israeli's eventually ended up in captivity in Egypt. God used Moses to bring them out of Egypt to the Promised Land, which is a large chunk of the Middle East."

"During the intervening years other issues developed between God and the Israelites. Finally he chose a boy named David to become king of Israel. David had his warts, but he was the greatest king the Israeli's had ever had and God decreed that the Davidic rule would last eternally. What that meant was that a ruler from the line of David would rule through eternity. That is how the birth of Jesus came about, through the line of David. Jesus was the sacrifice for all the sin of mankind, past, present and future. He is to set up his kingdom here on earth in something less than six years."

"Now when Jesus Christ was on earth he had followers called disciples. There were others called apostles, which means something like messengers from God. They wrote a bunch of letters to the churches that had been established in Jesus name around the Middle East during his life. These are the books of the New Testament. You see God made a change from the old way when Christ came into the world. The blood sacrifices were no longer required because Jesus had become the blood sacrifice for all mankind."

"The strange part of the story though is that the Prophets from the Old Testament days foresaw future events. For example, the birth and death of Christ were foretold some 3,000 years before the events took place. All the things that are taking place right now were foretold 5,000 years ago. The Book of Revelation in the New Testament is a chronicle of events now taking place. I can go to that book and tell you the exact sequence of what will happen between now and the time Christ comes again in less than six years."

"Have you heard all this before?" Connor asked.

"Not the way you tell it. It's like you know exactly what is going to happen from now till the end of time," Nancy cried.

"Everyone who can read can know that. It is all laid out in the Bible, exactly what is to happen and in what sequence. The only thing it doesn't tell is the timing between events. You know the hail and fire rain that happened recently was what the Bible calls the first trumpet judgement. It killed millions of people, mostly those who did not believe in God. The famine we are in was orchestrated by God as well. You see the majority of people alive on earth now don't believe in Him so he is punishing them for their sins."

"The next event to occur will be the seas and oceans turning to blood. One third of all marine life will perish during this judgement. After that rivers will turn to blood, making the water undrinkable. I could go on right to the end of the world as we know it, but if you can look at the events, relate them to the prophecy, and still not believe in God then there is no help for you," Connor finally wound down.

Everyone else had just listened as he spoke.

"I do believe. It's just that no one ever explained what it all meant," Nancy wailed.

"You have eyes, have you not? And you have a brain. Could you not take the time to try to learn why events happened?"

Connor was exasperated.

"My ministry, a direct calling from God, has led to the salvation of hundreds of thousands of people. I have been ridiculed, shot at, and every method at the disposal of Demir has been used to try to kill me. God has said that it will not happen, but many of my followers do not have the same assurance. Before I accepted this calling I was very squeamish about violence. Since all this started I have killed people without any mental qualms. We are in a fight against the vilest evil the earth has ever seen and it is a fight to the death. God will eventually win at the final battle, which some call Armageddon, but we still have a bit less than six years before that takes place, and yes it is foretold exactly what happens. Has this helped you understand the gravity of your situation?"

"Yes, yes, yes! I didn't know what I was doing, or I did know what I was doing but now realize that I was doing it for the wrong reasons. Please give me a chance to make up for it. I will do anything you ask."

"It's not what I ask, but what God asks. You must believe that God is the supreme ruler of the universe, that Jesus was His son, and that he came to earth to die for our sins. It is a simple formula but you must embrace those truths with all your heart and mind."

"What do you want me to do? I do begin to see that what you say is true but I would be lying if I said I embrace everything you say without studying the situation further," Nancy said, resigned to her fate.

"I can't afford to allow our location to be revealed to the Antichrist, so for better or worse we are stuck with you. Since it is obvious that you can't be released we will take you with us and assign someone to watch you all the time. Under no circumstances will you be allowed to work with our people until I am absolutely sure of your trustworthiness," Connor said.

"Do the rest of you have any reservations about what we are about to do?"

All answered verbally in the negative.

Connor had not become overly agitated, nor had he become violent during the confrontation with Nancy, but to the last person the group sensed the resolve and even ruthlessness beneath the surface.

Linda rode to Jerome with Connor and on the way told him that Nancy had pleaded that she was too broke to purchase an airline ticket to New York to make the meeting in BWI. "Thelma gave us all credit cards and I was with her the entire time from there on. She didn't use her cell phone, and she didn't leave any notes or anything for others I am sure. I don't know why I stuck so close to her, probably felt sorry that she was that broke, but I did. Do you suppose that might have been God telling me to keep an eye on her?"

"Stanger things have happened. We don't always know the mystery of God's ways, but He always knows what He is doing and uses whoever is in the right position to get the job done. It very well could have been God's way of keeping the secret secure."

"What are we going to do about her now?" Linda asked.

"We obviously can't turn her loose, but at the same time it is not right to keep people against their will. I suppose we will have to have someone with her all the time, and she absolutely cannot have access to a cell phone. I think she could be very useful to us in keeping our broadcasts secure but there are too many ways she could sabotage our efforts without our even knowing."

"It sounds like she doesn't really understand about God and the Bible. Maybe a few sessions with some of your earlier sermons will open her eyes to the truth."

"We can only hope that will be the case. I will explain the ground rules to her when we get to Jerome."

"How did you know about her?" Linda asked.

"I didn't, but I guess you could say God put the words in my mouth. I just had an irresistible urge to make the statement. It's funny in a way. God influences things in subtle ways at times. At other times he is so forthright that it's like being hit in the head with a brick," Connor said with a chuckle.

In the meantime, the conversation in the other vehicle, which Manny drove with the others as passengers, was along the same lines. One of the men said to Nancy, "I hope you realize what a predicament you are in. All the stuff you said at work about being a Christian was just a bald faced lie. How could you do something like this?"

"I said I was sorry, okay. I really don't know that much about Christianity. I just know that the OWC is the most powerful force in the world and to oppose them is folly."

"Boy, you really haven't read Revelation, have you?"

"I read some of it at the services we attended but I don't understand much of it."

"Like Mr. Frederick told you, all the events from now until the end of time are laid out in sequence. Demir is going to enjoy a lot of success during the next few years. He will kill many Christians who refuse to take his mark, which will probably be a tattoo of some sort on the forehead or back of the hand. God will allow the two witnesses in Jerusalem to be killed after they preach for three and on half years, exactly half of the tribulation period. The bodies will lie in the streets for three days and God will bring them back to life and they will ascend to heaven in plain sight of all those who support Demir. I don't know all of the things that are going to happen, or I know but don't understand them, but the final battle will be called Armageddon. I think I remember hearing that the actual battle site will be at a town in Israel called Petra, which is about 35 miles from Jerusalem."

"No matter how much it appears that Demir is going to be the winner, God will triumph in the end. After that Christ will return to earth and rule here for one thousand years. That's called the millennial kingdom in the Bible. After that, judgement comes, and the new heaven and earth will be created."

"What do you think he is going to do to me?" Nancy asked.

"He has every right to have you shot. I don't believe you realize just how many lives could be lost if you should have gone through with this crazy scheme. The numbers would be in the millions."

"Do you really believe that?"

"Yes. You realize that he is one of the two most influential Christians on the planet and that his preaching reaches millions every day. I'm sure Demir has hackers at work day and night trying to figure the best way to shut him down. That's why I agreed to come. I think we can be very instrumental in keeping the broadcasts going."

"What are you going to get out of this?" Nancy asked.

"It really doesn't matter. My days, like those of everyone on the planet are numbered. The number right now is less than six years. If you are talking about worldly possessions that is one of the false God's warned about in the Bible. The Bible says that man cannot serve both Him and money, or words to that effect. What I will really get is eternal life with God."

"What should I do now?"

"Just pray that you come to an understanding of the Bible and a belief in Christ. Otherwise you are damned to a life of eternal suffering. If you read Revelation you will see the truth of the prophecy, and that the events that have already happened are exactly what is prophesied. That should convince you beyond any doubt that we are on the right side. No matter what you decide, you can never be allowed to leave this place alive. If Connor doesn't kill you, I will. The stakes are just too high."

Nancy cried all the way to Jerome.

Chapter 20

When Connor got back to Jerome he got Lisa aside and told her about Nancy. "She will have to be watched constantly until she either comes to accept Christ, or we decide that she is simply too hard-hearted. Don't let her near a cell phone under any circumstances."

"You got it boss."

The mine shaft was now chocked full of equipment and furniture. Connor had thought that the mine would be musty and damp, but such was not the case. The low humidity outside, and the low moisture content in the soil kept the place comfortably cool and just a bit more humid than the outside air.

Larry had done a bit more to the cathedral room, as they had all come to identify what would become the major work area. He had chiseled out some stone to make the walls more uniform and built walls around a large part of the area. They really served no function but did make the place look a bit more like a regular office space.

The tunnel branch leading to the back entrance/exit had also been enlarged somewhat to allow people to more down it without bending quite as much. Wires in conduit lay along the outer perimeter of the passage. These would eventually lead to a satellite dish mounted some 100 yards from the cavern entrance around a bend in the landscape that hid it from view of those on the road to the west.

They had enough people with some knowledge of computers to start to lay out the work stations and mate the computer drives to the keyboards and printers.

It was only two days later when the first truck arrived. It held the stock of guns and ammunition. Most of the rifles and grenades they had taken from the OWC force were taken to the mine. Connor got the entire contingent together and told them, "Everyone will be armed with at least a pistol at all times. If you ladies are working the shops keep one handy near the cash register. I don't expect that we will be found out very quickly, but remember that most of the tourists coming through will be non-Christians. You must have firmly fixed in your minds that anyone not a Christian is the enemy. They might not look or act like it, but the very fact that they do not believe in God means they are a danger to us. I know that sounds very simplistic, but it is a fact. They have no idea that life on earth is on such a short string and if they even have a suspicion about what will be going on here, they will report it. Our operation will then be blown and we have to start from scratch again. Every time that happens we lose time and people, so be courteous but vigilant."

He continued, "Anyone needing weapons go to the truck down by the fire station and get what you need. Don't forget to make sure the ammo matches the weapon you choose."

One of the locals said, "You know we bill this as a mining ghost town and it wouldn't be out of order if all the men wore gunslinger belts and holsters as part of the ambience. It will make it simpler to get to them without having to conceal them. The tourists will think it is part of the bid to get tourists to town."

"That's a great idea. Where can we get enough belts and holsters for 70 or so men?"

"Most of us who live here have our own. There's a shop in Sedona that makes them special order. Maybe you can order them through one of the dummy corporations Sterling set up for the credit cards."

"Do you think you might be able to look into that and place the order?" Connor asked.

The man laughed. "Sure. You don't waste much time making decisions, do you?"

"I know a good idea when I hear one," Connor replied, laughing in turn.

"I would like to have church services for our group at least in the form of a morning devotional and a regular service on Wednesday's and Sunday's. I suggest we just meet in the open by the fire station until the weather gets too cold. Morning devotional at 8:00, regular services at noon on Wednesday and Sunday."

The next day the second truck arrived, this a regular semi. It was carrying the food. Even with the large number of people it took a long time to unload and get the cases of food to the proper location. Most of it was to go to the mine and the truck could not be driven to the mine entrance. The road was just not in shape to handle the large truck. They shifted the boxes to pickup trucks and used those to ferry the food to the mine entrance.

Not much had been said about the food situation, but the availability of fresh vegetables and fruits was almost non-existent. There was still canned food from the vast stocks before the rapture, but even that was beginning to dwindle rapidly with the onset of the drought and as a result of the first trumpet judgement. The OWC was handling the distribution of food in the major population areas, but in places like Jerome and other smaller towns all over the world, they simply didn't have the personnel to station people at every town and hamlet.

Instead, the people were supposed to come to the city distribution points for their allocation of food.

A third truck arrived before they had finished unloading the one with the food. This one was a U-Haul and they backed it up to the mine entrance and unloaded the furnishings and cots it carried.

While all this was going on, the computer troops were setting up the final configuration of what would be the broadcast studio. People also began to arrive. Most had caravanned across country in three of four car groups and housing assignments were made. The town gradually approached its population prior to the rapture.

Connor told Norm, "I would like to leave a skeleton crew at the old site and continue to operate it until it is discovered. Is there any way we can do that and bring this site on line at the same time?"

"Sure," Norm said. "The two are independent entities so it won't be a problem. I got together with the guys from NPIC and we designed a very elaborate system for the signals from here. They will need to get past over a dozen sites we are routing the signal through to even identify the originator. Then they will have to go through twice that many IP addresses to pin it down. Even if they do all that they will still not have the location."

"That's great. The more secure the broadcast is the better it will serve God's purpose. Are we ready to go here?"

"We've already tested the signal to the satellite and it seems to be working all right. We will check the other one out sometime today or tomorrow. I guess we are as ready as we will ever be. There might be some glitches but those can be worked out as they occur."

"Then plan on launching the site day after tomorrow. Let the site back east know that we will be broadcasting simultaneously for a few days to make sure the satellite system works properly."

"Once we are on the air I will change the data links on social media to redirect them to the new site instead of the old one," Norm said.

"You're the computer guy. Do whatever is necessary."

Lisa had been a constant companion to Nancy since her arrival and had spent a good deal of time studying the Bible with her. They had also watched several of Connor's earlier sermons that Lisa had saved on her computer and as they did they looked up all the references and Nancy began to see the light.

As they read through Revelation for perhaps the 4th or 5th time she said, "So according to the scripture the next thing to happen will be the sea's turning to blood?"

"That's correct, although other things could be happening simultaneously. Remember, the two witnesses in Jerusalem have the power to create pestilence, drought, and cause earthquakes, among other things."

"Is the part about the seas turning to blood literal? Will they actually be blood or just turn red and toxic?"

"I believe the interpretation is literal. I believe if you took a sample when it happened and had it analyzed it would contain the same make-up as blood," Lisa said.

"And that is supposed to kill one third of all sea life?" she queried.

"That's what the Bible says," Lisa responded.

"Why not all of it?"

"If I had to guess, which I do, I would say that the survival instinct will cause sea life close enough to rivers to seek safety there. The rivers and streams flowing into the oceans and seas will not be effected, so where the fresh water comes into the seas will provide some safe haven for sea life that can get to them. The fresh water will not turn to blood so the amount of fresh water entering the seas will grow greater each day and the safe haven will expand. That's just my interpretation of the reason, but only God knows why and how," Lisa said.

"It just sounds so unbelievable," Nancy said.

"Most of the things in Revelation do, but for almost two years things have happened exactly as the Bible said they would."

"You do believe that the people who disappeared all at the same time was the rapture, don't you?" Lisa asked.

"For something like that to happen with half the population disappearing at once means that something supernatural happened, but I don't know if I can reconcile that to everything that has happened since. Demir says that

God took all the people that disappeared because they had displeased Him. Why can't that be the case instead of the other way around?" Nancy asked.

"Because the Bible foretells the event in exactly the way it happened. That prophecy was written more than 2,000 years ago. God was displeased with the world, but not those who disappeared. That is why the times are so hard now and will continue to grow even harder. His punishment is being administered now on those who do not believe."

"If that's true, then why are Christians suffering too?"

"Doing God's will has never been an easy chore. All through the Bible His people suffered for obeying his calling. Our suffering on the earth is His way of testing our faith I think. We know that when it is all over that we will be given an eternal life in the most idyllic setting you could ever imagine. I suppose you might say that the tough times we go through here is payment in advance for what He is going to do for us. You have to remember that all of us who are believers now were not, until the rapture. All of us are learning as we go along."

Nancy didn't reply to that. One part of her wanted to believe but another part kept resisting. It was as the Bible said. Even those who heard and knew the truth of what was happening could still be persuaded by the Antichrist, and Nancy seemed to be one of those people.

Lisa told Connor that evening that she had given it her best shot but she didn't think Nancy was going to come to a belief in Christ.

They effected the switch over to the new equipment in Jerome and things went very smoothly. The last of the people from the eastern facility made their way to Jerome and everyone seemed to like the new set-up. Winter was not far away and the weather was beginning to change. Even in the hot summer, when the temperatures were over 100, after the sunset the temperature dropped

246

dramatically, sometimes as much as 35-40 degrees. Jerome was not very much above sea level but was just high enough to abate the temperatures somewhat.

It was late November when the second trumpet judgement occurred. Connor got a call from Ephraim, who told him of the event. The news stations started running stories about it shortly thereafter. It was worldwide and there was no way to hide it from the public, so like the first trumpet judgement, the news media reported on the phenomenon, though they didn't speculate about the cause or effect.

When an explanation came it was so far-fetched that the Christians wondered how anyone could believe it. According to the OWC the phenomenon had been caused by an alien chemical attack. The attack had been repelled by the OWC air force but not before the aliens dumped the chemicals in the world's oceans.

The story was totally ludicrous to Christians but the remainder of the population lapped it up like a cat would milk and praised the OWC for saving the planet.

When Lisa pointed out to Nancy that the Bible had stated what would come next she fell back on the OWC claim that it had been aliens.

The webcasts, both Ephraim's and Connor's, told the truth and gave the world the Biblical explanation. During that time both their signals were jammed and they had to switch to alternate channels, but it didn't stop them from telling the truth of the matter.

Connor auditioned the people at the site for announcing jobs on the webcast and chose three to do news and current events. The idea was to gather news to refute the claims of Demir and put out the real stories behind what the OWC was saying.

"My idea is to format it something like the Christian television shows did prior to the rapture. People have a right to know what is really taking place and I see this as the best method to get the word to them," he explained.

Connor did stints at irregular intervals to explain things that were happening and relate them to the Bible, but he also interspersed short sermons on Christian living and what God demanded of all who called him master of their lives.

He spent time talking about future events and how they would come about, what the effects would be, and what the Antichrist would be up to.

The efforts of Demir and his people to locate and shut down the broadcast were intensified.

Connor had a security force set-up and trained to respond to any attacks by OWC forces. He didn't figure they would have much chance against a frontal assault by much superior forces, but he wanted to instill a firm appreciation for the danger they were in.

Strangely enough, tourism had picked up and the shops they were manning only as a means of subterfuge turned a hefty profit. All the men wore holster belts weighted down with pistols and cartridges in the belt.

One day a patrol of OWC troops came to the town. The convoy consisted of three trucks with about 20 troops in each. They stopped near the fires station and used the restrooms. Then they walked around the town in groups of two or three. The sight of the cowboys wearing six-guns was so uniform that they didn't even pay any attention to them, probably thinking it was just for show. If they had thought for a minute that the weapons were the real thing matters could have gotten interesting. Some even bought souvenirs. The ice cream parlor did a booming business for over an hour and the group finally boarded the trucks again and headed over the mountains toward Prescott.

Connor had stayed out of sight, but watched the group warily. He breathed a sigh of relief as they departed.

He vaguely wondered if the OWC had somehow narrowed down their estimate as to their location and looked for Norm and the NPIC crew. "What do you think? Do they have an inkling about where we might be located?"

"I don't think so," Norm replied. "We don't have the satellite feed set up to accept queries, so if they find the signal all they will be able to do is jam it or take that channel down on the satellite. I think it was just a routine patrol."

The others seemed to agree and they continued to operate as normal, though with a degree of apprehension.

Connor was doing two sermons daily, one in the morning and one in the late afternoon or early evening. He had more than twenty ready to be aired, and though the sermons appeared to be live, they were in fact taped.

He made it a point to be on hand to answer questions after the taped sermons played to enhance the fiction that they were live.

Nancy asked Lisa if she would go hiking with her one day. It was just after the morning devotionals and Lisa asked another of the locals, a man, to accompany them.

The three set out to the south where the hiking was more uphill. They hiked perhaps a mile to a scenic overlook where the valley below could be seen clearly, with the red rock formations of Sedona predominant in the background. Nancy climbed across the guardrail and onto a boulder to get a better view. She gazed out over the panorama and commented about how beautiful it was. When she started to turn to come back she lost her balance. Before either of her companions could do anything she fell some twenty feet to the rocks below.

One look was all that was necessary to convince both that she was no longer among the living. Her head was twisted at an unnatural angle and she lay completely still.

Nevertheless, Lisa climbed down and checked her pulse, which was not there. She looked up and said, "She's dead. I think her neck was broken. What do we do now?"

"Go back and get some gear to haul her up. I imagine the reverend will want to at least give her a decent burial."

Was that God's way of taking care of a potential problem? Lisa wondered. Perhaps, she answered herself.

Chapter 21

Nancy's body was laid to rest in the local cemetery. The one thing that they all regretted was that they had not been able to get through to her with the good news of the gospel. When Lisa told Connor her thoughts about God taking care of the problem he emphatically agreed with her assumptions.

Things went smoothly in Jerome for a time. As to the remainder of the world, there were many more natural disasters that any of the group remembered for such a short time span. Earthquakes seemed to be occurring daily, typhoons, floods, and even volcanic eruptions at various locations were on the news almost continuously.

Mt. Aetna had erupted on the same day that Mt. St. Helens renewed her spewing of lava. A strong typhoon swept across the Japanese Islands two days later, killing thousands. A major flood in China had wiped out an entire city of nearly 100,000 people.

The Black Death, or Plague, had resurfaced in Europe and many people were dying from the disease. It was slowly spreading toward the Balkans and the Middle East.

Since they knew the cause of the disease, unlike the middle ages, when it killed so many, steps were quickly taken to arrest the outbreak and isolate those locations where deaths had been reported.

A major outbreak of Ebola killed over 20,000 in Zaire, and Scarlet Fever was once again detected in the United States.

One of these things alone could be seen as an anomaly, but three major diseases simultaneously that had all but been eradicated surfacing at the same time was too much to be coincidence.

Connor elucidated at length about this on his segments of the webcasts.

By this time Demir's forces had become outright hostile to anyone not clearly in his camp. Persecution of those even thought to be Christians had taken an upsurge and many were killed or run off their land by the people who lived among them.

It reminded Connor of the sectarian violence between the different branches of Islam of a few years previous. Neighbor against neighbor, and in some cases, father against son, or mother against daughter. People who didn't know the difference thought they were striving for a better life in their twilight years. They had no idea that they were living their twilight years.

Jerome had continued its existence as a tourist town and the tourists kept flocking through.

Food had become a bit more plentiful with a full crop during that summer. Still, the OWC controlled the distribution of what was grown.

Deer and antelope were still abundant in the areas surrounding the mountain range and the men took enough to provide meat for the population of Jerome. Enough vegetables were grown with irrigation in the lower elevations to provide most of their needs.

Through phone calls with Ephraim, Connor had learned that the two witnesses were still preaching to throngs of people too numerous to count. They were coming to Jerusalem from all over the world to hear them.

Many additional attempts had been made to kill them but the result was always the same, barbequed would-be assassins. Some were no doubt sent by Demir, but some were just disgruntled people trying to make a name for themselves, or outright lunatics.

That they were reaching a large number of people and bringing them to faith in Christ was self-evident. Ephraim's church rolls had grown to the point that it was difficult to keep track of them. Many of the converted went back to their own areas and spread the gospel in some manner there. The forces of Christianity were growing to a point that they would soon be able to hold their own against Demir's forces.

Connor felt that something big was on the horizon and it could only be the edict that Demir would issue for everyone to take his mark or die.

It was in the 26th month of the tribulation by Connor's calculation when the third trumpet judgement came to pass. A meteor so large that it shook the entire planet came hurtling from space and impacted in western Russia. The seismic activity was so great that it could not be measured on the equipment scattered all over the earth's surface. Buildings collapsed and roads buckled. Bridges were torn from their supports and the oceans and seas became a boiling cauldron of huge waves. This event would apparently release some mineral into the fresh water that would kill one third of fresh water life. The Verde River was near enough that they could go for a look at this phenomenon first hand, and many did.

Strangely enough, Jerome shook a lot but there was no major damage, nor was the mine damaged.

The earth's water became undrinkable and what was available quickly became a very expensive commodity. Water could be sold for as much as $100 for a glass in some places.

The water supply for Jerome was from a deep well and it seemed to suffer no ill effects from the event.

Scientists were scurrying to find some way to treat the water to make it drinkable but it took them almost two weeks to find a method, and then they still had to provide the necessary elements to combat the poisonous elements in the water. Many more died.

Gradually the water cleared again and became drinkable without treatment. However the tremendous damage to infrastructure would never recover completely. Travel by road for any great distance was unthinkable. So many bridges and roads were damaged that finding alternate routes would triple or quadruple expected normal travel times. In some cases destinations were simply impossible to reach.

This was in the United States. In other parts of the world, especially near the impact of the meteor, the damage was much worse. Moscow was almost totally leveled. Major cities in Europe suffered extreme damage and untold deaths resulted from the event.

Still, wouldn't you know, Demir blamed the meteor on natural causes, which was true to a certain extent, but Christians knew that it was actually the third trumpet judgement.

Even during the aftermath of one of the worst events in history, the Demir regime redoubled their efforts to eradicate Christians. Wholesale slaughter was occurring all over the world. OWC forces were going village to village, town to town, and city to city trying to identify and execute Christians.

The word got out very quickly via the webcasts of Ephraim and Connor. They warned their viewers that Demir's forces were on the warpath. Connor said in one monolog, "Christians are being rounded up and executed like the Nazi's rounded up Jews in Germany. He isn't bothering to take them to gas chambers. Anyone professing to be a Christian is either shot or beheaded on the spot. I know the Bible teaches love, but I refuse to go to the slaughter without taking some of the unbelievers with me. I tell you that God doesn't want anyone to be executed without resistance. If you have weapons, use them. This is now a fight for survival. Martyrdom doesn't mean submitting meekly. If you are killed fighting the forces of evil the reward is the same."

Ephraim broadcast much the same message. He warned people that it would not be much longer before Demir made his move on Jerusalem, and once that happened Christians would be hunted and slaughtered on sight. "When he institutes his decree to take his mark it will be much easier to isolate us, but let me warn you, do not take the mark, because if you do you are forsaking God, and that will lead to an eternity that you don't even want to contemplate."

As time passed and the midway point in the tribulation got closer and closer Connor preached about the specific part of revelation that dealt with the death of the two witnesses.

"The Book of Revelation is very specific about what will happen and when. Chapter 11: 3-12 tells the story. They will have preached for 1260 days before Christ allows them to be killed. If you use the rapture as the starting point of the tribulation the event will occur next September 14th. If you use the date when the treaty was signed with Israel, which is my interpretation from the Book of Daniel, then it will happen on October 23rd. On whichever date they are killed, they will lie in the streets of Jerusalem for three days. The city will rejoice and their bodies will be desecrated and violated. The corpses will start to stink but nobody wants them removed. They are symbols of the victory of the great Satan."

"But when they arise after three days for all to see, the city suddenly becomes the nemesis of Satan, for there is an immediate and sincere revival in the city. Multitudes come to Christ as the glorious event unfolds. That's in verse 13. John calls it a great revival. What these two accomplished during their 3 ½ years of preaching is nothing short of phenomenal. People from all over the world traveled to Jerusalem to hear them preach, and having heard them in person I know how persuasive their arguments were. That each person heard them in his or her own language attests at once to the supernatural nature of their presence. The times they had to defend themselves against attack are also straight from the Bible."

"However, before that glorious event, I believe the world will once more be subjected to God's wrath. The fourth trumpet judgement will see one third of heavenly bodies go dark. That includes the sun, moon, and stars. It will be so dark that you will not be able to see your hand in front of your face. Have you ever been in a basement without windows when the power went out? That's how dark it will be. You will only be able to discern pinpoints of faraway stars, and what little light reaches earth will not even be enough to choose your next step."

"Demir is going to desecrate and raze the temple. He will not leave a stone in place, but when Christ returns the temple will be rebuilt."

"After that comes a demonic locust plague. I don't know if this will be before the two witnesses are killed or after, but it is not going to be a very rewarding experience for those remaining. I don't believe Christians will be attacked by the locusts, but I am by no means certain. My advice when the judgement comes is to find a closed space inside and stay there until it is over."

"There are four more trumpet judgements and seven bowl judgements before the end, and each is worse than the one that preceded it. When Demir takes Jerusalem all Christians will be forced to flee. I believe most will go to the city of Petra. I am sure most of you know that is not far from Jerusalem. The Bible doesn't say this but my opinion is that most of the remnant who are in Jerusalem will be there and that they will receive divine protection from God. He has said that he will protect the remnant from harm until the end of the tribulation, so Petra seems to be the place where they will congregate. That's also where the final battle between God and the forces of evil will take place. I know that people don't want to hear about doom all the time, but that is all that is on the horizon until Christ comes again. Until next time let me leave you with this prayer."

Connor prayed longer than usual for the souls who were still lost that they would wake up in time to avoid the eternity that awaited them under Demir.

Chapter 22

The price on Connor's head was now up to ten million dollars. Sterling had left one of his business jets at Sedona for use of the group but no one had used it the entire time after they got everything in place.

Sterling had called on a regular basis and had made a couple of trips to the area but had only stayed long enough to assure that the group had all they needed.

He arrived the day after Connor had done the sermon about the coming death of the two witnesses. "I have turned over management of my empire to my second in command, minus the airplanes of course," he said. "I think I want to be here until after Jerusalem is taken. How can I make myself useful around here?"

"First by strapping on a gun belt. I suggest you change to Levis to fit in better before you do that though," Connor told him. "You might get together with our local security guy and have him show you our defenses and see if they can be improved. I think it's only a matter of time before they hit us hard."

Sterling did as Connor suggested. He was quite a sight. His hair was now almost completely grey and in jeans and cowboy boots with a gun belt strapped around his waist and a cowboy hat he looked like what most people think of when they think of the old west. He even had a red bandana tied around his neck.

Most of the defenses were oriented toward protection of the mine and Sterling pointed out that it might be a good idea to figure some way to bar access to the town itself. If OWC forces controlled the town then it would be a simple matter to direct their forces to the mine. Between the two they searched for some way to block the road on both ends in the event they should come under siege. A cement wall protected the road coming north down the mountain side. It was about 18 inches thick and Sterling thought that if the wall could be collapsed, at least a couple of sections, it would block the road from the south.

At the last switchback going out of town to the north was a stone building very near the road. The same could be done with the house. It would take a stick of dynamite in each place but they had people who knew enough about the stuff to plan on blowing those two locations if they were attacked. It was not going to keep trained soldiers from breaching the town, but it would slow them down somewhat, hopefully giving the remainder of the people time to get to the mine, where they would have a better chance at survival.

Sterling told Connor that the destruction from the meteor was horrendous in New York. "It's a good thing we didn't choose the second place we looked at for a base of operations. It is now only a bunch of rubble."

"What I believe is going to happen after Demir takes Jerusalem, is that all Christians are going to have to go underground. It is going to be difficult after the decree about taking the mark. With all the judgements that are coming I believe that is God's way of giving Christians some degree of protection. With all the misery they will be going through they won't have a lot of energy to devote to persecution," Connor said.

"What will you do when they discover this place?"

"Try to get as many people out as possible and then go to Petra. I believe you should do the same," he said.

"If I am indeed part of the Jewish remnant then I will survive to witness the final battle, and that is something that I really want to see," Sterling said.

"When I last talked to Ephraim he said things were getting tenser in Jerusalem. More violence against the church and more everyday rioting. Even the police are more apt to shoot first and ask questions later. He said that hundreds are killed daily. I can't imagine that it is much better anywhere else on the earth."

"Probably not. I know the same is true in New York, and probably most of the other major cities in our country. It's just as the Bible says it will be."

The situation got so bad in Israel that Demir decided that the Israeli's needed OWC assistance and sent 20,000 troops to Jerusalem.

To non-Christians it appeared that he was doing nothing more than assisting the Israeli's in keeping law and order, though that is something of a misnomer.

What he was doing was getting prepared for the siege of Jerusalem as the Book of Revelation foresaw. The Israeli army had forces garrisoned there, but most of their troops were spread around the country in other towns and cities.

Violence seemed to escalate instead of abate with the arrival of the troops and the situation continued to deteriorate daily.

More troops were brought in. Visitors were still flocking to the city to hear the two witnesses preach, even with the constant threat of violence. More and more burned bodies resulted from daily, sometimes even hourly attempts to silence the two.

The forty two month period of their ministry was coming to a close and they even mentioned this in their preaching.

Demir announced on television that it was his opinion that the two witnesses were responsible for the violence in Jerusalem and that it would be a good idea if Israel would close the city to tourists to try to deescalate the violent situation.

The Israeli's refused to do that and the status quo continued.

Each time Demir appeared on television he berated the Israeli's for not keeping order in the city. It should have been obvious to everyone that the same situation existed in most of the world's larger cities, but no one seemed to look at that aspect of the situation.

Demir was setting the stage for a full scale attack on Jerusalem and the Christians knew this.

When it appeared that Demir was on the verge of issuing the order for an assault, the lights went out.

One moment the sun was shining and the day looked lovely, the next moment everything was as black as the inside of a coal mine.

And it wasn't just the lack of light. Flashlights and automobile lights stopped working. Lighters would not light and matches would not strike. The blackness was total, except for distant flickers of stars billions of miles away.

Connor and Sterling had been walking along the street in Jerome when it happened. Both stopped, expecting the onset of darkness. It didn't happen. The day dimmed, much as when a cloud passes overhead suddenly signaling the onset of a thunderstorm, but when the intensity reached a level akin to a single lamp burning in a room the light stabilized. All around them was darkness, but in their immediate surroundings there was enough light to continue on their way.

It was strange to them to be walking along the street, able to see every step they took, while the world was in utter and total darkness.

"I wonder if non-believers will be able to see the light provided for us," Sterling voiced his thought.

"I don't believe they will. We will have to venture out and see what the situation is before too long."

More people came out onto the streets of the town, marveling at the total darkness of the noon-day sun.

Within minutes Connor's phone rang, as he suspected it would. It was Ephraim. "Is the same thing happening there? Can the believers still see?"

"Yes, but very dimly."

"It's almost comical watching all the people on the streets running into each other, walking into walls and cars, stumbling over curbs and even fighting in the dark. It seems nothing that would emit light works anymore," he said.

"This will give us a chance to get things done without OWC being privy to them," Connor said.

"That's true, but we don't know how long it is going to last."

"I should think it will last for quite a while. I don't believe God did this just to prove that he could. It is part of the judgements, so I think a lot of people will perish as a result of the darkness," Connor said.

As strange as it sounds, there were actually gun battles in the darkened world. Robbers still attempted to rob stores by touch, and some violent collisions of walking people resulted in killings by gunshot.

Even in the darkened conditions the two witnesses continued to preach, and Connor and Ephraim continued their broadcasts. They were not likely to get any non-believers as viewers, but some might listen to the messages.

World commerce came to a standstill and as the darkened conditions continued many people died because they could not be transported to hospitals. Others, who were short of food when the phenomenon started, perished while out trying to locate something to eat.

Television news stations stopped broadcasting and many of the radio channels went off the air simply because they could not operate by touch alone. Those which did stay on the air had very fundamental programming. The DJ's couldn't even identify what song was to play next.

Sterling and Connor flew to Jerusalem to confer with Ephraim. They simply gassed up the plane and took off. A stop in Washington, at Dulles airport provided gas, though they had to pump it themselves. Connor left money to pay for the gas under a brick near the fuel truck.

The next stop was in London, where they were met by more than 100 people, obviously Christians. They were offered food and drink and stayed for almost two hours talking with the group on the tarmac of the airport at Gatwick.

Connor left them with the entreaty to use the time wisely to get those things done that needed to escape detection by OWC forces.

They then flew directly to the nearest airport that would take the small jet in the area of Jerusalem and borrowed a car from a fellow Christian.

Connor didn't think it would be wise to try to drive around the streets of Jerusalem under the circumstances and borrowed two bicycles from a rack they passed. He called Ephraim and asked directions from where he was then located and within 20 minutes was in Ephraim's compound.

"You only have about a month left and Mordecai and Benjamin will have been here for 42 months. What are your plans?"

"I've already set up an alternate broadcast site in Petra. I think that is where most of the remnant will go. It stands to reason, since that is where the final battle will take place, and God has promised to keep us from harm. I imagine He will place a protective shield around the city, but that's just my opinion. What will you do?"

"Continue to operate as long as possible. We have no fallback position, so I will try to get as many of my people as possible to safety and then I imagine Sterling and I will come back to join you at Petra."

"I have been studying Revelation with particular emphasis on the sealing of the 144,000 and let me give you my take and see what you think."

"I believe that we have been under God's protection from the start, but the actual sealing will not occur until the Antichrist institutes his ultimatum that everyone take his mark. At that time a mark on our foreheads will become visible to other Christians but not to non-believers. Do you think that makes sense?"

Connor gave it some thought. "I suppose it could happen that way. I don't think God would have even had John mention the sealing if it was not some visible mark. Since none of us show anything now it makes more sense than anything else."

"Our Jewish leaders, even the non-believers, are very much afraid of what Demir is up to now. I have been hammering the point that he will violate the treaty and take Jerusalem in the very near future. MOSSAD has been trying to undermine OWC efforts without much success. The makeup of the work force is still divided between Christians and those in Demir's camp."

"And on top of that, our six nuclear weapons that we were allowed to keep are dispersed to different air bases and will be of little use when the real action starts. I suppose they could send the planes with them against Babylon, but Demir is too well protected for that to be a successful ploy. We are essentially defenseless. Troops from surrounding areas will be called in but I don't see them unleashing an artillery barrage against Jerusalem when the make-up is still 90 percent Israeli's. Demir has been shuttling more and more troops to the area and will guard the perimeter of the city while mopping up within the city itself."

"It's not going to be pretty. I wish there was some way I could help, but I don't see how it is possible," Connor said.

"You have done what God wanted you to do during these trying times, and I feel we will have much more work to do before the end."

The two only stayed for about three hours and headed back to the airplane. They returned the bicycles to the same rack they had taken them from and found the car they had borrowed. Within another hour they were back at the plane, which had been refueled and made ready for the return flight.

As in London, a large crowd had gathered. It was more than twice the size of the one at Gatwick and Connor spoke for almost thirty minutes. He cautioned that the Antichrist would take Jerusalem and require that everyone take his mark. "Under no circumstances are you to submit to the mark. That is the one thing that will undo your promised salvation. Resist as hard as you can, but refuse the mark, even unto death."

He went on to tell them what most already knew, that the witnesses would be killed and would be resurrected three days later, and prayed for their safety and devoutness.

The flight back was uneventful, though very long. Fortunately they had two pilots and didn't have the fatigue factor to deal with. By the time they got back they had only been gone for four days.

The darkness had lasted for 15 days and would continue for another week. Everyone was beginning to get on edge, wondering when it would end and what would happen when it did.

It was 23 days before the sun broke through the clouds again and people could once again see what was going on around them.

Demir wasted no time. Just as soon as the television stations were up and running again he came on television and decreed that the Israeli's had not lived up to their part of the treaty and declared it null and void.

Two days later the attacks against Jerusalem started. First a flight of OWC fighter/bombers flew over Jerusalem dropping bombs and strafing the city. The troops garrisoned in the city left their barracks in fighting formations and started to systematically place Jerusalem under siege. Israeli forces fought back bravely, even valiantly, but were pushed toward the center of the city.

It seemed the OWC strategy was to attack from all sides and push the opposition to the city center where they would mop up at their leisure. The air attacks continued, though there was stiff opposition from the Israeli air force. Both sides lost a large number of aircraft. The Israeli's did in fact try to nuke Babylon, but both planes with the weapons were shot down enroute to the target.

It only took OWC three days to subdue the city and the Israeli officials surrendered.

The two witnesses had been isolated near the Wailing Wall and more than 1,000 OWC troops surrounded them. They all fired as one upon a signal from the commander and the bodies of the two witnesses were riddled with bullets.

They didn't even check the bodies. Any living thing taking that many hits could not possibly survive.

You must remember that many of Jerusalem's inhabitants were still in the camp of Demir. They led marches past the two bodies and spat on them, kicked the bodies and wrote blasphemous slogans on their bodies with paint. Their clothing was ripped from their bodies and it was a great spectacle that went on day and night.

The Christians had begun to flee the city when the first action started, though Ephraim kept his broadcast going until OWC troops were at the door. His people were all armed and killed the troops in the immediate area and then started an orderly retreat away from the action. Some sought shelter with other known Christians, but Ephraim advised them all to make their way to Petra.

Demir had come to Jerusalem once it was secure and said that he would now rule his church from the most sacred site.

When the two witnesses were resurrected after the third day he was furious. It was at the stroke of noon that the bodies stirred and the people around them fell back in horror. The event didn't happen very swiftly. God wanted the population to witness his mighty power. The day darkened, except where the two witnesses were now floating above the city, casting a golden glow from God's power upon them.

All over the city people who witnessed the event fell to the ground and worshipped the living God, for only he could perform the miracle they were witnessing. Revelation says this results in a great revival in the city and no doubt that is the case.

As the two witnesses disappeared into the clouds a violent earthquake shook the city. Buildings crumbled and fissures opened in the paving.

Many people were killed, 7,000 according to Revelation.

Demir is even more furious at this and orders the temple completely and utterly destroyed. "Do not leave a stone in place," he told his disciples.

Chapter 23

Sterlings's pilot called from the airport in Sedona. When Sterling saw who was on the phone he had a premonition of OWC forces arriving. That is precisely what was taking place. Planeload after plane load of troops were disembarking and forming up near the airport.

A convoy of trucks arrived and the troops loaded up. Some of the trucks were towing artillery pieces, and at least two trucks were loaded with ammunition.

When the pilot told Sterling what was going on, he asked, "What do you want me to do?"

"Move the plane to Prescott airport. I imagine we are going to be in for a rough time here, but we will try to exit the area toward the south and cross the mountains. If we can make it to the airport in Prescott we will take off immediately. Be sure the plane is fueled and ready to fly."

He passed the word to Connor.

Connor got all the town's residents together. There were several tourists, who he told to leave town immediately or be prepared to face OWC forces.

"It looks like this is the showdown. Sterling's pilot called from the airport in Sedona and said that a large force of OWC forces, including artillery is on the way. I imagine we have about half an hour. I don't expect them to just ride into town. They will probably send out scouts to assess the situation first. Let's spread out around town at good firing locations. Blow the entrance to town when they get close. At least they will not be able to advance using the trucks for cover. Those of you who do not want to face them head over the mountains or disperse into the woods."

The word was passed to those in the mine to be prepared for an attack and people scurried about looking for good firing locations. Even the women broke out rifles and located firing positions on the upper floors of town buildings.

No more than a dozen elected to leave town and most of those were women. Connor told Larry to offer the people in the mine the opportunity to leave if they so desired before the action started.

Within twenty minutes the OWC trucks could be seen laboring up the grade to the town. When they got to an area that once was a schoolhouse but was now an art gallery, they unloaded and broke up into squads. The towed artillery was set up pointing toward the town proper and through binoculars men could be seen unloading ammunition for the big guns.

The approach was made single file along the road and the man who had been dispatched to light the dynamite was in place and on his cell phone with Connor.

"Don't wait too long. You need time to get out of there before they have time to recover."

"I'm on it. I would like to bury a few of them under the debris if possible."

"I repeat, don't wait too long," Larry said.

Not a shot had been fired, though everyone was in position, when the explosion occurred. They had miscalculated the amount of explosive needed on the high side, and when the house blew it scattered lethal debris almost 100 yards, mostly back toward the OWC troops, as the charge had been planted near the side facing the road.

The first squad of ten men all went down and half as many in the second file. While getting rid of the troops was nice, the ploy had been meant to block the road, and that had only marginally happened.

From there the OWC troops advanced under sporadic rifle fire from different points in the town. Any location high enough to provide a clear lane of fire was manned and the stone buildings provided adequate cover for the riflemen.

Within a matter of minutes the sound of artillery firing could be heard. The range was so close that it was not very effective and the trucks hooked up and moved the pieces back toward Cottonwood to more effectively use the assets.

Once the artillery had been moved the large shells started to rain down on the defenders. Using the artillery barrage for cover the OWC ground troops started to leap frog forward to the area where the debris blocked the road. Many used the huge chunks of stone and concrete for cover and started returning the fire of the Christian group.

As they skirted the roadblock and advanced farther toward the main part of town the defenders fell back to the mine.

Connor drove a car south to a parking area about half a mile from the back exit from the mine and returned to the mine.

Once inside he told everyone the situation. "This is a pretty defensible position, but they will eventually be able to root us all out. If you don't want to make this a last stand then I suggest you grab a weapon and head for the woods. Once it becomes clear that they will be able to breach the entrance I am leaving for Israel. I wish there was more I could do, but all I can think of is prayer."

He bowed and prayed for God's guidance and mercy on those who would surely die today. He asked for strength in their beliefs that no matter how tough the situation ahead that they would not waver in their faith.

Some of the men had fashioned positions on the hillside above the mine entrance and were picking the OWC troops off as they tried to gain access to the mine entrance.

The battle raged long enough for three additional truckloads of troops to arrive. It was obvious that they would not be able to hold out much longer and gradually the people withdrew to the back exit and melted into the surrounding woods.

Connor and Sterling made their way to the car Connor had appropriated and loaded three more people and headed across the mountains.

Connor told them, "We are headed to Israel. You guys are welcome to go along if you want."

The three were Larry, Norm and one of the NPIC people. All three agreed that Israel sounded good to them.

They got to the Prescott airport without trouble and within a matter of minutes were aboard the plane and ready for departure.

There was a short delay in getting clearance to take off but finally they were in the air.

"What are we going to do in Israel?" Larry asked.

"Whatever God directs us to do. It's a long way from over. I hate that things turned out this way for our people who have been so faithful, but we knew it was coming sooner or later, and I know most of them would rather go down fighting."

Connor took out his phone, ignoring the prohibition about cell phone usage on aircraft, and called Ephraim.

When the connection was made he said, "Well, they routed us out. Five of us are on the way to Israel. Figure out some way to use us when we get there. It's still a very long way from over and I know there's still a lot to do."

After he finished the conversation he put his seat back and went to sleep. The future could worry about itself for now.

www.ingramcontent.com/pod-product-compliance
Lightning Source LLC
Chambersburg PA
CBHW072208170626
46813CB00003B/846

* 9 7 8 0 9 9 7 8 9 4 9 0 5 *